PURGED

A Circle City Mystery

M. E. May

M&B

M&B Literary Creations

M&B Literary Creations

Copyright © 2014 by M. E. May

ALL RIGHTS RESERVED

Cover Art by Julie Kukreja, Pen and Mouse Design

Edited by Mary V. Welk

Printed in the United States of America
10 9 8 7 6 5 4 3 2

Books by M. E. May

Circle City Mystery Series:

Ensconced

Inconspicuous

Perfidy

Dedication

To my sister, Phillis White, whose love for
me has been a constant in my life.
During my years of experimenting with other religious
beliefs, she never criticized me, but showed me what a
Christian truly is through her example, not her words.

Acknowledgements

The *Circle City Mystery Series* would be nothing without those who serve and protect the great city of Indianapolis—the men and women of the Indianapolis Metropolitan Police Department. I am especially grateful to those in the department who have been willing to answer my technical questions about the IMPD's policies and procedures.

To my faithful friends and fellow authors, Tricia Zoeller and Sue Myers for their steadfast encouragement, I give my gratitude. Without the two of you, I might have given in when I became discouraged.

I wish to thank Mary V. Welk who did such a fabulous job of editing this novel. Her suggestions for changes, in addition to keeping me on the straight and narrow with grammar and punctuation, were vital to the success of this novel.

To my graphic artist, Julie Kukreja, who always creates such brilliant covers with just a few words from me, I give my deepest gratitude.

The most fabulous formatter in the world, Lara Hunter, also deserves my heartfelt thanks for doing such a wonderful job of getting my manuscript ready to print and to be submitted for eBooks.

Many thanks must go to my publicist, PJ Nunn of BreakThrough Promotions for taking some of the marketing responsibilities "off my plate" and helping me reach readers across the country.

Of course, I wouldn't be able to get through all the publishing highs and lows without my family—my husband, Paul and my children, Brian and Marie. Their encouragement and support mean the world to me.

"Do as you will, but harm none."

-Anonymous

Chapter 1

He could see the thirteen sinners dressed in flowing medieval dresses and cloaks of deepest, darkest obsidian, amethyst, and emerald. Oblivious to his presence, the women danced around the fire chanting and singing the devil's songs. In his anger, he vowed to make them repent, or he would destroy them one by one. Doug listened from his hiding place in the bushes, watching and waiting.

"Sisters, let us praise the Goddess on this Sabbat Samhain and be one with the Earth," cried a very tall woman in black. The hood of her cloak slid off her head when she raised her eyes and arms to the sky. Her long curly blonde hair glistened in the firelight as she danced and twirled. He was sure this one must be their leader. Everyone seemed to be following her.

The group chanted something about thanks to Mother Earth for her wonderful fruits. Why weren't they thanking God, the real true God, instead? Earlier they were beckoning the dead. Feeling his face flush with fear, he remembered his grandmother's claim that Halloween was an evil day—the devil's day.

"Blessed be," he heard the leader shout. "Thanks be to our ancestors for communicating with us tonight. Thanks to the Goddess for her many blessings of the Earth. Blessed be!"

"Blessed be," the others shouted.

"Let us go to our homes now and feel refreshed and one with the Earth."

The devil worshippers hugged and talked for much too long. Doug could not take them all at once. Afraid his mission could be thwarted if they left in pairs, he continued to peer at them while his gut knotted with impatience. One of the witches took a bucket of water and drenched the fire. Another came to help her stir it and douse it with another bucket to complete the job. The time was finally at hand, and many of them began to leave.

Doug's knees ached from kneeling in his cold damp hiding place. He hoped he would be able to walk once he had the chance to move. He mustn't fail, but must accomplish what he'd set out to do and make his grandmother proud.

Then the miracle he'd hoped for came to being. The leader stayed behind. He watched anxiously while she stirred the dirt and ash where the fire had been. Then she picked up a bag and shone her flashlight along the path leading to the parking lot.

Doug rose to his feet and slipped quietly through the woods to the trail he knew she must take. His heart thumped so loudly in his ears, he feared she might hear him coming. From his jacket pocket, he retrieved a small freezer bag containing the rag he'd prepared. At the sound of footsteps approaching, he hid behind a large oak.

"Oh," she said aloud in a joyous voice. "I feel clean and whole again."

When she passed him, Doug leapt from behind the tree and grabbed her, causing her to drop her bag and flashlight. Quickly he put the rag over her nose and mouth before she could let out a scream. She bucked like a wild animal trying to free herself. She kicked his shin and dug her fingernails into the skin on his right wrist exposed by the struggle. He held her tighter, ignoring the pain in his determination. Finally, the chemicals proved too much and her body surrendered.

He placed her on the ground and rubbed his shin, allowing himself to feel the pain. Knowing it would only be a bruise, he then checked his wrist. It bled, staining the sleeve of his coat, and he thought of the blood Christ shed for him. His own wounds would be worth it once he got her to confess her evil ways and denounce Satan.

Doug decided to check her bag to see what evil instruments it held. Inside, he found a long, sharp, two-edged dagger in a wooden case. The hilt was made of some sort of beast's horn. He must confront her about this instrument. How many sacrifices had she made with it?

Exhilarated, he put the dagger on top of the witch, picked her up, and carried her toward his car. He laid her on the ground a few feet from the parking lot and checked to make sure their two cars were the only ones left. The parking lot was empty of other vehicles, so he walked slowly to his, opened the trunk, and took out a large blue tarp.

Back with the witch, he tied her arms together with duct tape then wrapped her and her evil tool in the tarp. Doug smiled as he carried her back to his car and placed her in the trunk. He sighed and looked up to the heavens. "Thank you," was all he said.

Chapter 2

Sasha felt dizzy. Her head spun and ached as she tried to open her eyes. Nausea overtook her and threatened to erupt. Something was very wrong. Trying to move, she realized she was sitting in a chair bound by something wide and sticky which pulled at the skin and hair of her forearms. The attempt to open her eyes yielded nothing. She found a broad, scratchy cloth tied around her head which totally obliterated any light.

Fear pulsed through her. As her heart pounded, her head throbbed. She tried to focus her thoughts through the pain and remember what happened. She could still smell a hint of something sweet. Then it struck her—a man, there had been a man. He'd grabbed her and put something over her face and now she was…where? Then the creak of a door, footsteps, and panic caused her to try to pull herself loose from her bonds again.

"Ah, you're awake," he said.

The venom in his voice made Sasha tremble and stop struggling as his footsteps drew nearer. She wanted to ask him why he was doing this to her, but the tape across her mouth prevented it. Tears began to flow, soaking the blindfold, her chest heaving as she sobbed.

"Now, now, there's no need to do all this crying." He ripped the tape away from her mouth, causing her to jump and squeak in surprise. Her face stung once the shock faded.

"Who are you?" Sasha whined, turning her head in the direction of his voice. "What do you want from me?"

"I'm an angel."

She noted a change in his voice, an unexpected softness. "I thought angels were supposed to be kind and helpful. They don't kidnap and terrorize people."

"What do you know about it, devil worshipper? Sometimes angels do things that may seem cruel, but that is often the only way to bring God's justice upon those who defy Him. We must use whatever means we have to save your soul."

Her heart beat harder at his pledge to save her soul, no matter the cost. "Why would your god want to bring justice down on *me*, or to save *my* soul? I've done nothing to harm anyone."

"Because you are wicked. You and the other witches worship the devil. You must repent or be punished."

Her head throbbed again and her breathing became shallow with fear. Now Sasha understood. This religious fanatic had no understanding of her religion. Worse than that, this man used religion to give him an excuse to harm others. She knew enough about Christianity to realize he didn't even understand his own religion.

"I'm not a witch, and I don't even believe in the devil."

"Do not lie to me! I saw you dancing around the fires of Hell tonight, chanting and thanking some goddess."

He paused and Sasha heard him breathe in angry puffs. She felt his hot breath on her chin and smelled his perspiration and a hint of some sweet, cheap aftershave. Without warning, he ripped the blindfold from her head. She blinked from the sudden brightness of the sunlight peeking through the window. Then she saw his furious wild eyes and the sweat rolling down his forehead.

"If you do not confess your sins, I will have to bring justice upon you."

A flash of metal caught her eye and she screamed as a knife pierced her left thigh, spattering her own hot blood onto her face. "Please, stop! Don't hurt me anymore," she pleaded, her leg searing in pain.

"Then confess, witch, or you'll be put to death with your own evil instrument."

"You don't understand. I'm not a witch. I'm a Wiccan. We would never hurt any living creature, not even a blade of grass."

"Liar!" He plunged the knife into her right thigh.

Sasha screamed again at the excruciating pain. Warm blood flowed from her wounds down the sides of her thighs.

"I'm going to leave you to think about your fate. When I come back, I expect a full confession from you. When I get it, you will be set free."

Sasha closed her eyes and then heard the door slam.

"No," she screamed. "Don't leave me. Please! I'll do whatever you want, just don't leave me here alone."

There was no response from the man. He must have heard her. He couldn't have gone that far. She felt hot streams of blood continue to flow down the sides of her legs, pooling in the chair and soaking her skirt. Did he hit an artery? Would she be dead before he returned?

"Oh, sweet Mother of the Earth, help me!" Sasha shouted through her sobs of pain. She continued to scream until she was too hoarse to continue, and still no one came. Soon Sasha realized it was no use. She must be in a place where no one could hear her cries. Growing weaker by the moment, Sasha finally leaned back in the chair and gave up the fight.

Chapter 3

"I think it's right over here," said Zach, pointing to his left and walking a little faster through the woods.

April laughed, ran after him, and grabbed his arm. "I think you lured me out here under false pretenses."

"I suppose if we don't find the witches' den of iniquity, we could create our own." Zach started to grab her, but she was too quick for him.

"Oh no, you don't. We've got more hunting to do first. Didn't that friend of yours say it was near the creek?"

"He said it's a clearing about fifty yards from the fork in the creek." Zach squinted in a northerly direction and pointed. "There's the creek. If we follow it north, we should find the fork in no time."

Zack took her hand and led the way. He cleared their path of brush with his feet and held back tree branches so April could pass unscathed. Within ten minutes, they arrived at the water's edge.

"There's the fork," April shouted, her voice dripping with excitement.

Zach picked up the pace. When they reached the fork, he stopped abruptly and scanned the area. "I think we should head in that direction. See where the trees thin out?"

It took them hardly any time at all to cover the final fifty yards. When they broke through the last few trees and stepped into the clearing, Zach glanced at April. Her eyes were as big as saucers. Neither spoke at first. They merely looked around, taking in the strange scene. A fire pit stood in the center of the circular clearing. Leaves covered the area, but Zach found a line of rocks. He pointed them out to April and they both started to follow the line, clearing leaves as they went along. Soon they had enough of them cleared to see a pattern.

"This is a pentagram," said Zach. "It's a devil worshipper's symbol."

"Cut it out, Zach. You're just trying to scare me."

Serious and a little frightened, Zach frowned at her. "I heard witches gather at Halloween and do sacrifices around a fire. Look at this." He pointed to a rock formation. "This looks like some sort of alter."

"Damn it, Zach," said April stomping her foot. "Stop it! This isn't funny anymore."

"I'm not trying to be funny. I'm serious. I guess those witch rumors are true."

"I want to leave. This place is gruesome, and if you're right, it's probably cursed or something."

"Relax. It's two o'clock in the afternoon. These people only come out after dark."

"Screw you! I'm leaving."

Zach watched as April walked out of the clearing and back into the woods. As much as he wanted to stay and investigate, he saw her heading in the wrong direction. He let out a sigh, looked back at the site one more time, and turned to follow her. Before he took a step, he heard a blood-curdling scream coming from the path she'd taken.

"April!" he called, running towards the noise. He continued to call her name and follow her cries, ignoring the branches as they scratched his face and hands. He caught sight of his girlfriend sitting on the ground, shaking and sobbing.

"April, did you fall? Are you hurt?"

As he walked toward her, she put up her hands, panic on her face. "Stop! Stop! Don't or you'll trip over it, too." She pointed at the ground between them.

Zach cautiously walked towards the place April had indicated. There he saw a large pile of leaves and part of a human foot protruding from it.

He jumped back, his heart quickening. "Holy shit!"

"I thought it was a pile of leaves," she said, her voice trembling. "I wasn't paying attention and I tripped. I thought I'd caught my toe on a tree root. When I turned around, I saw that foot."

"It's okay, April."

"No, it's not okay! This is horrible. Do you think this was a human sacrifice?"

"I don't know. I didn't think witches performed human sacrifices. I thought they used animals." He walked around the body and offered his hand to April. "Come on. Get up off the wet ground."

He helped her to her feet and put his left arm around her, retrieving his cell phone with his right hand. "Alright, I have cell service here." Zach dialed 911 and held April close while she trembled and sobbed into his shoulder.

Chapter 4

Homicide Detective Chennelle Kendall arrived at the scene to find Patrol Officer Anne Samuels waiting just outside the crime scene tape. "Hey, Samuels, I haven't seen you for a while. How's it going?

"Don't ask, Detective Kendall," said Samuels.

"That bad?"

"Troubles at home, but not as bad as this poor soul." Samuels pointed toward the naked body of a woman Death Investigator Nate Spalding was examining.

Chennelle pulled out her latex gloves and put them on as she and Samuels approached the victim. "What we got here, Spalding?"

"White female. I'd guess her to be in her mid to late twenties. Whoever did this only covered her with leaves instead of trying to bury her. I've bagged the ones which covered the body for the lab. My guess, she was meant to be found."

"Any idea how long she's been out here?" Chennelle could see the body showed several nonlethal stab wounds, bruises, and burns—obvious signs of torture.

"Rigor's set in, and her liver temperature and lividity indicate she's been dead for less than twenty-four hours. I also found some maggot eggs already laid in the open wounds. If she'd been out here longer, those eggs would have hatched already. Of course, I don't think the victim was killed here."

"Why not?" asked Samuels.

Chennelle knew Samuels was getting ready to take the detective's exam and wanted to work in Homicide. She decided to guide her to an answer before Spalding said something flip and embarrassed the girl.

"Take a closer look at the body and surrounding area, Samuels." Chennelle allowed Samuels to move closer and waited a few seconds, watching her scan the woman from head to toe. "What *don't* you see?"

"No blood spatter in the area," said Samuels. "No pooling of blood around the body."

"Do you know what time it was when you discovered the body?" asked Chennelle.

"When I pulled my cell phone out to call 911, I saw it was 10:28," the boy responded.

"Did either of you see anyone else in the area?" asked Chennelle. Both teens shook their heads. "Are you sure?"

"We didn't see anybody, Detective Kendall," said Zach.

"We came up here because we heard a rumor that witches came here," said April, bursting into hysterical tears. "And it looks like it's true! Was she some sort of human sacrifice or something?"

April's terrified reaction stunned Chennelle for a moment. Where had the girl heard all of this garbage? She needed to assure them this was not the case.

"This could just be a campsite," Chennelle told them.

"I don't think so," said Zach. "We moved the leaves around the fire pit and looked. Someone made a pentagram with those rocks." He pointed at some smooth, rather large rocks set in a straight line.

"Even if it is a pentagram, statistics show even people claiming to be devil worshippers don't do human sacrifices," said Chennelle. She hoped this would diffuse the notion before these kids went back to their friends and had the entire northeast side in hysterics.

"At this point, we'd appreciate it if you would not discuss this with the news media or your friends," suggested Chennelle. "It will only cause panic."

"Don't you think people should be warned?" asked April with wide-eyed fear. "If these witches have decided they need to sacrifice humans, then people need to know not to come near this place."

"It looks like this woman was killed somewhere else and then disposed of here. I believe it's just a coincidence it was so close to this particular fire pit," said Chennelle. "Again, from what I've learned, witches and so-called devil worshippers don't perform human sacrifices. I'm afraid you two have watched too many horror movies."

April frowned at Zach then looked to Chennelle. "I suppose you're right. I probably let my imagination go crazy." The girl scowled at Zach again, indicating to Chennelle that she blamed her boyfriend for frightening her. "Do you have to tell our parents?"

"I'm afraid they already know," said Chennelle. "You're minors. The officers had to notify them and ask their permission to question you."

April moaned and walked away from Zach. Chennelle got the feeling this incident might be the end of their relationship.

"Can we go now?" asked Zach.

"As long as the officer has all your contact information, then yes," said Chennelle motioning for Patrol Officer Art Fleming. "I want Officer Fleming to escort you to your vehicle."

"I guess we don't have a choice." Zach looked up at Chennelle. She shook her head, giving him a reproachful look.

As the youngsters walked away, Officer Samuels approached. "Parelli has everything under control, and the body is on its way to the morgue."

"Once I get some photos from the CSI team, I'll start searching the Missing Persons database," said Chennelle. "I didn't want to tell the kids, but the Celtic tattoo on our victim's shoulder *could* mean she was involved in witchcraft. I know some of them hold to old Celtic customs. From what I understand, they celebrate Halloween like it's a new year's celebration."

"There are some partially burned logs in the pit," said Samuels. "Do you think our victim was here on Halloween, and then was grabbed before she could get to her car?"

"I think that's a good possibility," said Chennelle. "I'm going to need help with this investigation. Cases that deal with the occult are always a public relations nightmare. Barnes will be back from leave on Monday, and she's the best. I think I'll see if she wants in on this one."

"Is she doing okay?"

"Yes, she's doing really well. Barnes is a pro and knows the dangers of the job. Besides, it looks like she and Jacobs are back together. Love is always good for the soul."

"Sometimes," said Samuels, looking away.

"Down on love?"

Samuels blushed slightly. "A little. My husband, Aaron, can be hard to deal with sometimes."

"Sorry," said Chennelle, seeing the sadness in Samuels' eyes.

"Don't be. It will all work out. I do have two fantastic sons."

"There's always a positive side if you look hard enough."

Samuels smiled before turning at the sound of the search dog arriving. "I'd better get over there and help. Are you going to stick around?"

"Nah, there isn't anything else I can do here right now. I'm going home and send an email to Major Stevenson to ask if Barnes can be assigned to this case before he puts her on something else," answered Chennelle. "You go on...oh, and take care of yourself."

Chapter 5

"Hello, Grandmother," Doug said, walking in the front door, his arms laden with grocery bags. He saw her sitting in her easy chair watching one of her favorite evangelical preachers.

"It took you long enough," she growled, turning in her chair and glaring at him. "Or did you stop at some whore house along the way?"

"Of course not, Grandmother," he said, exasperated. "It's Saturday. The store was really crowded today."

"That's what your grandfather used to tell me." The look his grandmother gave him sent a chill down his spine. Then she turned her attention back to her television program. "Hurry up, it's already past noon."

"Sorry, Grandmother. I'll just put these things away so I can get started on your lunch."

"You do that. Make sure I get my medicine. I want some vegetable soup for lunch. You remembered to buy it, didn't you?" She turned her head again, eyeing him suspiciously.

"Of course I remembered it, Grandmother. You only reminded me twenty times before I left."

"Impertinent child," she mumbled.

Doug turned and rushed to the kitchen, hoping to avoid any further stinging comments. He pulled the groceries from their bags and quietly put them away. He would have preferred slamming the cabinet doors to rid himself of his frustration, but it would upset his grandmother, and her tongue would lash him more cruelly than ever.

If only Grandmother knew what he was doing to cleanse the world of filthy sinners, she'd be so proud. He would tell her all about it once he'd completed his mission.

"Where's my blessed soup?" she shouted.

"I'm fixing it now," he replied. After opening the can of soup, he poured it into a saucepan to heat on the stove. A microwave oven would be much quicker, but she wouldn't allow one in the house. His grandmother thought Communists invented them to radiate Americans so they'd all die from cancer. Doug was sure

Communists didn't invent the microwave and that many of them owned one, too. However, he knew arguing the point with her would do him no good. He must obey the Bible and honor her.

Once the soup gently simmered for a few seconds, he turned off the burner and poured it into her favorite bowl. Then he placed it on a serving tray with seven saltine crackers, a napkin, and a soupspoon. He took his grandmother's medications from the counter and placed them in a small dessert bowl. Blood pressure, cholesterol, blood sugar, water. He couldn't remember their proper names, but he knew them by what they were supposed to cure. A huge glass of water completed the tray.

"Here you go, Grandmother," he said, placing the ensemble on her wooden TV table and giving her his winning smile. Grandmother liked to eat where she could watch her programs. The television remained tuned into the evangelical religious channel all day and sometimes into the night.

"About time." Grandmother glared at him as she snatched up her spoon. "A person could starve around here with the likes of you to take care of them."

"Yes, Grandmother." He sighed and skulked back to the kitchen for a turkey sandwich. It was always best to eat alone and avoid Grandmother's many barbs. As much as he tried to ignore them, the pain was like a snakebite.

Soon it will be seven days, he thought, brightening his mood. After seven days, Doug could bring justice upon another sinner. Grandmother had often said the avenging angels needed to come and purge the world of the sinful. Sinners *were* becoming more abundant.

At age forty-seven, he heard the voice of God tell him this was his calling. This was why God had given him to this woman to train him up in the Word and why he must suffer at her hands. He would continue to cleanse and purge as long as his Master needed him. This was his destiny.

Chapter 6

"Anne," shouted Aaron Samuels entering the kitchen. "Where the hell is my debit card? I need some money. I'm goin' out with the guys this evenin'."

"How am I supposed to know where you put it?" Anne sniffed in disgust. She knew him better than that. He wasn't going out with his friends. Aaron was having an affair...not with a woman, but with a deck of cards. It would have been easier to deal with another woman.

"If you want gambling money, get a job," she said, glaring at him.

"Give me your debit card," demanded Aaron.

"No," Anne said forcefully.

"Then give me the cash in your purse."

"I gave you two hundred dollars on Wednesday, and this is only Saturday. Where did it all go, Aaron?"

"Expenses," he growled.

"What expenses? Booze? Poker?"

"I'm stressed," he countered. "I'm goin' out for a little recreation."

"Forget it. You've had your spending money for the week."

"Forget *you*, bitch," he said as he stormed out of the kitchen.

Anne turned back to the salad she was putting together. Looking out the window, she smiled at her sons who were playing catch in the yard. She was grateful they didn't have to hear this conversation. She tapped on the window, arousing their attention, and motioned for them to come inside. She and the boys were going to her parents' house for dinner this evening. Visiting with her mom and dad always made her feel loved and supported. They wouldn't ask about Aaron's absence because they knew. Michael, aged eight, and Justin, aged six, came flying through the kitchen, running to the back of the house to clean up. She didn't even have to tell them this time.

Anne looked up to the ceiling and asked God to help her. She'd only stayed in this loveless marriage for her sons. Boys that age needed their father, but did they really have him?

Chapter 7

"Good morning," said Homicide Detective Erica Barnes when Chennelle walked into the department. "I hear you requested my help with the female Jane Doe found on Saturday morning."

"That's right," said Chennelle. "I need the best, and that's you."

"You sure you're not getting stuck with the girl who lost her nerve?" asked Barnes.

"A mad man nearly killed you." Barnes' uncharacteristic lack of confidence surprised Chennelle. "I don't call taking some time off, losing your nerve. Besides, your father needed your help after his surgery."

"Thanks for saying that, Kendall. I'm not sure everyone agrees with you. I just hope you know I wouldn't come back to work if I didn't feel I was ready."

"Of course I do."

Chennelle had worked with Barnes in late May on the Emerson case. She'd often wondered if the killer had come after her instead, would she have handled it as well as Erica Barnes had.

"You went to southern Indiana to protect Mayhew's family from that nutcase a couple of months ago," Chennelle pointed out.

"All I did was enjoyed a mini vacation with them. Tyrone wound up the one in danger." Barnes shifted in her seat. "Well, looks like our shift supervisor has abandoned us."

Detective Brent Freeman and his girlfriend and county prosecutor, Natalie Ralston, had just departed on a two-week Caribbean cruise.

"He hasn't had a vacation for quite a while," said Chennelle.

"How much you want to wager they're engaged by the time they get back?"

"I only take sure bets."

Barnes laughed. "So, tell me about this Jane Doe case. I'm ready to sink my teeth into something."

"We think she's involved in one of those witchcraft groups," said Chennelle. "The body was found only about two hundred yards from a clearing where we discovered a stone altar and a pentagram made of rocks. Of course it's weird because we can't find any evidence she was killed anywhere near where we found her."

"What makes you think she's part of a witch's coven then? Couldn't the location be a coincidence, or could one of *the witches* have killed her?"

"Human sacrifice is off the table. There was no human blood found on the altar, which would be the obvious place to do a sacrifice. As a matter of fact there was no blood at all on it."

"And, our vic's a witch because…?"

"The victim had a tattoo of a Celtic knot on her shoulder."

"Oh, then she's probably not a witch, but a Wiccan," said Barnes, shrugging her shoulders.

Barnes' response surprised Chennelle. "I've heard of Wiccans, but don't know much about them or how they differ from witches."

"Wicca is more of a religion. They believe in a goddess who is part of nature. Their motto is to never do harm to any living creature and to keep nature sacred. They were probably the earliest ecologists."

"So they're not into doing spells?"

"I think they use candles and do some sort of spell work, but it's their oneness with nature that makes them different. I'm pretty sure the idea of Mother Nature is a reference to their goddess. We really should do more research on it if you think this could have something to do with her murder."

"Did I hear you two talking about our Jane Doe?" Their commander, Major Robert Stevenson, walked into the room. "By the way, Barnes, welcome back."

"Thank you, sir," said Barnes. "And, yes, we were discussing Jane Doe. We think there may be a subculture involved, perhaps Wicca or witchcraft."

"People are already stirred up about this," said Stevenson. "We just got word that a church group from the northeast side is having kittens over it. They've been after us for months demanding we disband this group of witches, and *stop their evil* from spreading."

"Great," said Chennelle. She knew that when religion became an issue, things could get sticky really fast. "Do you have the name of this church, sir? If Jane is a witch, or a…." She snapped her fingers trying to remember then looked at Barnes.

"Wiccan," said Barnes.

"Of course."

"Come with me," said Amber as she gestured for the detectives to follow her.

Windowless and very plain compared to the shop, Amber's office contained the standard five-drawer vertical filing cabinets, a desk, and three chairs. The bulletin board hanging above her desk featured several post-it notes, a calendar, and a few photos of what Chennelle guessed to be customers.

"Have a seat," Amber said, pointing to the two side chairs while claiming the desk chair for herself. "First of all, I don't think we've had the pleasure." She extended her hand to Chennelle.

"Detective Kendall," said Chennelle, shaking the other woman's hand. She sat down and opened her purse to remove the photos of Jane Doe.

"Amber," said Barnes, "I'd like for you to take a look at the photos Detective Kendall is holding and tell me if you recognize the person. I want to warn you, this woman is deceased."

"What makes you think I might know her?" asked Amber.

"She has a tattoo of a Celtic knot," said Chennelle as she showed Amber the photo of the victim's shoulder.

Chennelle saw the shopkeeper shake, as though a cool breeze had blown through the office. She glanced up at the detective, her expression one of obvious apprehension.

"This next photo is of our victim's face," said Chennelle. "Her skin color will be grayish, she's been washed clean of makeup, and her hair is combed straight back. Are you ready to take a look?"

Amber nodded and reached out to take the photo. She continued to look into Chennelle's eyes as the photo came to rest in her hand. Then she closed her eyes momentarily. As she brought the photo up toward her face, she opened them.

Gasping, Amber dropped the photo. She raised both hands to her face, covering her mouth, and cried out, "No, it can't be!"

Barnes jumped out of her chair and touched Amber's shoulder. "So you know this woman?"

Amber nodded, one hand still concealing her trembling lips, the other hand planted on her stomach. Chennelle felt sure the woman was about to vomit. Bending over, Chennelle picked up the photo and quickly put it back into her purse.

"I'm sorry, Miss McManus," she said. "I realize this is quite a shock, but we need to know the name of this woman. We want to notify next of kin and start working on a motive so we can find out who killed her."

Barnes rubbed Amber's back. "Put your head between your knees and take some deep breaths."

Amber bent over, breathing slowly in and out. Then her body began to shake and she began to cry.

Chennelle glanced over at Barnes, hoping she could get Amber to gain control. They needed that name and the names of anyone Amber thought had a reason to harm their Jane Doe.

Gabriella walked in looking concerned. "Amber, I…." She knelt down in front of Amber and took her hands. "What is it? What has happened?"

"It's Sasha…" was all Amber could squeak out before she resumed sobbing.

"Can you give us Sasha's last name," Chennelle asked quickly before Gabriella lost control as well.

Instead of crying, Gabriella stood up with a shocked expression on her face. "Winston," she said, and then sat down hard in the chair previously occupied by Barnes.

Chennelle decided Gabriella was more capable of answering questions at the moment. She let Barnes comfort Amber as she proceeded to pull a pen and notepad out of her jacket pocket. She wrote down the name of the victim."Gabriella, may I have your last name, please."

"Lopez," the woman answered. "How did this happen?"

"I can't give you details right now, but I can tell you that Miss Winston was murdered."

Gabriella closed her eyes and turned her head. Chennelle feared the woman would lose her focus. She had to talk fast.

"Miss Lopez, can you think of anyone who might want to harm Miss Winston?"

"Sasha was wonderful—funny, kind, always laughing. I can't think of anyone who would want to kill her."

"This is not happening," said Amber, her face soaked with tears. "We just saw her on Sabbat Samhain."

"What's that?" asked Chennelle, looking at her partner.

"Halloween," said Barnes. "It's a celebration of the harvest, right?"

"Yes," said Gabriella. "There's more to it than that, but I'm sure you don't want a lesson in Wiccan rituals."

something that night you thought of as trivial. For instance, the car you saw, Gabriella."

"We will," said Amber, her reddened face turning angry. "I want this bastard put away."

"So do we," said Barnes.

Chapter 9

Chennelle returned to the office with her partner and filed the proper paperwork in order to gain entry to Sasha Winston's home. She also looked up David Wagner's information and tried to contact him, but had to leave a voicemail asking him to call her back. While she was doing that, Barnes put out a BOLO on Sasha's car since it wasn't found in the parking lot near the crime scene.

Once they had the warrant, she and Barnes met Patrol Officers Gavin Lloyd and Angela Sanchez at the Franklin West Condominium Complex. They canvassed Sasha's neighbors before examining the condo. Those who were home said Sasha was a wonderful neighbor. None of them ever heard any kind of disturbance coming from her place. Luckily, they also found someone with whom Sasha had entrusted a key, so they could enter without damaging the door. Chennelle asked Officer Lloyd to continue to speak with neighbors while Officer Sanchez accompanied the detectives to Sasha's home.

"Let's glove up," said Chennelle. "We may want CSI to come out later if we find anything suspicious."

All three women entered the condominium, each moving in a different direction of the living area.

The furniture looked contemporary. A black leather couch accented with deep purple pillows stood against one wall. Multiple candles, several magazines, and tasteful lamps decorated the cherry wood tables. It certainly didn't look like the den of a devil worshiper as the Avenging Angels Church had implied.

"We're looking for clues as to friends, family—anyone who may have known Sasha," said Chennelle. "Try to find an address book, letters, anything that could help us. If there's a computer, we'll have forensics pick it up for the geeks to look over. I'll start in the master bedroom. Barnes, you take the kitchen, and Sanchez, you finish in here."

Chennelle entered the master bedroom to find a very feminine setting. The woman was really into purple. This seemed more like a room for a preteen girl, not a grown woman. A brass bed with a white ruffled spread and canopy with purple rosebuds took up most good night sleep tonight. This case is going to zap all of our energy."

"I couldn't agree more."

Chapter 10

"That knife you talked about is called an athame," said Chennelle as she scrolled through the information on her computer screen. "As you said, it's a two-edged knife used as a symbol of God and is used in various rituals like casting a circle—whatever that means. It's also used to cut on a spiritual plane, not a physical one."

"Wonder what the autopsy will tell us," said Barnes. "I wish we could have found more at the crime scene. He may have used her knife on her. Dr. Patel should be able to tell us if she thinks a knife like this could have made Sasha's wounds."

"If we find it, there would be no doubt," said Chennelle "I'm sure Forensics would find her blood and DNA on it."

"I can't find a knife for you, but I believe we have your missing auto," said Detective Trevon Adams from the Robbery Unit. "Your BOLO turned up a vehicle owned by one Sasha Winston being driven by two rowdy teenage boys. They aren't saying much to us, but maybe a couple of homicide detectives will loosen their tongues."

"Were their parents called?" asked Chennelle.

"Yes and both sets of parents are disgusted with the boys," said Adams. "This isn't their first scrape with the law. There will be a rep from DCFS with each of them. Dale Farnsworth is seventeen, he's in room two. Greg Keller is sixteen, he's in room one."

"I love a challenge," said Barnes. "Which one do you think will crack first?"

"My money's on the sixteen-year-old," said Chennelle.

"I would tend to agree with you," said Adams. "However, the seventeen-year-old seems more shaken up."

"I'll take Keller," said Barnes. "It's been way too long since I've been in an interrogation room. I'm ready to kick some ass."

Barnes took off for interrogation room one leaving Chennelle with Detective Adams. They looked at one another and Chennelle's heart raced just a little. His warm brown skin and intense dark eyes bored into her soul.

"How've you been?" asked Adams in a low soft voice. "I miss you."

"I'm fine, and I'd better get going," she said, looking away. "I've got a suspect to question."

She started to walk away, but he took her arm, stopping her flight. "Come on, Chennelle. Meet me for dinner after work. We can get past this misunderstanding."

Chennelle stopped melting and stiffened as heat rose in her face. She pulled her arm from his grasp and glared at him.

"*Misunderstanding?* So you're saying that I misunderstood the night I got off work early and came by to surprise you and got the surprise of *my* life."

He lowered his voice to a whisper. "No baby. That was a mistake. She don't mean nothin' to me."

Chennelle continued to glare at him. At that moment, she wanted to punch him in his lying mouth and break all his pearly white teeth. She looked around to make sure no one was listening to the conversation.

"Number one, don't you baby me, Trevon Adams. Number two, I obviously *don't mean nothin' to you either* or you wouldn't have slept with the bitch. Now, I'm going to go interrogate our joy rider and find out what he knows about my case."

Chennelle walked away from him knowing he was eyeing her backside. She felt like a fool because she knew he was a player before she decided to go out with him. Obviously, she fell into the same trap so many people do in relationships. She thought she'd be the one to change his wandering eye. This was something she'd warned her sister about and then she'd forgotten to heed her own advice.

Of course, Adams wasn't important now. Her case needed to be her main focus. Dale Farnsworth was waiting.

Chapter 11

As she stepped into interrogation room two, she could see what Adams meant about the kid. He was rocking in his seat, repeatedly placing his hands first in his lap and then on the table. The child services representative looked as though he was ready to slap the boy.

"Hello, I'm Detective Kendall. I'm here from Homicide."

"Homicide?" shouted Farnsworth. "We didn't kill anybody! We just found the keys and took the car, that's all we did. We was walkin' in the woods and found a bag with the keys in it. Then we found the car abandoned in the parking lot, so we decided to drive it around, that's all. I swear it. We didn't kill anybody."

"You might want to stop talking now, Dale," said his rep.

That was easier than she'd expected. She should have taken bets on how much time it would take to get the confession.

"Thank you for straightening that out for me," she said. "Your name is Dale Farnsworth, is that correct?"

"Yes," he said meekly after getting the nod from his rep.

"Okay, Dale. May I call you Dale?"

"Yes."

"What day did you find this bag and take the car?" asked Chennelle.

"We cut classes and went hiking through the woods Friday afternoon," said Dale. "Then when we were goin' back to my car, we saw this bag on the ground maybe a hundred feet from the parking area."

"What did the bag look like and what else was in it?" asked Chennelle.

"It was black canvas; something like somebody would take to a gym. Only it didn't have gym clothes in it, just a bunch of weird stuff."

"What do you mean by *weird*?" she asked.

"There was a short broom that looked like somebody strung it together. Then there was a stick that had ribbons tied on it, a pouch of colored rocks, a wallet, and the car keys. Oh, and some matches and a thing that looked like a tiny caldron, like you see in the movies only really little."

"Did you find a fancy knife?" asked Chennelle.

"No," he said, looking thoughtful. "We didn't find any knives in it. The only other thing in there was some wooden box."

"What did you do with the bag?" she asked.

"It's in the back seat of the car," he replied. "We only took the cash and the keys out of it and then threw it in the back seat."

"Thank you, Dale," she said. "You've been very cooperative."

When Chennelle stepped out of the interrogation room, Barnes and Adams were waiting for her. She'd really been hoping Adams would have gone by now.

"So much for Adams' judgment of character," said Barnes, giving him a look of exasperation. "The little dick lawyered up as soon as I stepped into the room. Said he wasn't going to say anything to the cops. How'd it go for you?"

"All I had to do was say *homicide*. The kid fell apart and gave me a detailed confession," said Chennelle. "He said they found her bag on the ground near the parking lot. Did your guys find a black canvas bag in the back seat, Adams?"

"They did. It's been turned over to Forensics."

"Did anyone find a knife in the car?" asked Barnes.

"Not to my knowledge," said Adams. "We didn't do much with the car. We left that up to the lab rats."

"Okay," said Chennelle. She gazed momentarily into Trevon's intense eyes. "You'd better get in there while he's still singing."

Chennelle walked past Adams, gently brushing his arm with hers. She nodded to signal Barnes to follow her, still feeling Trevon's eyes on her.

"What was that?" asked Barnes. "Is he still trying to get back on your good side after what he did to you?"

"Don't worry," said Chennelle, her facial muscles tense from trying to hide her feelings. "He can talk all he wants. He's not getting me back into his bed."

"Glad to hear it." Barnes' scowl gradually faded. "Are we heading for the morgue?"

"I think we'd better," said Chennelle. "Let's find out if our killer decided to use an athame on a physical plane instead of a spiritual one."

Chapter 12

Chennelle found the forensic pathologist, Dr. Padma Patel, with Sasha Winston on her table when they arrived at the morgue. After she and Barnes put on protective gear, they entered to find Dr. Patel examining the stab wounds.

"Hello, Dr. Patel," said Chennelle. "What do we know so far?"

"I found fourteen superficial stab wounds to the top of her legs and arms and the front of the torso. I would suspect the killer used these minor wounds to torture her. They would have been painful, but not life threatening," said Patel. "Then we have some deeper wounds on the thigh of both legs. These were very forceful, but nonlethal. Either blow could have caused her death had they come any closer to the femoral artery in either leg."

"So what was the actual cause of death?" asked Barnes.

"The killer took a large knife and drove it into the center of the victim's chest, breaking the sternum and plunging it directly into the heart. This individual must have been very strong to accomplish this, and the knife—or possibly a dagger—must have been made from very sturdy material."

"When I was doing my research, it said an athame is usually made of steel and is at least one-eighth-inch thick," said Chennelle. "The case for it was found in her bag, but the athame is missing. Can you tell whether it was a one or two sided blade that cut her?"

"The larger wounds make it harder to tell," said Patel. "Rarely does one pull a blade out exactly as it went in. However, the smaller wounds are sharply defined, so they seem more deliberate. The killer may have withdrawn the knife slowly since the bruising on certain areas of the arms, legs, abdomen and chest indicate she was bound very tightly."

Dr. Patel moved to a stab wound on the leg and spread it for them to see. "Take a look here. This wound is more jagged, so she probably jerked during the knife's insertion. However, this laceration on her shin—" She pointed to another wound located between the bruises on her knees and those on her ankles, "—indicates a smoother cut."

Chennelle looked closely. "So, could this have been made by a double edged blade?"

"I believe so," said Patel. "See how the ends of this wound are almost identically thin? This means the two edges of the blade were similar in design. If something with one sharp edge had been used, one end of the wound would have been thicker than the other."

"So this bastard used her own knife to torture and then kill her," said Barnes. She glanced at Chennelle. "Do you think he kept it as a souvenir?"

"Who knows what these nut jobs think." Chennelle felt a slight shiver, as though a cool breeze had touched her. "Of course, you would know."

"Yeah, but Emerson was delusional," said Barnes. "This guy is deliberate."

"Anything else we should know?" Chennelle asked as she turned back to Dr. Patel.

"The branding was definitely done post mortem," said Patel. "Also, the body was washed before it was taken to the woods. Once he stabbed her heart, there would have been an excessive amount of blood. She had to have bled out somewhere else and the blood rinsed off before she was moved."

"According to Mark Chatham, CSI found very little blood on the ground," said Chennelle. "They're testing it to make sure it belongs to the victim. They also believe she was dumped less than an twenty-four hours before those kids found her."

"Ah, yes, I would agree," said Patel. "There was very little insect activity and no wounds from animal bites. There's one more thing. When I cleaned under her fingernails, I came up with skin. I think she took a good DNA sample for us when he first grabbed her. I've sent the nail scrapings to the lab."

"Thanks, Dr. Patel," said Chennelle. "Time for Barnes and me to go have a little talk with the boyfriend."

Chapter 13

Doug left the coffee shop at 4:30 p.m., which gave him enough time to follow Toni Kelso home from her job at Benson's Jewels. He'd met her there a month ago when he stopped to have some links taken out of a new watch. Then he'd seen her among the other witches last week, and he knew God had sent him to Benson's so he would know how to find her when the time came.

He'd been very careful to make certain Toni's schedule didn't deviate from day-to-day. There was too much to do to be careless.

In his research, he'd found Toni to be single with no children. She had recently moved here from Los Angeles. He supposed the latter was a voluntary step closer to redemption as L. A. contained some of the most evil people in the world. At least, that's what his grandmother always said.

Apparently, very much a creature of habit, Toni pulled into her driveway at exactly 6:05 p.m. He wondered how frustrated she must be when anything changed her every day routine, such as road construction. It must drive her mad to be stuck in traffic. Of course, he'd only been following her for three days.

He drove past her house as her garage door closed. On the seventh day, Toni would meet the avenging angel. Doug would take her to his special place and use the blade he had taken from the first witch. It was the only thing he'd kept from her bag, which he'd regretted. Not thinking, he'd thrown the bag aside and it was gone when he took the witch back to the woods. He hadn't asked her name, but God would know it when she stood before Him.

Grandmother would question him if he came home late. Doug decided to stop at the store for her favorite ice cream. This would throw her off and he might even get a thank you for being so considerate.

He hurried home to find her sleeping in her chair, television blaring with thou shalts and thou shalt nots. Doug walked softly to the kitchen, hoping not to wake her. Perhaps he could get her dinner ready before she woke and realized he was late.

He'd barely had time to set the ice cream in the freezer when she started bellowing at him.

"Is that you, wretched child?" she screamed. "Where have you been and why haven't you made my supper?"

"I had to run an errand, Grandmother," he shouted to her.

"Likely story, young man."

The growl in her voice reminded him of an angry wolf. If not for the commandment, "Thou shalt honor thy father and thy mother," he might have abandoned her years ago. She could be so unpleasant. However, Doug knew he had to suffer in this life to obtain his reward in the hereafter, so he tolerated her personality, which seemed to worsen as she aged.

"I want that ham you promised me," she yelled. "Hurry up, I'm starving."

"Yes, Grandmother, it will be ready in just a few minutes." He sighed. All of the pain and humiliation would all be worth it when it was his turn to see the face of God.

Doug quickly warmed the slice of ham she'd requested. The leftover green beans and mashed potatoes were heated in less than two minutes and her meal ready in less than five. He put it on a tray with her evening medication and went into the living room.

Grandmother was rocking back and forth in her chair. "'Bout time, boy."

"I was a little late today because I stopped by the store to get your favorite ice cream for your dessert tonight."

"Really?" she asked, her eyes transforming into angry slits as she glared at him. "You could have called me to tell me you'd be late. There some harlot at the grocery who has your eye? It shouldn't take you an hour and a half to go to the store after work."

Not wanting to say something that might give her an excuse to continue to complain, he simply nodded. It was always best to agree with her whether she was right or wrong.

He sat quietly on the couch watching her eat and thinking about his plans for Toni Kelso. He supposed that a harlot had caught his eye, but not in the context his grandmother imagined. A harlot and evil devil-worshipping witch was on his mind. She was a glutton too by the looks of her. Gluttony was a deadly sin as well. Poor Toni had much to repent.

"Are you listening to me?" shouted his grandmother, pulling his mind to the here and now.

"I'm sorry, Grandmother. I was thinking about work."

"What's there to think about? You just stick some coffee in a coffee maker with some water and turn it on."

Grandmother truly didn't understand what an art it was to be a barista. Nor did she understand that this was a job where he could flex his hours to take care of her needs.

"Did you need something?" he asked.

"I need for you to take this blasted tray away and bring me some of that ice cream. May as well get a reward for waiting here starving while you run all over town."

"Of course, Grandmother." He took her tray and went back to the kitchen. He shook his head, smiling at what she'd just said. Sometimes her exaggerations were quite funny. In a roundabout way, he was sure she was saying thank you.

After preparing the dish, he took it to her, handed it off, and then kissed her cheek. She waived him off, but he could have sworn he saw an inkling of a smile.

"I'm going to go take a shower," he said. "I'll check on you when I get out and help you get ready for bed."

Her mouth full of ice cream, she simply nodded.

He walked down the hall and turned to look at her before he went into his room. Although she was harsh, he did love her. She *was* his mother, the only mother he'd ever known. He was sure she meant well; some day she would see her real reward for raising him and preparing him for his destiny.

Chapter 14

Anne Samuels blew out a breath and sighed. It had been a long day after very little sleep the night before. After the fight with Aaron on Saturday night, and then again on Sunday afternoon when he finally showed up at around two o'clock, she was exhausted. She'd called the neighbor to see if the boys could stay a while longer so she could stop by her parents' house. She'd made a decision and needed to talk it over with her mother.

Pulling up to the red brick house on Kessler Boulevard, she noticed her father with his leaf blower moving leaves into a pile. It was so loud; he didn't hear her coming and jumped when she tapped his shoulder.

"You tryin' to give your dad a heart attack, young lady?" he said, breathing heavily.

She threw her arms around him and he dropped his leaf blower. "I love you, Daddy."

"Hey, what's brought all this on?" he asked. "You all right? Everything okay at work?"

Anne was pretty sure he knew, but was giving her the opportunity to tell him only if she wanted to do so.

"I'm fine, work's fine," she said, giving him her best fake smile. "Is Mom home? I need to talk to her about something."

"Last I saw her she was in the kitchen bakin' cookies for my grandsons," he said. Then he took her by the shoulders and his hazelnut eyes bored into hers. "Honey, you know you can talk to me, too. If you need anything, and I mean anything, you let me know. Okay?"

"Sure, Dad," she replied, breathing a little deeper to keep her tears at bay. "I'll catch you on my way out."

"Try not to sneak up on me next time." He smiled at her and bent over to pick up his leaf blower. The noise immediately commenced.

Walking around to the back of the house, Anne noticed the last remnants of soft red petals clinging to a rose bush. She remembered the day they'd planted it. Anne and her brothers had given it to their mom for Mother's Day many years ago. She didn't appreciate her mom as much back then. It took becoming a mother herself to understand what hers was trying to do all those times Anne had felt so mistreated.

"I was wondering what made your dad take a break," shouted Mildred Francis Russell from the back steps. "Come on in here so we can hear each other."

Anne followed her mom into the house, through a utility room, and into a kitchen that smelled like heaven. The smooth aroma of brown sugar and chocolate made her mouth water. She stepped over to the cabinet and grabbed a small plate and a glass for milk. Then the timer went off.

"Let me get this last batch out and then we can talk," said her mom.

Anne poured herself a glass of milk and sat down at the old beat up oak table. She put two warm chocolate chip cookies on her plate, ate both of them and downed the milk before her mother could even turn around. She half rose, reaching for more, when her mother walked over and smacked her hand.

"You'll spoil your dinner," she said, motioning for Anne to sit down. "Now, let's get to what was so important you had to stop by here. And, by the way, cookies won't make it better. They'll just make you fat."

Anne nodded, feeling like a child again. She guessed she'd always be their baby. Her mouth had gone dry. Jumping up from her chair, she went to the refrigerator and pulled out a bottle of water. She could feel her mother's eyes on her as she returned to the table and sat down again.

"Mom, I've made a decision," said Anne, her voice cracking. "I hope you won't be upset. I know you and Daddy have been together forever, and you always taught me that marriage is a lot of work, but...."

Anne's voice didn't want to work properly. Taking a drink of water and then a deep breath, she continued without looking at her mother. "Things aren't working out very well at home. Aaron won't quit gambling. The boys are noticing his lack of concern for them. He's verbally abusive to all of us. I don't think it's good for them to live like that."

Hesitating, sure her mom would be upset if she actually said the word divorce, she dared to look up. To her surprise, her mother

"Like I told you," said Barnes in a louder voice. "You need to leave, *now*. No more smart-ass comments or I'll find a way to make an obstruction charge stick."

Roman gave Barnes the once over, sneered, and then headed out of the dining area. He grabbed his coat from the hall closet and slammed the front door behind him.

Chapter 16

"Nice guy, your dad," said Chennelle as soon as the dust settled from Roman Wagner's noisy departure. "Why don't you go wash your face and take a minute, and then we can talk?"

David nodded and walked to the back of the apartment.

"Geez, what a jerk," Barnes whispered. "I'm going to go over and see Pop and give him a big hug after this."

"Yeah, maybe I'll give my dad a call, too," said Chennelle. "I haven't talked to my parents for a while. I guess I'd better quit taking them for granted."

Moments later, David returned to the room slump shouldered and looking defeated. Chennelle felt sorry for him because he lost someone he loves and then gets nothing but more grief from a father who supposedly loves him.

"Where were we?" he asked.

"I think we should start with your accusation," said Barnes. "What's going on in this church you mentioned?"

"The Avenging Angels Evangelical Church has only been in the area for about five years. I was still in college at the time, so I only went there when I came home on breaks. I don't know exactly why my parents decided to switch churches."

"Go on," said Chennelle.

"My mom got breast cancer two years ago."

His pause and sigh were obvious signs that he didn't want to start crying again. Chennelle nodded to encourage him to continue.

"The church kept telling Mom and Dad that God would save her. Well, He didn't. My mom died a year later."

"And you blamed the church?" asked Barnes.

"No. I was pretty mad at God though."

"That's a normal reaction," said Chennelle. "This doesn't explain why you think the church had something to do with what happened to Sasha."

"After we buried my mom, I stopped going to church. That really upset my dad," said David. "Then one day, I attend this Earth Conference. I'm taking a break in the hotel coffee shop when in walks Sasha—the most beautiful woman I've ever seen." He paused and shook his head. "I'm sorry. I know I need to get to the point."

"We understand," said Barnes. "Her loss is still very fresh, but if you move up to where the trouble started, we'd appreciate it."

"Sasha was very honest with me. She told me right away about her Wiccan religion. I didn't really care, because I was falling in love with her. Then she told me about this new church that was protesting her....uh...."

"Coven?" asked Barnes.

"Yeah, that's it. They were protesting her coven's existence, claiming they were a bunch of devil worshippers."

"A lot of people don't understand the peaceful nature of the religion or the fact that they don't believe Satan exists," said Barnes.

"Right," said David, his voice rising. "I tried to explain this to my dad to see if he could get the church to lay off. That only made things worse. He started claiming that she'd *bewitched* me and now the devil had me in his clutches." David's laugh was marred by pain.

"Can you give us a location for this church and maybe the name of the pastor?" asked Chennelle.

"I sure can. The pastor's name is Jeremiah Green. I don't have the exact address, but it's located not too far from Geist. I'm sure they're listed in the phone book or on the Internet."

"Not a problem," said Barnes. "We'll locate them. Thanks for your help, and I'm very sorry for your loss."

"Thank you, Detective," said David. "Just find out who did this. Sasha didn't deserve to die like that."

"We will, Mr. Wagner," said Chennelle as she rose to leave. "You give us a call if you think of anything else we should know."

"No problem," he said, handing the detectives their coats.

When they were on the other side of the door, Chennelle looked at Barnes and said, "This is going to be a public relations nightmare, you know."

"When it comes to religion, everyone gets involved," said Barnes. "It *can* get ugly."

"Well, let's hope our fabulous PR sergeant can handle this nightmare for us, because I'm not looking forward to this one."

Chapter 17

Chennelle yawned as she poured her first cup of coffee for the day. She'd overslept, so there was no time to have a decent cup at home. This would have to do. Not a good start to a day she already dreaded.

"Good morning," said Barnes cheerfully, grabbing a cup.

Chennelle peered at her. "Have a good night?"

"I don't kiss and tell." Barnes poured the brew and crinkled her nose. "If this stuff gets any thicker, it'll be espresso."

"You're not trying to change the subject, are you?"

"Of course, not," said Barnes, taking a sip and wincing.

"Doesn't matter. Just don't ever take up poker as a profession because your feelings are written all over your face."

"I can put on an unemotional face when the need arises. I'm sure you'll agree when you watch me question Reverend Jeremiah Green. I just hope Meghan's prepared for the fallout from this case."

"I sent her an email this morning warning her, but I'm not worried. Sergeant Baxter is great at public relations." Frowning, Chennelle leaned back against the counter and sipped her coffee.

"What are you thinking?" asked Barnes.

"It's not so much thinking as dreading," Chennelle responded. "I called Reverend Green after I got home last night. I made an appointment for us to see him at 10:00 this morning. There's something about him that's...I don't know...eerie."

"Does he sound like Vincent Price or something?"

"Barnes, you crack me up."

"Yeah, I'm hilarious. So what's so *eerie* about this guy?"

"I just have the feeling we won't get any straight answers. He's charming...you know the type. It's like he could talk just about anybody into doing anything."

"A psychopath?" said Barnes.

Chennelle shook her head while smiling at Barnes. "I don't think I'd go that far, but there is a resemblance."

Barnes cocked her head to the side, one eyebrow raised as she gazed at Chennelle.

"I know I'm not explaining myself very well," said Chennelle. "It must sound crazy."

"It's woman's intuition. A girl's best friend…if we listen to it."

Chennelle pulled her lips down in a grimace. "I hear what you're saying. Every time I ignore that *little voice*, I live to regret it."

"Well then, let's sit down and prep for this interview," said Barnes. "It's going to be a doozy."

Chapter 18

"Doesn't look like much, does it?" said Barnes as she pulled into the parking lot of the Avenging Angels Evangelical Church. "Looks more like a garage."

"I heard it was a small place. Maybe it's all they can afford," said Chennelle. "Looks like the house is in the back."

She pointed to a small bungalow-style home that couldn't have more than two bedrooms. It was red brick with pots of mums lining the sidewalk leading from the driveway to the front door.

Barnes parked the car and grinned at her partner. "Well, here goes nothing."

When they exited the vehicle, Chennelle noticed the front curtain move as though someone had peeked out at them. She was correct because the front door opened before they reached it. There stood a very thin, gray-haired woman. She couldn't have been more than fifty-something, yet she dressed as though in her eighties. Her frumpy housedress and apron gave her the appearance of a country wife.

"Are you Mrs. Green?" asked Chennelle.

"Yes, and you must be Detective Kendall," she said.

"This is my partner, Detective Barnes. We have an appointment to speak with your husband this morning."

"Oh, yes, I know all about it." The woman's voice came across as sweet as honey. "Won't you come in? I've made coffee and baked homemade cookies for you."

"Thank you," said Chennelle, glancing at Barnes. Chennelle assumed this lady didn't get out much or have many visitors. She was much too anxious to please.

"Have a seat on the couch, Detectives, and I'll tell the Reverend you're here."

When she disappeared down the hallway, Barnes turned to Chennelle. "She calls him the Reverend? I'm all for respect, but holy crap, this is a little out there."

"I know what you mean," Chennelle whispered. "Reverend Green must run a tight ship."

Both Detectives sat up straighter and stopped talking when heavy footsteps sounded in the hallway. In walked a gray haired, gray bearded man, stocky in appearance and bespectacled with stark black glasses that made his features appear harsh. His wife followed him. Chennelle rose and Barnes followed suit.

"Reverend Green, this is Detective Kendall and this is Detective Barnes," said Mrs. Green with a sweeping hand motion, as though they were prizes on a game show. "I'll go get the refreshments." She bustled off to what Chennelle assumed was a kitchen.

"Ladies, please be seated," the reverend said in a commanding voice.

They sat back down on the couch while he took the armchair across from them, staring at them in silence. Chennelle began to squirm, uncomfortable under his gaze. She'd known this wasn't going to be an easy interview, but you'd think a preacher would be more polite.

After a moment or two, Reverend Green spoke. "You said you had a matter of great importance to discuss. How can I help you?"

"As I explained to you on the phone, a woman's body was discovered in the woods near Geist Reservoir," said Chennelle. "This person was part of a Wiccan coven."

"Ah, yes," said Reverend Green. "Roman Wagner called me to tell me of this tragedy. His son was…involved with her."

Chennelle gave Barnes a quick glance before continuing. "I met Mr. Wagner when we visited his son's apartment to ask a few questions. He seemed quite pleased that Sasha Winston was dead."

"I think you misunderstood," said the reverend. "Granted, Roman is a very passionate person. After losing his wife to cancer, his whole life began to revolve around David and the church. He was terrified when David took up with this woman."

"According to David, Sasha had never tried to sway him towards her religion," said Barnes.

"But we all know that when someone falls in love, the object of his or her affection has a good deal of influence on future decisions. Since he was in love with Sasha, David might have converted to her…*religion*…to please her."

"Here we go," said a cheerful Mrs. Green, carrying a heavy looking tray into the room. It held a silver coffee urn, sugar bowl and creamer, and three china cups. "Please help yourselves,

Detectives. I baked those sugar cookies early this morning just for you. Here let me pour. What do you like in your coffee, Detective Kendall?"

Chennelle gave Mrs. Green a smile. "We both take our coffee black, Mrs. Green."

"You must try some of my cookies, too," Mrs. Green said, handing a cup of coffee to Chennelle.

"My dear," said the reverend. "These young ladies did not drop by for breakfast. They have a job to do."

Mrs. Green looked abashed. Her cheery smile faded and her gaze fell to the floor as she nodded. She quickly poured coffee for Barnes and the reverend, adding sugar and cream to the cup she handed to her husband. Afterwards, Mrs. Green stood behind the reverend's chair as though waiting for further instructions.

"Thank you, Mrs. Green," said Chennelle. In defiance of Reverend Green's putting his wife in her place, she took a bite of cookie and then placed the remainder on her saucer.

"It has come to our attention that you and your followers are very well aware of the Wiccan coven," said Barnes. "We were told that you've been calling our headquarters with complaints against these women."

"Our church has only been here for a few years. In that time, members such as Roman Wagner have become very concerned about the devil worship happening in the community. We became even more concerned when Roman's son became involved with one of them."

"We're going to need names, Reverend Green," said Barnes. "Someone left a message on this woman indicating this is a religious vendetta. We need to speak with everyone who has displayed animosity toward these women."

"Devil worshippers," he said. His words were like ice.

"A human being is dead, Reverend," said Chennelle, becoming more irritated by the minute. "No matter what you think of her religion, Christianity teaches that murder is a sin."

"I really don't see how my giving you the names of our parishioners will help. All our members are wonderful and faithful Christians. They would not have handled this problem by killing."

"Then there's nothing to worry about, is there?" Chennelle noticed that Mrs. Green was looking quite nervous. "We believe

Sasha Winston was killed October thirty-first or November first. Can you tell us your whereabouts during those two days?"

Reverend Green stood abruptly. "How dare you imply I had anything to do with this!"

Chennelle raised an eyebrow at Barnes, then stood up with Barnes following suit. Mrs. Green looked terrified.

"We didn't accuse you of anything, Reverend," said Chennelle, trying to keep her temper in check. "However, we do have to be thorough. Eliminating suspects is as much a part of the job as finding them."

"He was with me those two days," said Mrs. Green. "On the thirty-first, we did our weekly hospital visits. On the first, the reverend was in his study working on his Sunday sermon. He was in there all day, except for meals of course."

"If that's all, I'm a very busy man," her husband said through pursed lips.

"What about that list?" asked Barnes as she handed him her business card. "You can send it to us via email if you like."

He snatched it from her, turned, and walked down the hallway.

The three women stood in silence for a moment, Mrs. Green watching the hallway. She turned to the detectives.

"I'm so sorry," she whispered. "He's been a little stressed out lately. He's really a very nice person…deep down."

"Don't worry about it, Mrs. Green," said Chennelle. "We've had worse conversations."

"I bet you have," Mrs. Green responded, regaining some of her cheerfulness. "Would you like to take some cookies back with you? The reverend doesn't need to be eating them."

"Sure," said Barnes. "Shall we wait here?"

Mrs. Green nodded. She rushed to the kitchen and returned with a storage bag full of cookies. She must have already had them packaged to go.

"Thank you," said Chennelle as they approached the front door. Then she gave Mrs. Green one of her cards. "If you ever need someone to talk to, give me a call."

Mrs. Green smiled and nodded.

When Chennelle saw that Mrs. Green had closed the door, she turned to Barnes. "What a jerk. You'd think a preacher would be more cooperative."

"Most of them are," said Barnes. "Thing is, preachers are humans, too. They have the same flaws as other people. Not sure how guys like him can talk about the things Jesus stood for one minute and be hateful the next."

"The Jesus I know wouldn't act like that," said Chennelle.

"Precisely."

Chapter 20

It took Chennelle's best efforts not to gasp when she saw Lucas Knight. Balding and gray, Knight sat bent over in his wheelchair, frail and non-threatening. She wondered why his neighbor had been so anxious to give them the impression that Knight was harassing her victim.

Chennelle glanced up at the camera. Barnes was watching the video feed on her computer and Chennelle wanted to make sure the camera's green light was on. It was.

"I'm Detective Kendall, and you are Lucas Knight?"

The feeble old man slowly raised his head and frowned at her. His gray, bloodshot eyes stared at her momentarily before he spoke. "Yep."

Chennelle switched her attention to the forty-something, blue-eyed blond woman sitting next to him. "I understand you're his daughter."

"Yes, my name is Jennifer Black. I'm not sure why you needed to speak with my father. He couldn't have had anything to do with that poor girl's murder."

"I understand your confusion, Ms. Black..."

"Mrs. Black...."

"What difference does it make, girl?" said Knight, suddenly springing to life. "Call her Jennifer and you won't have to worry about all that crap."

Chennelle looked at Jennifer, whose face had flushed with embarrassment. She nodded her assent and the detective continued.

"Jennifer, we always talk to people who may have known the victim, especially neighbors. They may have seen something or someone we need to look into in order to get a complete picture. Knowing the victim is very important in discovering who may have killed her."

"Okay," said Jennifer. "Are you up to this, Father?"

"Hell, yeah I am. Stop treatin' me like an invalid."

Lucas Knight certainly did nothing to dispel the grumpy old man stereotype. Chennelle hoped her parents wouldn't take on this personality in a few years.

"Mr. Knight, we understand that your condominium is across the street from the one owned by Sasha Winston. Did you know her?"

"Yep. She was a pretty little thing. Brought me some herb tea once, said it'd help my arthritis. It worked, too."

He paused, his features dropping into sadness. This wasn't at all the expression of a man who would have treated Sasha Winston badly. Quite the opposite, he seemed to be quite fond of her.

"Did you see her very often?"

"Used to until Miss High and Mighty here and her husband told her to stay away."

"Why would you do that, Jennifer?" asked Chennelle.

Jennifer glared at her father and adjusted herself into a straighter, more defensive sitting position.

"That girl was giving him all sorts of home remedies—teas, incense, and some sort of rocks that were supposed to cure what ailed him."

"And they was workin', too," shouted her father.

"Those things weren't working. She was brainwashing you," said Jennifer, visibly upset. "He stopped taking some of his medications."

"Poison, you mean," said the old man.

Jennifer closed her eyes long enough to have counted to ten. She took a deep breath and looked more composed when her eyes opened.

"This woman was convincing my father that his medications were not good for him. I asked my husband to do a background check on her and found out she's into some sort of New Age religion."

"Wiccan," said Chennelle.

"That sounds right," said Jennifer. "My husband and I belong to a church in the area."

"Idiots," said Lucas.

Jennifer again closed her eyes briefly, but then continued. "My husband and I spoke with Reverend Green. He told us she was a witch and a devil worshipper. He said to keep Father away from her."

"Did you say Reverend Green?" asked Chennelle. "Are you a member of the Avenging Angels Evangelical Church?"

"I'm not arguing with you," Anne said firmly. "I'll call you when I know something definite."

Anne turned her back to him and started to leave, but he was on her in seconds. He grabbed her by the arm and roughly turned her to face him.

"You ain't going anywhere," he said. "I'm going out tonight. It's your turn with the kids."

"Let go of me, Aaron," said Anne in her most authoritative voice. "This is an emergency. I have to go. Now, for the last time, let go of my arm."

He let go, pushing her into the wall. "Fine, go then." Turning, he went back to his chair and commenced his drinking.

Hoping that the shouting didn't disturb Michael and Justin, she decided to take a peek in their rooms to make sure they were still doing their homework. They were, thank goodness.

"Hey, guys," she said, drawing their attention to her. Trying not to look upset, she said, "I have to go to the hospital. Grandpa's been in a car accident."

Justin's mouth dropped open and his pencil fell from his hand.

"Is he going to be okay?" asked Michael.

"They're doing surgery on him right now, so I hope so. Grandma's really upset right now, so I'm going to go stay with her until he comes out of the operating room. I need for you to be my little men now."

Both boys jumped to their feet and threw their arms around her. It was all she could do not to start crying.

"I need for you to finish your homework. Then, take your baths and get ready for bed. Try not to bother your dad."

"Okay, Mommy," said Justin, his big brown eyes searching hers.

"That's my man," she said and hugged him again. "Now, please go to bed on time, even though it might be hard to fall asleep. I'm not sure how late I'll be, but I'll check in on you when I get home."

"I won't let you down, Mom," said Michael.

Anne kissed her sons and escaped their view before the tears started to flow. She grabbed her keys, purse, and coat and left for the hospital. Her only prayer was that she made it there in time.

Chapter 22

Chennelle felt a wave of weariness as she turned the key in her door. Starting the day with the nasty reverend, then watching Anne Samuels' suffer the pain of a failing marriage was enough to exhaust anyone. However, her day hadn't ended there.

She and Barnes were having a difficult time contacting the church members the reverend provided to them. She wondered if he'd contacted them first and suggested they not speak to her. She had a feeling Charles Black was the type who'd have a lawyer in tow. With nothing but Lucas Knight's allegations about a son-in-law he obviously couldn't stand, they had nothing to hold him on. Of course, he'd be smart to give them his alibi, and a good attorney would advise him to do so.

Deciding there was no need to dwell on a day that was slowly fading away, she tossed her keys on the end table and hung up her coat. Then she grabbed a bottle of Chardonnay from the kitchen on her way to her garden tub. She would soak away her troubles with bubbles and candlelight while sipping wine and listening to her favorite soft jazz music.

She was listening to the soft sounds of Al Jarreau while preparing for her stress-free evening when her cell phone started ringing. "Please don't let it be work," she said aloud.

Looking at the caller ID, she grimaced. It was Trevon Adams. No way was she answering any of his calls tonight. He just wanted something he couldn't have. The minute she gave in to him, he'd go looking for another conquest. If he kept calling her, she'd have to go to Major Stevenson and file a complaint. She really didn't want to do it, because the minute you filed a harassment complaint, people started acting as though you're the one who's done something wrong. If he'd only do something in front of a witness, it would be so much easier.

The phone stopped ringing and the bubbles were growing. Chennelle popped the cork on her Chardonnay and poured. That first sip delighted her tongue and tickled on its way down her throat. She set the glass on the edge of the tub, turned off the water, and stripped off her clothes while swaying to the music. After lighting the candles, she turned off the overhead light and slipped her right foot into the tub. It was perfectly hot. The smell of lavender filled her nostrils as she pulled in her left foot and sank into the tub.

"What could be better than this?" she said as the heat filled her tired muscles with relief.

Then it happened again. Her cell phone began to ring. "Son of a...," she growled as she grabbed her phone from the tub side shelf.

"You need to stop calling me, asshole!"

"Chennelle?" said the small, sweet voice of her mother.

She couldn't believe she hadn't looked at the caller ID this time. "Sorry, Mama. Trevon is trying to get back into my good graces."

"I see."

Her mother went silent for a moment. Chennelle knew there was some thinking going on whenever there was silence. "Mama?"

"Yes, dear."

"Did you have something you wanted to talk about?"

"Of course I did," she said in a rather testy tone. "Your father and I will be celebrating our fortieth wedding anniversary next month. Your sister wants to have a big to do, but your father isn't too happy about it."

"I thought Papa loved having big family gatherings."

"Big *family* gatherings, yes. However, Saundra wants to have it at some big venue and invite the whole world."

"Oh," said Chennelle, guessing that her running interference between Papa and Saundra was about to be requested of her.

"Can you talk to Saundra? She'll listen to you. We just need her to tone it down a bit."

"Who's paying for this party?"

"She says you and your brother are helping her, because you are all our children and should show us the respect we deserve by throwing a great event."

"In that case, I'll get on it. Don't worry, Mama. I'll find out what she has in mind. You know I can bully Carl into anything, so tell Papa I'm taking care of it."

"Thank you, sweetie," she said, relief in her voice. "I knew I could count on you. I'll talk to you later."

"Sure thing. Love you."

"Love you, too," said her mother before hanging up.

Chennelle set her phone aside and immersed herself in bubbles again. She took a huge swig of wine and tried to relax. After some dinner, she would call Saundra. Her sister's husband was an attorney and they had plenty of money, but she and Carl weren't quite that lucky. Carl worked for a construction company and made a good wage, but had three children and a wife. He didn't have the kind of money Saundra wanted to spend.

"Family," said Chennelle as she raised her glass as though toasting them. "Can't live with them, can't shoot them."

Chapter 23

Anne studied her mother's worried face as she sat at the end of a rather uncomfortable couch in the surgery waiting room. When Anne arrived over an hour ago, the prognosis didn't look good. Most of her father's ribs were crushed, and there was a lot of internal bleeding. They said his heart wasn't touched, but they were afraid his lungs and other vital organs could be damaged. They definitely needed to remove his spleen.

"Hey, Sis," said Grant as he and Jeff came in from getting coffee. "Two creams, two sugars, just the way you like it."

Anne took it gladly. Being the eldest, Grant always seemed to be the one holding everyone up in a crisis. Jeff, on the other hand, was always the prankster. He gave their parents fits when he was growing up. However, tonight Jeff seemed very reserved and mature. He held a cup of coffee out to their mother, who shook her head.

"I'll just set it here on the table in case you change your mind," he told her.

Anne closed her eyes momentarily, thinking about what she'd almost done before receiving the phone call about her dad. After Aaron's reaction to this situation, she knew she'd have to go through with the divorce just as soon as she got through this current crisis.

She opened her eyes when she heard someone new enter the waiting room and call out her mother's name. He was tall, freckle-faced, and dressed in green scrubs. Anne stood quickly and joined her brothers alongside their mother.

"I'm Mrs. Russell," said her mother in a weak voice. "How is Peter?"

Anne could tell by the solemn look on the doctor's face that the news wasn't good. He came to her mother and knelt down in front of her, taking her hands.

"Mrs. Russell, I'm afraid we couldn't save him. He had too many internal injuries to survive. He was a fighter, though. He managed to live on the operating table for much longer than we expected once we got into his chest cavity."

Her mother sat there unable to speak. A blank look came over her face, as she seemed to stare through the doctor, not focusing on anything in particular.

The tears began to stream down Anne's cheeks as reality set in. She closed her eyes and tried to visualize him the way she'd seen him yesterday. He was happy and busy without a care in the world. Her father was gone. How could this be?

"So, doctor," said Grant, his voice cracking, "what do we do next?"

"You'll need to call the funeral home of your choice and make arrangements to have him transported. They will help you through the process of getting paperwork, etcetera."

Grant simply nodded. Anne could see the pain in his eyes, but she knew he'd never break down, especially in front of their mother.

Jeff, on the other hand, got up and walked to the other side of the room wiping his face. Anne had never seen him lose his cool. She walked up behind him and rubbed his back. He turned to her, threw his arms around her, and started to sob into her shoulder. She buried her face in his chest and did the same. Two people lost in sorrow.

She heard the doctor tell her mother how sorry he was one more time before he left the room. Anne pulled away from Jeff, grabbed some tissues from the nearest desk, and shared them with him. Then she turned to her mother, who was still staring straight-ahead and unfocused.

"Come on, Mom," said Grant, taking her arm and trying to get her to stand. "There isn't anything else we can do here. Let me take you home with me tonight."

Their mother finally looked up into Grant's face. "I want to go home, to my own home. The one I shared with your father for over thirty years."

"I know, Mom. But you shouldn't be alone tonight," he pleaded.

"Looks like I'm going to be alone for a lot of years to come, Son. May as well start now."

"Mom," said Anne. "Please don't stay at the house tonight. If you do, none of us will sleep worrying about you."

Her mother sighed, which was a pretty good sign that she was resigned to give in to whatever Anne suggested, even if she didn't like it.

"Okay, I'll go home with Grant tonight, but I want to go home tomorrow."

"It's a deal," said Grant. "We'll stop by your place and get an overnight bag. Then I'll call Father John and let him know what's happened."

"I should have called and asked him to come," said their mother in a panic. "Your father didn't receive the last rites."

"Mom, this is a Catholic hospital," said Anne. "If they think someone is bad enough to pass away, they call one of their priests. I'll check, but I bet it was done before he went into surgery."

"Would you, dear? I'd feel much better if I knew." Her mother frowned. "I wish I'd called Father John, though. It was just such a shock."

"Don't worry," said Grant. "God's not going to keep Peter Russell out of Heaven because of a technicality."

"I guess you're right," his mom said. "Your father was a very devout Catholic. I'll see him again."

"That's right," said Jeff. "Now let's get you out of here so you can get some rest. I'll come by and take you to breakfast. Then we can all meet at your house and start talking about what you want to do for the funeral."

"We'll all be there," said Anne, patting her mother's arm. "Does ten o'clock work for everyone?"

The boys nodded, but Mom was back to gazing into space.

"Don't worry, she'll be okay," said Grant. "We'll see you at ten tomorrow morning at Mom and Da...Mom's house."

Anne nodded and left her brothers to convince her mother it was time to go. Once she told Aaron about the divorce, she would move in with her mom and take care of her. She and her sons would bring new purpose to her mother's life. However, it would have been better if her dad was there, too.

Chapter 24

"Let's talk about it tonight," said Barnes. "I like that place off Meridian. It's easy access to downtown."

Chennelle eyed Barnes patiently as she waited for her phone conversation to end.

"Love you, too. Talk to you tonight."

"Ben Jacobs, I presume," said Chennelle, grinning at Barnes. Erica Barnes and Sergeant Ben Jacobs had been an item for a couple of years now and were getting ready to make the big move. "Finally going to get that place together?"

"Looks like it," said Barnes. "I think Pop's been a little anxious to see us settle down. He wants to make sure I've *got someone* before he leaves this world."

"From my experience with your dad, he'll be around for a long time."

"You've got that right," laughed Barnes. "Since Mom passed away, I think he's been worried he won't get to experience walking me down the aisle or seeing any grandkids."

"Who's walking down the aisle?"

Chennelle turned to see Trevon Adams coming from the back of the room. "Nobody," she said stiffly.

"No need to be hostile," said Adams, throwing up his hands defensively. "Since I've heard you've taken an interest in Patrol Officer Samuels, I thought you might want to know that her father was killed by a drunk driver last night."

Chennelle's chest constricted and she looked away. She couldn't help but feel a surging anger as she thought about how much this woman was already going through. Now to lose her father in such a senseless manner....it wasn't right.

"Did they catch the driver?" asked Barnes.

"Yeah," said Adams, disgust in his voice. "Some rich bitch from Carmel who'd had a few drinks with friends after work. They were on 96th Street when she crossed the yellow line right into him. Of course, as with most drunks, she came out with only minor injuries."

"They've arrested her, haven't they?" asked Chennelle.

"Not yet. They're taking their time, but I'm sure they will. Just because he was retired didn't make him less of a cop," said Adams.

"Damn straight," said Barnes, an angry frown creasing her brow.

Chennelle stared into the distance, not sure what to do for Anne. She could hear Barnes and Adams speaking indignantly, but didn't comprehend what they were saying. Her only concern was for Anne Samuels. Between the husband and now losing her father, how was the poor thing going to study and pass her detective's exam.

"Okay, you two," said Chennelle, snapping back to the moment. "Barnes and I have a murder to solve. I'm sure we'll hear something about arrangements later."

"Okay, just thought you'd want to know." Adams turned away, looking like a hurt puppy, and walked towards the Robbery Division.

"I think you hurt his little feelings," Barnes whispered.

"He'll get over it," said Chennelle. "What's up next on our agenda?"

Before Barnes could answer, Sergeant Meghan Baxter walked up to them.

"The preacher you two interviewed yesterday is here with a few of his flock. They want to talk to you as a group."

"Are you freakin' kidding me?" asked Chennelle. "We don't do group interviews."

"That's the only way they'll talk to you," said Baxter.

"Where are they?" Chennelle puffed out a long breath in exasperation. This coming on top of the news she'd just received about Samuels was not the way to start the day.

"I put them in the large conference room on the third floor," said Baxter.

"There are that many of them?" asked Barnes.

"The preacher, his wife, and five parishioners." Baxter paused. "I think I should be in there with you."

"Sounds like a good idea," said Chennelle. "The more witnesses we have to this conversation, the better. Besides, you handle pain-in-the-butt people all of the time. I'm sure you'll keep Barnes and me in line."

Baxter laughed. "That's what I do best. Let's get this over with and hope for some useful information."

Chennelle and Erica rose from their desk chairs and followed Baxter to the elevator. Rolling her shoulders, which were already stiff with tension, Chennelle realized today wasn't going to be any better than yesterday.

Chapter 25

When they entered the conference room, Chennelle recognized three people—Reverend and Mrs. Green, and Roman Wagner.

"Hello again, Reverend Green," said Chennelle. "I'm sure you remember Detective Barnes, and you may have briefly met Sergeant Baxter from the Public Relations Office. Good morning, Mrs. Green." With a nod in Wagner's direction, she continued, "I met Mr. Wagner at his son's home a couple of days ago."

Mrs. Green rose quickly. Apparently, it was her job to do introductions. "These are our church board members. To my immediate right are Mrs. Nora Putnam and her son Curt Putnam. Across the table from me are Mr. Jack Calder and Mr. Charles Black." Mrs. Green sat back down just as quickly as she'd stood, her duties complete.

Chennelle's eyes focused on the infamous Mr. Black. She'd be doing some one-on-one with him later.

"We want to get this done as quickly as possible," said Reverend Green gruffly. "These folks are very busy. They are aware of the situation with these...*women*...and are willing to speak with you openly about their feelings."

"We're very grateful for your cooperation," said Sergeant Baxter. "Of course, you all know that Sasha Winston was murdered and left in the Geist Reservoir woods this past weekend. No matter what her religious beliefs, she didn't deserve to be tortured and killed."

Chennelle saw Mrs. Green and Mrs. Putnam cringe at what they'd just heard. Perhaps they didn't realize the full extent of what happened before today.

"We would never condone this means of ridding the world of devilry. Then we'd be no better than they are," said Jack Calder. "We would talk to them and try to persuade them to see the light."

"That's right," said Mrs. Putnam. "No one deserves to be murdered. Although, I thought devil worshippers performed sacrifices and stuff."

"No, Mrs. Putnam," said Chennelle. "One thing you need to realize is that the religion these women are practicing isn't devil worship."

"Any worship other than to the one true God *is* devil worship," said Reverend Green angrily. "If you do not believe in God, you believe in the devil."

Chennelle did all she could to keep from showing her anger. Not having much of a poker face, she breathed deeply and began again.

"I realize you have your opinions on this subject, Pastor, but the people who practice this religion do not make sacrifices of any kind—animal or human."

"Hmph," said Reverend Green.

"Do any of you know of anyone who might want to physically harm these women?" asked Barnes.

Each person looked to the other, except for Reverend Green, who was glaring at Chennelle. Like a flock of sheep, it was as though they weren't able to speak without the shepherd's permission.

"Well, is there anyone in your congregation who might take the step of murder to rid the world of these so-called sinners?" asked Chennelle, her patience wearing very thin.

"I can't imagine anyone from our church doing such a thing," said Curt Putnam. "There are some folks who are really upset about those witches meeting in the woods. But kill them? I don't see it."

"What about you, Mr. Wagner?" asked Chennelle. "You seemed almost overjoyed that Sasha was dead when we talked to you at your son's place the other day."

Roman gave her a quick, sharp look that set her teeth on edge. He surely wasn't going to deny what he'd said that night. What was going through that prejudiced little mind of his?

"I was trying to get my son to see reason," he said at last. "He was grieving for someone who wasn't worthy of him. She was leading him astray."

"And you didn't decide to take matters into your own hands and *help* him by taking her out of the picture?" asked Chennelle, staring deeply into Roman's eyes.

"This is preposterous," shouted Reverend Green. "Roman Wagner is a fine Christian man who was concerned for his son's soul. He tried and tried to convince David that he was heading in the wrong direction, so why shouldn't he try to bring the boy back into the fold once she was gone?"

"Even fine Christian men are human and find themselves in situations where they might do something desperate," said Chennelle, now focused on the preacher.

Reverend Green's face turned beet red. It appeared he wanted to blast Chennelle again, but was thinking it through.

Baxter must have seen a blow up on the horizon, because she quickly picked up the conversation. "Okay, let's take a breath and take a look at this from the police department's point of view. We have a young woman who was tortured and murdered. A religious message, which we cannot disclose at this time, was left with the body. Your congregation has been known to oppose the activities of these women, so naturally the police need to talk to people who have been vocal about the *witches,* as you call them."

"I see what you mean," said Mrs. Green, surprising Chennelle since the woman rarely spoke. Even her husband seemed startled, but didn't say anything to her.

Reverend Green stood. "I think we're done here."

"First," said Chennelle. "I'll need for each one of you to give us a statement as to your whereabouts on Halloween, since that is the last time anyone saw or heard from Ms. Winston."

Reverend Green's face appeared to redden even more. His blood pressure must have risen to dangerous proportions.

"This helps us eliminate people from our suspect pool," said Sergeant Baxter. "Once we've checked your stories, then we shouldn't need to meet with you again."

"Well, then," Reverend Green huffed, "I don't see any reason why we shouldn't all cooperate. I don't want to put our congregation through any further heartache over this matter."

"Thank you," said Baxter.

One by one, Erica and Chennelle took down the statements of each person. They then dismissed them all, with the exception of Charles Black.

"Mr. Black, I'd like for you to go with Detective Barnes," said Chennelle. "I'll join you in a few minutes."

Reverend Green immediately confronted Chennelle. "What's the meaning of this? You've already taken Charles' statement."

"We have information suggesting that Mr. Black was spying on Ms. Walsh."

"You must be joking," he said.

"When it comes to murder, I never joke."

Chapter 26

On her way to the interrogation room, Chennelle spotted Barnes outside of number three talking to Major Stevenson.

"About time, Kendall," said the major. "I saw Barnes here bringing Charles Black up to question him. You should know, he's the mayor's nephew."

Chennelle rolled her eyes. She couldn't help herself.

"I know, Kendall. I don't like it either." Major Stevenson paced back and forth a couple of times before stopping, his eyes fixed on Chennelle. "You two need to go into the observation room. I'm taking this one."

"But, sir…," Chennelle started to say.

"Barnes has already briefed me on your conversation with his wife and father-in-law. I think I'm capable of handling the interrogation."

"Yes, sir," said Chennelle, stinging from his words. She and Barnes went to the observation room and watched as Major Stevenson settled in, placing a folder Chennelle hadn't noticed before on the table.

"Wow, I must really be in trouble to have the head of Homicide question me," said Black.

"Drop the smart ass remarks, Black. This is very serious."

"Alright, I didn't mean anything by it," said Black, raising an eyebrow. "I don't know what more I can tell you that your detectives don't already know."

"Oh, I think you need to explain why you would spy on our victim for your pal, Roman Wagner. We haven't heard your version of the story."

"His son was involved with someone Roman didn't like, so I said I'd watch her when we went to check on Lucas. It wasn't a bad gig. She was nice to look at."

"I thought I told you no smart ass remarks," barked Stevenson.

"Look, Rob, you know I'd never stoop to murder."

Hidden behind the one-way glass, Chennelle scowled. "He's not just the mayor's nephew, Stevenson knows him."

"Seems like that would give us an advantage," said Barnes.

"We'll see."

"Right now, I'm Major Stevenson to you and you're on a very short persons of interest list."

"Do I need an attorney present?" asked Black, the silly smirk fading from his face.

"I don't know, do you?" Stevenson leaned toward the other man.

"I wouldn't want Stevenson looking at me like that," said Barnes.

Chennelle agreed, but wasn't sure where this was heading. Although by now, Black had to realize how it would look if he didn't answer the question.

"The woman was dating my friend's son. He was concerned about what would happen to the boy's soul if he got serious about her. He just asked me to keep an eye out for David."

"Is that all?"

Black's jaw dropped and Chennelle could have sworn she saw a bead of sweat shining on his upper lip.

"Rob, you can't be serious," cried Black. "I'm a good friend to Roman, but I'd never do anything illegal."

Major Stevenson didn't say another word. He simply opened the folder and showed Black some of the crime scene photos, one by one. Chennelle noticed the photo with the brand wasn't there.

"What the...is this her?" asked Black. Then he began to wretch and Stevenson put the photos back in the folder.

The major got out of his chair and grabbed a trashcan just in time for Black to vomit in it instead of on the floor. He held Black's shoulders and looked towards Chennelle and Erica.

"He's not our guy," said Barnes. "He wouldn't have made it past the first stabbing without throwing up all over her."

"Yeah, but that doesn't let Roman Wagner off the hook," said Chennelle. "If anything, Black admitting he was watching Sasha Winston for Wagner makes for a stronger case against him."

The door opened and the major entered. Chennelle hadn't realized he'd left the other room.

"Here's your file, Kendall," he said.

"I guess you knew exactly how to get him to talk," said Chennelle. "I'm sorry about before, I...."

He held up his hand, silencing her. "Frankly, I'd have been a little concerned if you hadn't said something. Nobody likes to have someone else jump in on a case they've been working their butts off to solve—even if that someone is their boss."

Chennelle would have cringed at that last statement had she not seen Stevenson's impish smile. She'd discovered early on that this was a symbol of trust and encouragement coming from him.

"Carry on," he said, and left them.

Chennelle took one glance back at Charles Black, who was now red-faced and sweaty but no longer puking.

"You heard the man," said Barnes. "It's time to carry on."

Chennelle looked at her watch. "We have just enough time to grab some lunch and then head over to Barbara Dodson's house."

"Where do you want to stop for lunch?"

"I'm sure we'll find plenty of fast food joints on our way to the northeast side."

"We'll just stop when we get the urge," said Barnes.

"Okay then, let's start carrying on with our carrying on."

Barnes simply shook her head and led the way.

Chapter 27

Barbara Dodson had agreed to meet Chennelle and Erica at her home at 3:00 p.m. As they pulled into the long, circular driveway, Chennelle couldn't help but be a little intimidated by the size of the place. She stopped the car, put it in park, and looked at Barnes.

"I guess this is how the other half lives." Barnes smiled at her. "Can't wait to find out what they do for a living."

They exited the vehicle and strode up to the door. Chennelle heard a lovely melody announce their arrival when she pushed the doorbell. Moments later a stout woman opened the door.

"May I help you?"

"Yes," said Chennelle. "I'm Detective Kendall and this is Detective Barnes. We have an appointment to speak with Mrs. Barbara Dodson."

"She's expecting you. Come right this way." The woman stepped to one side to give them room to enter, then shut the door and passed in front of them. She led them to a living area with a floor to ceiling fireplace made of stones, and some of the plushest furnishings Chennelle had ever seen.

After the woman left them, Chennelle turned to Barnes. "Good grief. If I sit down on anything in here I may sink so low I'll never be able to get up."

"I guess there is something to be said for being too comfortable," said Barnes.

Chennelle walked towards the fireplace to examine the photos lined up on the mantle. One photo in particular caught her attention. There were several women in it all dressed in hooded capes. She wondered if these were the members of the coven. On closer inspection, she noted that one woman looked very much like Sasha Winston.

"Hello, Detectives."

Chennelle turned to see a woman in her early forties wearing a royal blue dress and heels. Her mane of shimmering auburn hair and pale flawless skin gave her a polished beauty. Her crystal blue eyes were striking and entrancing.

Chennelle pulled herself into the moment. "Mrs. Dodson?"

"Oh, I'm so sorry, how rude of me. Yes, I'm Barbara Dodson, and you are?"

"Detective Kendall, and this is Detective Barnes. We understand you own the property that includes the woods where we found a young woman who'd been murdered."

Barbara frowned. "Yes. That was Sasha Winston you found. I can't believe anyone would hurt her, she was so sweet and kind."

"Unfortunately, Mrs. Dodson, this happens much too often to very good people," said Chennelle.

"Please, call me Barbara. Do you think this has something to do with our religion?"

"We aren't sure at the moment," said Chennelle. She didn't want to disclose the fact the word *FORGIVEN* was branded on the victim's chest. "However, we would like to ask if you or any of your other members have received any sort of threat."

"I haven't, and none of my coven members have said anything about threats. So again I'll ask you, do suspect this has something to do with our religion?"

"There was a message left with the victim that we cannot disclose to anyone outside of those investigating this case," said Chennelle. "We have to explore all possibilities. It may have been someone she dated in the past who wasn't happy with the breakup. Someone she didn't even know could have been stalking her. That's why we have to talk to everyone who knew her, so we can get a picture of her life and discover who might have done this to her."

"But it is ironic that Sasha would be tortured and killed right after our Samhain ceremony, and then brought back and dumped near our ceremonial area."

Chennelle simply nodded. It was ironic, and also very possible the killer was sending this group a message.

"We understand a church group has been very vocal about your activities," said Barnes. "Has anyone from that congregation approached any of you?"

Barbara gave a snort of laughter. "They're harmless. I get a letter about once a month from their board, begging us to come back to God. There isn't anything threatening in these letters. I think they sincerely fear for our souls."

Chennelle and Erica glanced at one another. Chennelle knew most congregations were full of sincere, good people. However, every now and then someone who was already unstable would take the Bible and use it to fit his or her radical agenda. She had a feeling they were dealing with a person who fit in this category.

"I'm sure that's what they intended," said Barnes. "But there are people whose minds don't work that way. There have been many cases of unstable individuals who don't think their religious establishment is working fast enough to rid the world of evil. They use this as an excuse to take matters into their own hands."

"But we're not evil," said Barbara.

"We know that," said Chennelle. "But unfortunately, there are others who don't. They think you are witches and worship the devil."

"That's insane," Barbara said, sitting straighter and looking offended.

"Yes, it is," said Barnes. "The problem is that people don't take time to thoroughly study the religion they oppose. They usually go off what they've heard from others, starting in childhood. Then there are those who would commit murder for their cause. This type doesn't think like we do. They take what they've learned from other biased people and decide to use it as a mantra for a mission from God."

"From what I understand, their God would never tolerate such things," said Barbara. "Their Jesus came to Earth to show them that God was merciful and that we should treat others well."

"We could debate this for a long time," said Chennelle, "but for now, we need for you to warn the other members of your coven not to go anywhere alone. They need to be aware of the possibility that your group has been targeted."

"Are you serious?"

"Very serious," said Barnes. "We hope this isn't the case, but we'd rather make sure you're all aware of the possibility so you can take precautions."

"I appreciate that," said Barbara, pausing for a moment. She stood staring at the floor. "I'll call a meeting tonight to let them know."

"Excellent," said Chennelle. "Any chance you have those letters from the church?"

"No, I threw them away."

"If you get any more of them, please notify us right away," said Chennelle, rising and handing a stack of business cards to Barbara. "While you're speaking to your group tonight, ask them if they've gotten any threats. Many of us get that feeling of being watched and don't pay attention to it. Have them start watching for cars or strangers who seem to be everywhere they are. If members are being stalked, this will be a good way to find out. They should then contact us immediately."

"I appreciate you coming by today," said Barbara. "We will be more vigilant from now on."

She escorted the detectives to the door. As they heard it close behind them, Barnes said, "Aw, man. I forgot to ask her what they do for a living."

Chennelle lifted an eyebrow, smirking at her. "Google it," she said.

Chapter 28

It had been only a week since Samhain. Barbara Dodson felt it imperative to call the coven together before their scheduled Saturday meeting. They needed to discuss what happened to Sasha and to perform a protection ceremony. The basement was prepped with the usual necessities—athame, candles, bell, and broomstick. For good measure, she'd placed a sage stick in the small cauldron to light once all had arrived. They would burn it to ward off evil.

Barbara had just pulled on her emerald green robe when the doorbell rang. She'd given the housekeeper the night off, so she had to answer it herself. Deciding to be cautious, she peeked through the peephole and saw the faces of Carmen Cortez and Bella Fuller.

"Come in, my friends," said Barbara, holding the door open for them. As she turned to shut it, she saw four more women coming— Cathy Grindle, Maci Bradley, Victoria Barker, and Gabriella Lopez.

"Let's all go into the living room and wait until the others arrive." Barbara gestured to her right.

"Barbara, did those female detectives come see you?" asked Gabriella nervously. "One of them knew Amber when they were in high school. I just can't believe Sasha is dead."

Barbara put her arm around Gabriella's shoulders and pulled her into a hug. "Don't worry. Tonight we'll talk about how to stay safe. We'll burn the sage to push the negativity from our presence. We shall burn our black candles and ask the goddess for guidance and to keep us safe from unseen forces, our blue candles for hope, and the red for strength."

Gabriella's smile looked half-hearted. The doorbell rang again, but Barbara let Maci answer it. Four more robed women entered the room.

"It's time for us to start," said Barbara, glancing around the room. There were only ten others. "Where is Toni?"

There were shoulders shrugging, heads shaking, and much murmuring. No one answered the question, so Barbara walked away and dialed Toni's cell number. It rang until the voicemail message came on. She hung up and tried again. The voicemail came up again, but this time she left a message.

"Toni, we're already short one in our circle. We really need you, so please try to get here as quickly as possible."

When she returned to the room, Barbara could see ten concerned and frightened faces. "I'm sure she'll be here soon. Let's go down and make sure everything is ready. We'll wait another ten minutes. If she isn't here, we'll create the circle without her."

They all followed Barbara down to the basement. Not wanting to create a panic, Barbara gave each member a task. Her own stomach was churning. She hoped Toni was just running late. She asked the goddess to keep Toni safe.

Chapter 29

Toni Kelso awoke with her head spinning. She was sitting in a hard chair. Barely able to open her eyes, she felt herself sway to one side. She jerked up straight, having met some sort of resistance. Her vision blurred when she opened her eyes. There was a shimmering light to her right and a shadowy figure.

"Where am I?" she asked, slurring her words as though drunk. However, she didn't remember consuming any alcohol. "Who are you and what's going on?"

"I'm the one who's going to save you."

The male voice was deep and quiet. It was a voice she thought she'd heard before, but from where? Toni squinted in his direction. "I can't see you very well. What do you mean you're going to save me?"

"Actually, I won't be saving you, God will. I'm merely his instrument."

She squinted harder and shook her head, hoping it would clear up. Her vision began to improve a bit and she saw the glint of a blade reflecting candlelight. Opening her eyes wider, she stared at it, her pupils finally able to focus. A good look at the handmade handle brought recognition, and her chest constricted with fear. This was the athame that belonged to Sasha Winston.

"Where did you get that?" she asked, even though she already knew the answer.

"I found it on a witch."

"She wasn't a witch!"

"She...so you admit you knew the wicked soul who owned this blade?"

Anger and terror fought in her head. She wanted to throttle him, but was strapped to a chair. Her only concern at the moment was how to get out of this alive.

"Toni, I've been watching you for a while now. You go to the woods and meet with the other witches. You gyrate and pray to some goddess who isn't the true God. You've sinned and need to repent."

She looked into his cold gray eyes and felt a chill that made her shiver from head to toe. His expression was determined. Toni was sure this man wouldn't listen to her explanations of her religion. This guy must have gone off the deep end. Most Christians were very good to her; nobody she'd ever met before would have gone to these lengths to try to convert her.

"So, you know I'm a Wiccan. Then you'll know I love nature and I don't worship the devil or anything."

"You...," he said with a fearsome sneer before pausing briefly, "...you *are* a witch. You have broken God's laws and must confess. If you don't, you'll go to Hell."

Toni screamed as she felt the knife slowly enter her left hand. "Stop, stop!"

"Are you ready to confess your sins?"

"Why are you doing this to people? Jesus doesn't like it when humans harm other humans."

His startled expression took her by surprise. She could feel the warm blood from her hand seeping through her pants leg.

"You think you know what Jesus would do?"

"I've studied the Bible. Jesus treated his worst enemies with kindness."

"So you believe in Jesus?"

"I believe he existed."

His voice boomed as he said, "But do you believe that Jesus is the one true Son of God, and that only through his blood can you be saved?"

"I don't know."

The man screamed like a wounded animal and brought the knife across her throat.

She stared at him suddenly realizing where she'd seen him. Trying instinctively to bring her hands up to her throat, she remembered they were bound. It was no use. She couldn't speak or scream, only feel her blood as it flowed down her chest and sprayed the room with every heartbeat. Toni could hardly keep her eyes open now. The pain began to fade as light-headedness assaulted her senses. The last thing she heard was the man's whispered confession.

"Forgive me for losing my temper, God. I could not save her."

Chapter 30

Chennelle had only been in the office for about fifteen minutes when she received an urgent call from Barbara Dodson. Apparently, one of her coven members, Toni Kelso, didn't show up for a meeting the night before, so Barbara went to the woman's house to check on her. Toni's car was in the driveway, but Barbara couldn't get her to answer the door, and all of her calls were going to voicemail.

Chennelle told Barbara not to attempt to enter the home. She was going to send out some patrol officers and then she and Detective Barnes would be there as soon as possible.

As Barnes pulled up to the house, Chennelle noticed Barbara Dodson pacing back and forth on the sidewalk and Patrol Officer Donovan Bays banging on the front door. He turned and walked toward them.

"Still no answer?" she asked Bays, even though she knew what he was going to say.

"No, Detective."

She noticed he looked rather grim. "Did you look in the windows?"

"I saw a purse and keys in the living room," he said. "All indications are she's in there."

"We're going to have to break in." As much as Chennelle hated to destroy someone's property, the fact that Miss Kelso wasn't answering the door or the phone was a bad sign.

Chennelle and Barnes drew their weapons and signaled for Bays to begin. He put on his leather gloves and used his nightstick to break out a pane of glass in the window next to the door. Once he removed the broken glass, it was quite easy for him to reach in and unlock it.

As Bays had said, a purse and keys rested on top of a People magazine laying on an oak coffee table in the living room. The silence of the house was palpable.

To the left of the living room ran a hallway. Chennelle signaled for Bays and Barnes to go down and check those rooms. She went straight ahead towards the dining room. Only three chairs stood around the table, which seemed odd to her. Then she inhaled it, an all too familiar metallic smell. Turning to her right, Chennelle noticed the opening to the kitchen. Inside, she found the source of the odor. A young woman sat in the missing chair, her neck severed so deeply it was a wonder it hadn't come off. Her blouse and bra straps were pulled down over her shoulders so her chest was exposed above her breasts.

"Barnes, Bays," she shouted, lowering her weapon as she stared at the word UNFORGIVEN.

"We got nothing back in the— Holy crap!" Barnes said, coming to an abrupt halt.

"Doesn't look like he took the time to torture this one," said Chennelle.

"Guess I'd better get the crime scene tape and start a log," said Bays as he joined them. "What should I tell her friend?"

Chennelle rubbed her eyes, then said, "Nothing. I'll come with you. Barnes, call the office. Ask for another patrol car, the death investigator, and a crime scene team."

Barnes nodded and Chennelle followed Bays outside. Barbara was leaning against her car, but took a step forward when she saw them coming.

"She's dead, isn't she?" said Barbara, her eyes tearing and her face screwing up in pain. "I knew I should have checked on her last night. It wasn't like her not to show up without calling us."

"If you'd checked on her, he might have had two victims instead of one." Chennelle smiled at Barbara.

"I want to see her."

"Mrs. Dodson, I can't let you do that. Our death investigator has to look at the body, take photos, and get her ready for transport. When she arrives at the morgue, they will need to collect evidence from her and take more photos before anyone outside of the department can see her. The fewer people who go near her at this point, the better."

"I didn't realize."

"Does she have family in the area? We need to get in touch with them before the news media gets hold of this. Even when we refuse to give them information until notifications are made, they often show the home or give an address, which gives the family enough information to realize what has happened."

"Toni moved here from Los Angeles a year ago. I met her mother and step-father when they visited her this summer," said Barbara. She opened her purse and pulled out her cell phone. "Let's see now."

Chennelle pulled out a pad of paper and a pen, ready for the information.

"Here it is. Her name is Zelda Franco and here is her number." Barbara turned the cell phone so that Chennelle could see the number. It was difficult to focus on it as Barbara's hand was shaking slightly, but Chennelle managed.

"Thank you, Mrs. Dodson. I think it best that you go home now so we can do our job and catch whoever did this."

"Okay.... Oh, and the ladies who did show up last night are well-informed about your suspicions that our coven could be a target. This just substantiates your theory. I'll make sure they know if you'd be so kind as to let me know when Zelda has been informed."

"I'll be glad to do that. All of you should be on high alert."

"Thank you, Detective Kendall." With that, Barbara turned and headed for her car.

Chennelle watched her go, and then she jumped, startled by Officer Bays' booming voice.

"Detective.... Sorry, I thought you heard me coming."

"That's okay, Bays. What do you need?"

"Could you help me stretch out this tape? As you can see, they sent me out by myself today since Samuels is on leave, and I think the news media's arriving."

She turned to see an ABC van pull up to the curb. It wouldn't be long before the other television stations followed suit. "Sure. Barnes is in there taking a preliminary look at the scene, but we can't do anything extensive until the others arrive. The neighbors are already looking out the windows, so we'd better get this up."

Chennelle took one of the rolls of crime scene tape and a couple of posts and started at the mailbox, enclosing the yard to the right while Bays went left. As she trekked along performing this boring but necessary task, all she could think about was Toni Kelso and the word branded across her chest. Sasha apparently cooperated in order to be forgiven. What had Toni refused to do in order to be marked differently?

Chapter 31

It had taken the majority of the day to process the Kelso crime scene. D. I. Spalding confirmed the cause of death as exsanguination from the wound to her neck. Again, Chennelle wondered what Toni Kelso could have said to piss this guy off and cause him to kill her so quickly. The only other injuries they could see were a shallow wound to her hand and a few bruises.

Chennelle had managed to get in touch with the victim's mother soon after Kelso was found. Zelda Franco had taken the first flight out of Los Angeles, and was now on her way to the station.

Barnes had volunteered to stick around, but Chennelle insisted Erica keep her plans with Ben. This wouldn't take long and Chennelle was the lead detective on this case. Besides, she didn't want to stand in the way of true love or the chance for her friends to get their first apartment together at a great price.

Sitting back in her chair, Chennelle closed her eyes trying to think of something appropriate to say to Kelso's mother. The conversation they'd had earlier was short because Zelda wanted to get her flight booked. It must have cost her a fortune to buy tickets for a same day flight.

She thought about what she'd want to hear under these circumstances. She'd want people to tell her it was a mistake. It was somebody else, not her daughter. Even though she wasn't a mother herself, she couldn't imagine how the death of her child under any circumstances would be bearable.

Opening her eyes to the sound of footsteps, Chennelle turned in her chair to see Officer Lane escorting a short, plump woman dressed in jeans and a colorful blouse. Thinking this must be Zelda Franco, Chennelle stood.

"Detective Kendall, this is Mrs. Franco," said Lane. "She said she has an appointment with you."

"Thank you, Officer Lane." Lane left and Chennelle pointed to her side chair. "Please, have a seat, Mrs. Franco."

"I want to see my daughter."

"Mrs. Franco, maybe you should wait until tomorrow. You've had a long trip and…."

"You're damned right I've had a long trip. I want to see her. She's my only daughter and I want to make sure you have the right person."

Chennelle had been right to think Zelda Franco would want to confirm this truly was her daughter. This must be the first step to acceptance.

"Alright, let me call the morgue so they can get her ready and I'll drive you there."

* * * * *

Chennelle had offered to take Zelda to dinner before they went to the morgue, but she had refused. She'd said she wasn't hungry, and wasn't sure she'd ever be able to eat again. This was probably wise in the end, because viewing a dead body tended to make some people lose whatever they've recently eaten. Chennelle was simply trying to be polite and make sure Toni Kelso was in the best shape for viewing.

Zelda had been very quiet during the ride over, but Chennelle knew she'd need to ask a few questions. She decided to do so while they waited in the morgue reception area.

"Mrs. Franco, I hope you are up for a few questions. The more I know about your daughter, the easier it will be for me to discover who did this to her."

Zelda nodded, but continued to stare at the doorway into the back room.

"Do you know of anyone who might have wanted to hurt your daughter—an old boyfriend, a rival of some sort?"

"My daughter was shy and, as you saw, rather chubby," said Mrs. Franco, still staring at the door. "She didn't have any boyfriends to my knowledge. Her friends were those in her coven."

"Has Toni always been of this religion?"

"Her father used to take her to a Methodist church back in L. A., but I've always taught her about Wicca. That's why he divorced me. He didn't like my religion. He even tried to get custody of her, but the judge didn't buy it because I didn't object to him teaching her Christianity."

Chennelle thought this might be significant in what happened to Toni. If she defied her killer by showing him she knew as much as he did about religion, he might have become angry and silenced her.

"My daughter found comfort in Wicca. She was very fortunate to meet Barbara Dodson. She treated her as she would her own daughter."

The doors opened and a morgue attendant nodded at Chennelle. She rose, and so did Zelda. They followed the attendant into the viewing room.

When the curtain opened, Chennelle heard Zelda give a little gasp. Zelda's eyes filled with tears and she pressed her hand to her mouth. The attendant had done a wonderful job, covering Toni's body with a sheet up over the wound in her neck. There was only a slight bruising on her right cheek. She looked a little gray, but peaceful.

"That's my girl," said Zelda. "My sweet girl. How exactly did she die?"

"The perpetrator cut her throat."

"Did she suffer?"

"The death investigator said it would have been quick and relatively painless," said Chennelle. She actually had no idea how long the death had taken or if there'd been much pain, but she wasn't going to put this woman through any more tonight.

"Thank you, Detective Kendall. Can you call Barbara? She said she'd come pick me up from the station when I was done."

"Of course, I will."

They went back to the waiting area and found that Barbara Dodson had already arrived without Chennelle's call.

"I found out your flight had arrived and called the station. They told me you came here. Oh, Zelda, I'm so sorry."

Zelda flung herself into Barbara's waiting arms and the women sobbed on one another's shoulders.

With Zelda safe in Barbara's care, Chennelle walked out to the parking lot. As she got into her car, she felt the sting of sympathetic pain and began to cry. Two really nice women, loving, kind, who would do no harm to any living thing, murdered ruthlessly. She had to work fast and furiously to make sure this didn't happen again.

Chapter 32

It had been twenty-four hours since the discovery of Toni Kelso's body. The autopsy wouldn't be ready until Monday afternoon, but it was obvious the victim bled out after having her head nearly cut off.

This had been one hell of a week, especially hard due to the death of Peter Russell. The weekend wasn't going to be much better. Today Chennelle was having lunch with her sister to discuss their parents' anniversary party. At least she would have Sunday to relax before the Monday morning funeral mass. She felt a pang of guilt at dreading the meeting with her sister when Anne Samuels would be putting her father to rest in a couple of days.

Saundra had asked Chennelle to meet her at the Carolina Grill in Zionsville at 11:30 a.m. Her sister lived about a mile from the restaurant. Saundra always expected Chennelle to make it more convenient for her.

"You don't have anyone to look after," Saundra would say.

Since her sister and brother-in-law had no children yet, she wasn't sure what Saundra was doing all day to *take care of* Terry. However, she wasn't going to argue with her. Letting her have her way about the restaurant put Chennelle in a better position to negotiate the cost of the anniversary party. When she'd talked to her brother yesterday, he had already told her he wasn't going to be able to fork out thousands of dollars for something his parents didn't want. She hoped he'd back her up when push came to shove.

Chennelle allowed the waiter to seat her, because despite the fact that she lived farther away, she knew her sister would be late. It was already 11:45 a.m. and no Saundra. Occasionally she'd look up from the menu and glance at the door, irritation raising her blood pressure. She didn't want to be scowling when Saundra arrived, but was having difficulty keeping her cool.

The next time she took her gaze away from the menu, she saw Saundra sauntering towards her wearing a lovely black pantsuit with a peach silk shirt and carrying what looked like a briefcase. She looked like she was going to a job interview, not lunch with her sister. Chennelle suddenly felt self-conscious about the blue jeans and green cable knit sweater she was wearing.

"Hello, sweet sister," said Saundra in her most enthusiastic tone of voice.

This immediately put Chennelle on her guard. A greeting like that could only mean Saundra already made the plans and had no intention of compromising. This was going to be a pain. She decided her stomach would be too tense for the chili she'd thought of ordering.

"Hey, Sis," said Chennelle.

"I have the most fabulous ideas." Saundra opened her briefcase and pulled out a manila folder. "Here, take a look at this."

Chennelle opened the folder before taking a sip of water. When she saw the figure at the bottom of the page, she choked and spit water everywhere.

"Chennelle!" said Saundra in low voice, hoping not to rouse attention.

However, it was too late for that. Chennelle was coughing into her napkin one second and trying to dab the water off the contents of the folder the next. Her face hot with embarrassment, she finally got control over her coughing fit and tried some more water.

"Are you alright?" asked the waiter. "Can I bring you anything? Perhaps another napkin."

Chennelle nodded and he hurried away. She looked over at Saundra, who was hiding behind her menu. The only comfort afforded Chennelle was that her sister also appeared totally embarrassed and uncomfortable.

After clearing her throat and taking a couple more sips of water, Chennelle was finally able to talk. "Saundra, there is no way we are going to have this at Stonegate. It's a beautiful place and is great for weddings, but Carl and I can't afford the budget you've proposed."

Saundra slammed her menu onto the table, but didn't speak right away, because the waiter had returned with another napkin for Chennelle and a pitcher of water to refill her glass.

"Are you ready to order?"

"I think my sister may need a few more minutes to look over the menu," said Chennelle, not taking her eyes off Saundra.

"Very good," he said before turning and walking to another table.

She could have sworn her sister trembled a little, perhaps in an attempt to regain her composure. After a deep breath, Saundra said, "How many fortieth anniversaries are our parents going to have?"

Chennelle raised an eyebrow and continued to stare at her sibling. She wasn't going to answer such a stupid, rhetorical question.

"One, Chennelle, only one," said Saundra heatedly. "We owe it to them to make this an event they'll never forget."

"Even if they don't want an event this extravagant?"

"Mother says they don't want it, but once it's over they'll be so happy we did this for them."

"No, they won't, Saundra. If you do something this big, you risk Papa not coming at all."

"That's ridiculous. He'll come if you ask him. He always listens to you."

"I spoke to Mama a few days ago. She called to ask me to make sure you don't plan anything big because Papa is totally against it."

Saundra slammed herself into the back of her chair. She was actually pouting as she did when they were kids.

"Saundra, look. It's not that this isn't a wonderful idea, but Mama and Papa don't want it. They would be furious if they thought Carl pitched in this much money—money that he could have used for his children."

"Well, then he can pay what he thinks he's able and you and I will split the rest."

"Absolutely not," said Chennelle, gazing intently at Saundra. "I don't make enough money in five years to pay my part for this venue. We need to do something simple. They have a nice party room right here we can use. We keep it to immediate family and in-laws only."

"Here—family only. What kind of celebration is that?"

"The kind our parents will enjoy and we *all* can afford without going into debt for the next twenty years."

"Give me my folder," Saundra said abruptly, her eyes still fierce with anger. Chennelle passed the still damp folder to her and she stuffed it into the briefcase. "I've lost my appetite."

"Come on, Saundra, stay. We can talk to the people here about the cost to have the room."

"I'm not in the mood. I'm going home." Saundra stood so quickly, she nearly knocked over her chair.

"Saundra," said Chennelle, but her sister's back was already turned to her and she was walking hurriedly towards the door.

"Is she not staying for lunch?" asked the waiter, startling Chennelle.

"No, but I'll go ahead and order. How about the chicken taco salad?"

"Ah, a very good choice. I've had that one myself and it's delicious. Anything else to drink?"

"No, water will do."

He nodded and walked to the kitchen area.

What was she going to do about Saundra? What would she tell her mother about Saundra's behavior? Tracking criminals was almost easier than dealing with her sister.

Her salad arrived in record time.

"Is there anything else I can get for you?" asked the waiter.

"How about a personality transplant for my sister?"

He simply smiled at Chennelle and walked away.

Chapter 33

It seemed like a million years ago that Anne had sat at her mother's kitchen table with her brothers and planned this day. In reality, it had only been four days. She now sat watching her mother, who was standing by the casket patting her father's hand. Anne couldn't bear to touch her father's ice-cold hand. That would make it too real.

The outpouring of love for her father was wonderful, but she couldn't even remember who or how many had shown up for the visitation the evening before. Police officers and their families had turned up at her mother's house every night since it happened with condolences, flowers, and food.

Parishioners from St. Joseph Catholic Church were also very kind in dropping by to console them. Her mother had been a member of that church all her life. They had asked that donations be made to the church in lieu of flowers, but people still couldn't stop themselves from filling the place with beautiful bouquets and hearty plants.

Anne and her sons had stayed with her mother over night. Aaron was supposed to be here by now, but hadn't shown. For all she knew he was sleeping off a night out on the town. She actually hoped he wouldn't show up, because he'd only do something to embarrass her in front of her family and colleagues.

"Mom," said Michael gently.

"Hey, sweetie," she said and pulled him into a hug.

"Mom, are you okay?" he asked, which made her squeeze him tighter.

She released him and looked into his big brown eyes. "I am doing okay, but it hurts. I'm going to miss your grandpa so much."

At this, both sets of eyes filled with tears. Michael ran over to get the nearest tissue box and brought it to Anne.

"Where's your brother?" she asked.

"He wanted to stay with Uncle Jeff in the family room. I think seeing Grandpa like this kinda scares him."

"Then it's okay for him to stay with Uncle Jeff for now."

"Mom, if Grandpa isn't here anymore, where is he?"

"His soul went to Heaven."

"How do you know?"

"I'll answer that one for you." Mildred had apparently decided to join them. "If your mother took you to church more often, you wouldn't have to ask that question."

Anne knew her face had just reddened, because it felt quite warm. She knew her mother was right. Because of Aaron, Anne had neglected to take her sons to church with any consistency. She realized this could be why Justin was frightened. He didn't really understand it either. This lack of religious education would stop immediately.

"Your grandfather was a wonderful, good Christian man who helped others his whole life. That's how I know he's in Heaven," said Mildred. "I watch my children and grandchildren and the goodness he instilled in each one of you, and that's how I know he's in Heaven."

"Thanks, Grandma," said Michael. "I think I'll go tell Justin and maybe he won't be so scared anymore."

"Sounds like a good idea," said his grandmother. Then she looked at Anne, her deep brown eyes glistening. "You've done a wonderful job with your boys, despite Aaron's attitude. I'm very proud of you, and so was your father. Now that he's gone, I can tell you this. No matter how hard of a time he gave you when you first decided to go into the academy, he was so proud of you, Annie. He just gave you a hard time because he was scared."

"Because I'm a woman."

"No," she said with a short laugh. "He would have done the same thing if the boys had decided to take that route. He knew how much I worried about him and the danger he was in every day. I'm sure he thought my anxiety would end once he retired."

Mildred turned her gaze toward the casket. "I wasn't worried about him anymore, and looked what happened."

Anne put her arm around her mother's shoulders, pulled her close, and closed her eyes. Mildred began to weep as Anne let her own tears flow down her cheeks. This was the first time her numbness had subsided since that awful day, so she could allow herself to feel the pain.

* * * * *

The mass was beautiful and meaningful. So many of her father's colleagues had asked if they could say a few words; it caused the service to last about an hour longer than normal. It was worth it to hear the heartfelt praise of those who'd worked with him all those years. Now Anne was simply pacing through her parents' home, trying to smile at those who had come by to make sure they ate something and to do their best to comfort the family.

As she had expected, Aaron didn't show up at the church. She didn't even bother to call him to ask if he was okay. At this point, she didn't really care. Her only problem now was how she was going to tell him that she and the boys were moving in with her mother permanently. He wouldn't be pleased to find out his only source of income was about to disappear.

Anne looked to her left and saw Chennelle Kendall talking to Trevon Adams. Chennelle didn't look very happy, so she decided to go over and interrupt them.

Anne touched Chennelle's arm, which was very tense. "Thank you for coming. I'm sorry we haven't had much of a chance to talk."

Chennelle's demeanor did a one-sixty as she gave her attention to Anne. Her eyes softened into pools of pity and she drew Anne into a hug. "No need for you to apologize. There were a lot of people for you to deal with today. But, Anne, if you need anything, anything at all, please call me."

"Sure. I really appreciate the offer."

"I know you've been studying for the detective's exam. If you want to take a break and wait for next time, I can make the recommendation."

"Absolutely not," said Anne. "My father would kick my butt if I let this keep me from taking that exam."

"Then, if you need someone to help you study, give me a call," said Chennelle.

"I'd be glad to help you, too," said Trevon.

Standing with her back to him, Chennelle rolled her eyes.

"Thank you both. I just may take you—"

A crash behind them cut her sentence short. It was Aaron, and he looked drunk. He was stumbling and knocking things over. Ben Jacobs grabbed Aaron's arm to prevent him from going to the ground, but Aaron jerked away and mumbled something Anne couldn't understand. Everyone was staring at him.

"Aaron," said Anne. "What are you doing?"

"I've come to shhhow my dear fatherrr-in law my respecs," he said, barely understandable through his drunken, slurred words.

"Coming in here drunk isn't very respectful," said Anne. "Sit down and I'll get you some coffee."

When she reached for his arm to guide him to a chair, he took a swing at her. He missed, but her avoidance caused her to lose her balance and fall to the floor. Chennelle and Erica were at her side in seconds to help her up. Before she knew it, Trevon had a struggling and cursing Aaron pinned to the floor.

"What's going on here?" said Anne's brother Grant as he entered the room.

"Seems your brother-in-law is disrespecting your sister in her time of grief," said Trevon. "Lloyd, you're in uniform. Do you want the pleasure of taking this guy in for attempted assault and drunken disorderly?"

"Sanchez and I are about to go on duty," said Lloyd, signaling for his partner to join him. "We'll be glad to take him off your hands."

"That's not neces—" Her husband cut off Anne's sentence again.

"Shut up, bitch," Aaron screamed. "This is all your fault!"

"You need to quit while you're ahead, numbskull," said Trevon taking Lloyd's cuffs and securing Aaron's hands behind his back.

Anne had actually started to tell Lloyd he didn't he have to take Aaron in, but now she'd changed her mind. If he was in a jail cell, it would take him days to post bond, and she certainly wasn't going to do it. In the meantime, she could move all of hers and the boys' things out of the house and get a restraining order.

"You're gonna let them take me away," he screamed. "Where are my boys? I want to see 'em."

"Get him out of my sight," said Anne.

Trevon got off of Aaron and pulled him to his feet. Lloyd and Sanchez each took one of Aaron's arms and led him out the front door while he continued to scream obsenities.

Ben tossed his keys to Erica. "Adams and I will follow the squad in. Come pick me up in about a half hour. We should have him booked and resting in County by then."

Erica nodded, then turned to Anne. "Are you alright?"

"The only thing that hurts right now is my pride," she said. "Where are the boys?" Anne was suddenly terrified that they had seen or heard this whole thing.

"Jeff took all of the kids to get ice cream," said Grant. "They were getting pretty bored and I think Jeff was starting to feel a need to get away from all of this."

"I'm so sorry," said Anne. "Where's mother? I don't want her upset by this."

"About twenty minutes ago, I gave her one of those sleeping pills the doctor prescribed. With any luck she'll have slept through the whole thing."

Anne turned to thank Erica and Chennelle for taking care of her and found they were gone. She turned back to her brother.

"They went out the back door," he said. "I think they wanted to give you some space. You look beat. Why don't you go lie down, too."

"Sounds good, but I want to wait for Michael and Justin to come back."

"Annie, you won't be much good to them if you're exhausted. I can't leave without my two, so I'll be here to take care of things. Don't look at me like that. You go upstairs and I promise I'll send Michael and Justin up as soon as they get back."

"Pinkie swear?" she asked, extending a hooked pinkie finger.

He smiled at her and hooked his pinkie in hers. "Pinkie swear."

They released their fingers and she headed for the staircase. Grant was the patriarch of the family now and he'd never broken a pinkie swear promise in his entire life. She'd succumb to his request because she knew she could depend upon the man her father raised.

Chapter 34

Chennelle walked into her condominium and kicked off her high heels before she even closed the door. This had been an emotionally exhausting few days to say the least. First, there was her sister's outburst in the restaurant, then laying one of her own to rest, followed by the ever-popular drunken idiot. Dr. Patel had promised to have the autopsy report on the Kelso case ready for her tomorrow morning. At this point, a nice quiet autopsy report sounded mighty fine.

She'd never met Aaron Samuels until today. When colleagues complained about their spouses, she usually tried to give the other party the benefit of the doubt. In this case, however, Anne was being kind in her description of her husband.

After leaving the Russell household, she met Erica at the station to give their eyewitness accounts of Aaron's behavior. When they were walking towards the booking room, they could hear Aaron screaming and cursing at the top of his voice.

"You can't do this to me," he'd said. "My lawyer will chew you up and spit you out for this."

Adams and Jacobs kept quiet; the more Aaron talked, the deeper he sank into trouble. She had to admire their self-restraint because she was ready to punch him.

Now it was time to try to salvage some relaxation from this crazy weekend. She dug her toes down into her plush gray carpet and worked out the cramping tight shoes had caused. When she reached her bedroom, she started stripping off clothing piece by piece and tossing it haphazardly on the floor. By the time she walked into her bathroom, she was naked. On the back of the bathroom door, she found her nightgown and fluffy purple robe hanging from a hook. The silky sky blue nightgown slid over her body, creating a sensation of soft hands caressing her frame. She shivered at the coolness of it, but soon cured that with the warmth of her robe. Off to the kitchen for a glass of wine and a bit of cheese with crackers.

Chennelle had just settled down in her favorite chair and had barely had a sip of wine when her phone rang. Caller ID implied it was her brother-in-law, Terry. A twinge of panic stilled her lungs. Terry rarely called. She started breathing again and answered.

"Terry, is something wrong?"

His laughter filled her ears. "I know I don't call often, but does everyone have to think there's some great catastrophe when I do?"

"Yes, you have to admit hearing from you personally is highly unusual."

"I suppose you could be right. However, the only catastrophe I want to talk about is the one I averted. Apparently, my darling wife called Carl after she rushed home from the luncheon with you on Saturday."

"The luncheon we didn't have, you mean."

Terry chuckled again. He was a jolly sort. "Yes, I guess so. From what I understand, she was pretty riled up by the time she got hold of Carl. Anyway, he asked for my help in, shall we say, tempering my wife's enthusiasm in planning this gala event for your parents."

"And were you successful?" asked Chennelle, hoping the skepticism didn't show in her voice.

"I do believe I was," he said. "She had apparently told Carl of your proposed *idiotic* idea to have an intimate family only dinner at the Carolina Grill instead of her proposed and very reasonable soiree at Stonegate. When Carl heard the price, he sided with you. By the time I got home she was totally unhinged."

"So what happened? Did you have to throw a bucket of ice water on her?"

Terry burst out laughing. Chennelle hoped her sister wasn't around to hear this conversation. If she was livid Saturday night, this would send her over the edge.

"No, no," he said, catching his breath. "I just listened to her rant until she fizzled out. Then I pulled out my *understanding husband hat* for a while and comforted her. Once she seemed primed to listen, I explained to her that this whole thing is supposed to be for her parents and that we should go visit them on Sunday and find out what they wanted."

"She went for that?"

"Hook, line and sinker," he chuckled.

"Did she listen to them?"

"After I put on my *lawyer hat* and helped them argue their case, she finally caved. They loved the idea of having family only in the restaurant and they compromised by telling her she could fill the room to its fifty person capacity with aunts and uncles and a few close friends. She decided she was fighting a lost cause."

"Way to go," she said, very impressed by his expertise. She probably should have gone to him in the first place. "Is she still mad at me?"

"No, because the other part of the compromise was that she would be in charge of the planning."

"That's no compromise as far as I'm concerned. If she wants to do the planning, I'm all for it. I've got a pretty nasty case right now that may be a serial killer. We've got two victims from the same Wiccan coven and I'm afraid there will be more."

"I sure am glad I went into real estate law instead of criminal law," he said. "The pay is better and I don't have to defend sleazy characters I know are guilty."

"I hear ya, bro. Thank you for getting this mess in order. I owe you one."

"After that, I think you owe me more than one."

This time Chennelle laughed. "Good night, Terry."

"Good night, Chennelle."

Chapter 35

Tuesday morning, Chennelle walked into her office barely able to remember how she got there. She was still drained from the weekend and Monday's craziness, but happy her brother-in-law had convinced Saundra to chill out. Dropping her purse on her desk, she noticed a folder from autopsy labeled "Kelso, Toni."

Chennelle heard footsteps and looked up to see Barnes and Adams coming toward her. Adams had an official document in his hands.

"You look like hell," he said.

"Thanks," she said sarcastically. "What brings you to my side of the street?"

"Here's the official statement from the Samuels' attempted assault and public intoxication for you to sign."

"*Attempted assault?*" said Chennelle.

"That's all the prosecutor can go for since he didn't actually touch her," said Barnes. "Adams tried to find a previous arrest, but there wasn't one. If he's ever tried this before, it was never reported."

"Too bad he didn't try to hit me," said Adams, puffing out his chest. "I'd have at least knocked his ass out cold for a few hours. The way it looks now, he'll probably make bail and only get a hefty fine."

"Maybe the judge will hold him when he finds out he isn't working," said Chennelle. "I don't think Anne will bail him out."

"I would hope not," said Barnes. "He might have friends or other family who will help him, though. There's a public defender over there with him now."

"What a scum bag. I hope somebody warns Samuels that he might get out today," said Chennelle, her brow furrowed. She hoped Anne had gone over and grabbed her things out of the house and talked to someone about a restraining order. If he took a swing at her once, he'd do it again. She took the report and signed it.

"Okay, ladies. I've got to turn this in and then get back to good old robberies and burglaries. Ya'll have a nice day."

Chennelle watched as Adams' fine behind moved away from her. If he wasn't such a player, she might have been very happy with Trevon Adams.

"What were you reading when I came in?" asked Barnes.

"I just opened the Kelso autopsy report. Apparently, Dr. Patel completed this over the weekend."

"Anything we didn't already know?"

"No," said Chennelle, shaking her head and opening the folder again. "Cause of death was the slit throat. The only other injuries were from Kelso trying to pull her arms free from the duct tape and a bruise on her right cheek. The branding was done post mortem, just like with Winston."

"Did she have any defensive wounds?"

"No, and there is a tox screen pending, but I'd think she'd have defensive wounds if she'd been able to fight back. I wonder if he's using chloroform. It's almost impossible to detect once someone is dead."

"Looks like this Wiccan coven *is* being targeted," said Barnes, plopping down in her chair. "I wonder what good old Roman Wagner was up to that night."

"I've been wondering the same thing. Maybe we should give him a call."

"We can see what he has to say about his pal, Charles Black, too," said Barnes.

"I'm sure Black's already told Wagner he confessed to the spy game."

Barnes sniffed. "No doubt, but it will be interesting to see what sort of crap he tries to sell us."

"It certainly will," said Chennelle. "I'll call him right now."

Chennelle grabbed his number out of the file, picked up the receiver and dialed.

Chapter 36

When Chennelle called Roman Wagner's cell number that morning, she was surprised to find him home instead of at work. Had he called in sick because he'd had an exhausting weekend of witch hunting?

Roman agreed to allow her and Barnes to come to his home to talk. Chennelle didn't tell him about Toni Kelso, so he most likely thought this was about Sasha Winston—unless he was the killer.

"I'm sure glad the news media hasn't made the connection about the Wiccan coven yet," said Barnes. She shivered and pulled her jacket collar up as the cold November wind whipped around her, stirring up a plethora of color from the ground around her feet.

"They'd have a field day with it, wouldn't they?" Chennelle pushed Wagner's doorbell. "I only hope they don't find out until after we've found the perpetrator."

She heard footsteps as someone approached the door from the inside. It swung open and there stood Roman Wagner looking pale and tired. Perhaps he was actually ill.

"Come in, Detectives," he said weakly.

The hardwood floors appeared dingy, and Chennelle thought she could have written her name in the dust on the small table in the foyer. Roman was apparently not much of a housekeeper. She thought about the fact his wife had died a few years ago. She wondered how shiny everything might have been when she was here to care for it.

They followed him into a living room which was unusually dark for mid-afternoon. The curtains were drawn, and only the light of a table lamp dully illuminated the room. Roman sat down in a recliner, but did not lift the footrest, nor did he offer them a seat. Chennelle and Barnes glanced at one another, then sat down on the couch nearest their host.

"As you can see, I'm not at my best," he said. "Has there been something new in Sasha's case? I'd really like to finish this so I can get on with my life."

Chennelle's jaw tightened. Sick or not, this man was insufferable. She pulled in a deep breath, hoping her anger wouldn't show during questioning. Looking at Barnes, she blinked assent for her to begin. Chennelle pulled out her notebook to write down the conversation.

"Mr. Wagner, we know about your feelings toward Sasha Winston. If we didn't, we might not be here," said Barnes with her best smile.

Roman sat forward in a more aggressive position. "What do you mean by that, young lady?"

"Detective, sir. You should call me Detective or Detective Barnes."

He smirked and repeated the question in a slow, sweet, mocking tone. "What do you mean by that, Detective Barnes?"

"What I mean is that your attitude towards Miss Winston brings you under suspicion for her death," said Barnes. "We checked out your alibi for the night of October thirty-first and early morning hours of November first. I'm afraid it doesn't check out. The people you said you went bowling with told us that you were all together that evening, but that you left the bowling alley at ten o'clock. Sasha didn't go missing until after midnight."

"I told you…" He paused and coughed deeply. "…I came home and went straight to bed."

"Unfortunately, there isn't anyone who can corroborate your story, Mr. Wagner."

Chennelle looked up from her notes, waiting for Roman to answer Barnes' question. His paleness had given way to a slight flush—fever or anger? He grabbed a glass of water from the table and drank deeply from it, then put a lozenge of some sort into his mouth.

"I guess that is unfortunate since I live by myself," said Roman. "My son should have been here with me. If it wasn't for her, he wouldn't have gone out on his own."

"I'm not here to discuss what she did, what he did, or what you did in regards to your relationship with your son, because you made it quite clear when we met, that you didn't like her."

"Lady…I mean, Detective. If people went around killing everyone they didn't like then we wouldn't have any problems with overpopulation and starvation. Those left would probably get along fine because they like everybody."

"Really," said Barnes, raising an eyebrow. "Sort of like the *meek inheriting the Earth?*"

"Ah, you have read your Bible," he said. "So, then you know that it also says *thou shalt not kill*. God Himself gave that law to Moses and I would never break it."

As Chennelle glanced up again, she saw the stubborn sincerity in Roman's face. She was anxious to see his reaction when Barnes started asking about Kelso.

"All of that aside, we do have something other than the death of Sasha Winston to discuss with you today."

"Shoot," he said, and then laughed. "Not literally." His laughter only started him on another coughing jag.

Chennelle and Barnes waited for Roman to get control again. With pen poised, Chennelle stole a glance toward her partner; her jaw seemed tenser now. Once Roman stopped coughing and had another long drink of water, he looked to Barnes for her next question.

"We understand you and Charles Black are good friends," said Barnes.

"You know we are, so there's no need to beat around the bush. When I found out his father-in-law lived across the street from Miss Winston, I asked him to keep an eye out for my son."

"Why?" asked Barnes.

"I was worried about my boy—end of story."

"Mr. Wagner, where were you last Thursday evening?"

"The same place I was the previous Thursday, bowling. I bowl on a Thursday night league."

"So, you're telling me your alibi is the same as for the night of October thirty-first?" asked Barnes.

"I just said that, didn't I? Why do I need an alibi for this past Thursday? Somebody else snuff it?"

"As a matter of fact, someone else *did snuff it*." Barnes paused while Chennelle watched for the information to sink into Roman Wagner's hard little head.

"Mr. Wagner, did you know a woman named Toni Kelso?" asked Barnes.

"I heard that name on the news this morning. Is she one of them witches, too?"

"They're Wiccans, Mr. Wagner," said Barnes, appearing to be losing her patience. "Did you know her or ever meet her in your encounters with Sasha Winston?"

"No," he said, scowling at her. "If you're here to accuse me of another murder, you can just get your butts out of my house, because I ain't talking to you anymore without my lawyer."

Chennelle and Barnes stood. There was no use trying to ask him anything else now that he'd requested the presence of an attorney.

"If you change your mind, you know how to reach us," said Barnes. "We'll have DNA results in soon from the bits of skin that were found under Sasha Winston's fingernails. We're pretty sure she clawed this guy before he subdued her. That should give us some conclusive evidence as to the killer's identity."

Roman rubbed his left wrist.

Chennelle saw this and wrote this action in her notes. There would definitely be a DNA search warrant in this man's future.

"See yourselves out," he growled.

They turned and left the way they'd come. Chennelle made sure the door was locked before she closed it.

"Holy crap," said Barnes. "He isn't just prejudiced against *witches,* he has no respect whatsoever for women."

"I noticed, but I'm not sure he's the one."

"Don't you think it's odd that both of these murders have taken place on his bowling night?"

Chennelle did think it was odd, but was it because he was their killer or was it just a coincidence?

Chapter 37

Doug had finished washing the dinner dishes while listening to his grandmother mumbling hallelujahs during her favorite evangelic program. It was after eight o'clock now and time for her evening medications. He neatly put them in the dish as usual and placed it on the tray with two saltine crackers and a glass of water. She claimed the crackers calmed her stomach.

He walked over to her chair and saw she was nodding off to sleep. He hated to wake her, but she needed to take her medication on time, and sleeping in the chair wasn't good for her back.

"Grandmother," he said quietly, touching her arm.

"What?" she shouted. "Oh, it's you. Wasn't Reverand Beacin wonderful tonight?"

"Yes, Grandmother. Now you must take your medicine and go to bed. You don't want to wake up with a cramp in your back, do you?"

"Don't just stand there, boy. Give them here."

He lowered the tray and she took each pill one by one, swallowing each with a gulp of water. Then she ate her crackers slowly, which he often felt was done to test his patience. Once she was finished, she pushed forward in her chair and reached for her walker.

"Would you like for me to help you to your room, Grandmother?"

She turned her head, scowling at him. "Do I look like an invalid to you? I'm not so bad I can't get to my own bed at night."

"Of course you're not an invalid. I didn't mean to hurt your feelings."

She laughed, not with joy but with cynicism. "I'm a lot tougher than you think, boy. It takes a lot more than that to hurt my feelings."

He knew quite well that she was tough. She'd raised him from infancy to be what he was today. Would he have had the guts to fulfill God's plan for him had he not had her influence?

"Okay, Grandmother. I'll clean this up and come to say goodnight in a few minutes."

He watched as she slowly lifted herself from the chair. Doug had offered to buy her one of those recliners that tips forward to make it easier for her to get out of it. She'd flatly refused and said it was for lazy people. As soon as she was steady with the aid of her walker, he turned to take the tray back to the kitchen. He'd leave it there until morning.

After turning off the television and saying goodnight to his grandmother through her bedroom door, he went straight to his room with a surge of excitement flowing through his body. It was time to plan his next purging.

He unlocked his bedroom door and looked down the hallway as though expecting someone. Entering quickly, he turned and locked it again.

On Doug's wall above his dresser was a huge bulletin board filled with photos, most of which were on the right-hand side. On the left, under an index card with the word PURGED written on it were two photos. One was of Sasha Winston. He'd taken that one during one of their meetings in the woods last summer. The other of Toni Kelso, which he'd taken as she'd left work last month.

He walked over to the board and touched the photo of Sasha, feeling a great sense of relief. The word FORGIVEN was written in red marker across it. He had accomplished his mission with that one. Toni's photo, however, caused a pang of grief in him. It was marked UNFORGIVEN, a reminder of his failure.

Opening a dresser drawer, he looked at Sasha's dagger. He thought about how well it had worked to bring about Sasha's confession. Looking at it he remembered the anger he'd felt—no, the rage—when the second witch dared to tell him he wasn't a good Christian. He'd been very patient with Sasha and didn't understand why he wasn't the same with Toni.

"Maybe I should have prayed more," he muttered. "Even Jesus got angry and that's what He did. He prayed more. He asked for forgiveness for losing His temper in the temple. That's what I'll do."

Doug fell to his knees and prayed in a whisper. "Please forgive me for my impatience. Be merciful to the witch, Toni Kelso, as she had no time to confess. If I hadn't lost my temper, she might have found forgiveness." He paused as tears of guilt filled his eyes and flowed down his cheeks.

He stood and took another photo from his board. "Help me to be more patient with the witch Carmen, for she must repent and be purged of her sins."

Pinning the photo on the left side of the board, Doug ran a finger down the woman's cheek. How lovely she was with her long, silky black hair and deep brown eyes.

"No," he shouted, pulling his hand away as though he'd been burned. "Even her photo bewitches me."

He turned away, closed his eyes tightly, and tried to rid her from his thoughts. She'd be meeting her friends at the coffee shop on Wednesday, as she always did. He'd listen in and decide how best to take her.

For now, Doug needed to rest. No more mistakes or the punishment would be severe.

Chapter 38

It was nearly eight-thirty at night and Anne wanted to finish packing up her things. Trevon Adams had called her earlier and told her the charges the prosecutor was willing to take on. Since this was his first offense, Aaron's bond would be small. She assured Adams that she wasn't going to post it, but no telling who he'd contact to help him out.

"Michael, Justin, are you about finished?"

"Yeah, Mom," yelled Michael.

The boys had been set the task of packing up their toys and any other belongings they wanted to keep. She'd already taken out four boxes, wondering how two young boys could have accumulated so much.

Anne had just taped up her last box when she heard a thump behind her and turned to see not her sons, but Aaron slumped against the doorframe. She took a step back, heart thumping with a sudden jolt of fear.

"Well, well," he said, obviously drunk. "Where do you think you're going?"

"The boys and I are going to stay with my mother for a while. She needs us."

"*She* needs you? And what about me? Who's going to take care of me?"

"You, Aaron. You'll take care of you."

Aaron took a step toward her, his eyes in angry slits and pointing his finger at her. "You're my wife. It's *your* job to take care of *me*."

"It's the twenty-first century, Aaron," she said, exasperated. "I'm not your mother."

"Don't you bring my mother into this, you stupid bitch. My mother would never have treated my father the way you treat me."

She stared at him defiantly, even though her heart was about to leap through her chest. "I really don't care, Aaron. Go live with her if you need a caretaker. I have a full-time job and actual kids to take care of."

More swiftly than she could have expected, he was on her. He grabbed her by the shoulders and flung her to the bed. Then he jumped on her, holding her arms down and sitting on top of her.

"You're my wife," he said through gritted teeth. "You'll do as you're told. Now let's take off these blue jeans so I can show you who's boss around here."

"You're drunk."

"I may have had a couple of drinks, but then again, I need a drink or two to live with the high and mighty Patrol Officer Anne Samuels."

Aaron bent down, still sitting on Anne and holding her arms above her head. His breath stank of whiskey and cigarettes. She turned her head to avoid a kiss and he squeezed her wrist tighter. When he tried again, she spit in his face.

He let go of her left wrist and hit her across the face with his fist. Dazed, her blurry vision revealed he was unzipping her jeans. She tried to move, but was disoriented. Then the second blow came to her right cheek; this time it was the back of his hand.

Aaron rolled her over; she knew what he was going to do. He'd done it to her once before. Every time she tried to get up, he pushed her down again. Her head was spinning and she was afraid she would pass out. Then she remembered the boys.

"Get off her," Michael shouted.

"Hey, Michael," said Aaron. "Get back to your room and unpack. This is adult stuff."

Anne tried to see Michael through her swollen eyes. Then she heard a zipper and felt Aaron tug at her jeans.

Again, Michael shouted, "I said get off her. You're not going to hurt my mom."

Aaron got off, giving Anne a chance to push up from the bed a little, her head pounding from the blows. Now she could see Michael and he was holding her Glock.

"You wanna be a cop like your mommy?" said Aaron in baby talk. "You sayin' you don't want to be like your old man?"

"No, I don't want to be like you," shouted Michael. "Get out of here and leave us alone."

Aaron took a couple of steps toward Michael. Anne tried to move off the bed, terrified that Aaron would get the gun and shoot them all. She closed her eyes in pain as she fell to the floor.

"Mom!"

"I'm okay, baby. Daddy's going to leave now."

"The hell I am," screamed Aaron as he turned toward her. He raised his fist to strike her again, and then she heard the blast of the gun.

Chapter 39

Chennelle watched as the first ambulance left the scene with a screaming Aaron Samuels inside. She had received a call from Major Stevenson telling her there had been a shooting at Officer Samuels' house and that the victim was screaming that it was an attempted murder. He wanted her and Barnes on the case since they were familiar with the Samuels' family situation.

"I'm fine," said Samuels to a couple of paramedics trying to get her to cooperate. "I need to see my sons."

Turning toward the second ambulance, Chennelle walked over and tapped the paramedic on the shoulder. "Give me a minute with her," she said. Chennelle wanted to vomit at the sight of Anne's face. Aaron had blackened both of her eyes, the left one swollen shut.

"Detective Kendall, I need to see my boys. I need to know they're okay." Anne started to cry.

"Anne, I'm not going to let you see Michael or Justin until you pull yourself together. Do you hear me?"

Anne looked up and nodded, wiping away her tears, her chest heaving with the effort.

"Take some deep breaths now." Chennelle rubbed her shoulders, waiting for her to calm down. "That's right. Now, tell me what happened."

"The boys and I were packing up the rest of our things when Aaron showed up. He was drunk...he...he...said we weren't going anywhere. Then he...he came at me and threw me on the bed. He was going to...r...r...he was going to rape me." She burst into tears again. "He didn't even care that the boys might see what he was doing to me."

Chennelle rubbed Anne's arm gently. "Where was your gun?"

"I'd just gotten it out of the safe and had put it in my purse on the dresser by the bedroom door. I...I...didn't think Michael knew what to do with it. How did he load it?"

"He didn't. The cartridge was still in your purse. It appears you forgot to empty the chamber, so there was one bullet in it."

"Oh no, how could I be so stupid? What's going to happen to Michael? What will they do to my son?"

"Luckily, Michael had told Justin to call 911 before he went to try to rescue you. The first responders got here just after the shot was fired. Michael kept telling them he had to stop his dad from killing his mom."

"My poor baby. This isn't right, Chennelle. It's just not fair."

"No, it isn't. But here's what you are going to do. You're going to stop crying and then I'll have Barnes bring Michael and Justin over here. I'm sure they're as worried about you as you are about them."

"Okay."

"The way you look is going to be bad enough, but you and I will assure them that you're going to be okay, but you need to go to the hospital."

"I can't go to the hospital, they need me. I can't leave my boys."

"Anne," Chennelle said, frowning at her. "You are going to do what I tell you to do. This man punched you really hard. You need to have x-rays to make sure there aren't any broken bones, and I doubt you've avoided at least a slight concussion."

Anne nodded. It was hard to tell what her expression was with all that swelling.

"When you leave for the hospital, Barnes and I will talk to the detective they sent over from the Juvenile Branch about taking your boys over to your mother's house. We'll explain what happened and ask that she have one of your brothers meet you at the hospital. I'll have your mother stay with me while the juvenile officer interrogates Michael. After what all of us witnessed on Sunday and after Aaron's actions tonight, no one in their right mind would bring charges against Michael."

"Okay."

"I've already talked to somebody from Sexual Violence. Detective Pat Flannigan will be there to take your statement and CSI Sophia Parelli will take photos of your injuries and other evidence from your clothing, fingernails, etc."

"Aaron never said who posted his bond," said Anne in a much calmer voice.

"Some friend of his, or should I say ex-friend once we arrest Aaron for assault and battery and attempted rape. The judge will throw the book at him this time."

"Maybe it was worth getting punched then," said Anne a small, painful looking smile forming.

Chennelle waved at Barnes. The next thing she saw were Anne's sons running toward them.

"Slow down fellas," said Chennelle. "Mom's pretty sore, so be careful."

"Mom, are you okay?" said Justin, shaking slightly. His eyes widened as he caught full sight of her injuries.

"I've been better," she said.

"Mom, I'm so sorry," said Michael, bursting into tears. "I didn't know it was loaded. I wanted to scare him. I wanted him to stop hurting you."

Anne pulled her eldest son to her and then Justin tried to put his arms around both. They all cried for a few minutes.

Chennelle felt like an intruder, but she had to make sure Anne went to the hospital for treatment as soon as possible. "Okay guys, your mom needs to go to the hospital for some tests. We want to make sure she doesn't have any broken bones."

Justin looked at Chennelle and back to his mother in horror. "You're not gonna die like Grandpa did, are you?"

Anne gasped and grabbed her youngest son by the chin. "Look at me. This isn't anything near as bad as what happened to Grandpa. These nice paramedics can only do so much out here, but they want to make sure I don't have any injuries to my bones or my eye. It's just a check up to make sure there isn't something in my head that needs fixing."

"Okay, Mommy," said Justin, relaxing his shoulders.

"Detectives Kendall and Barnes will take you over to Grandma's. She's going to be very upset about all of this, so you have to take good care of her for me, okay?"

Both boys nodded.

"Michael, I want you to answer all of detectives' questions honestly. Nothing bad is going to happen to you, I promise. Grandma will have Uncle Jeff or Uncle Grant come and get me at the hospital, so don't worry about me."

"It's time to go now," said Chennelle. "Give your mother a very gentle kiss and then go back to the car with Detective Barnes."

The boys did as instructed and waved at their mother until they disappeared into the back seat of Barnes' vehicle.

"Thank you," said Anne as the paramedics helped her into the back of the ambulance and had her lie down.

"Take care, Samuels," said Chennelle. "Don't worry about your sons, they're in good hands."

Anne gave her a thumbs up just before the driver closed the doors and headed for the cab.

A tear trickled down Chennelle's cheek. She wiped it away and walked to the car. It was time to keep her promise.

Chapter 40

"Coffee, I need more coffee," said Barnes, literally dragging her feet across the room. "Yesterday had to be one of the longest days ever."

Chennelle definitely agreed. It had taken her most of the morning to finish typing her notes from their interview with Roman Wagner and then type up the report she was just finishing on the incident at the Samuels' residence.

She and Barnes had stayed with Anne's mother, Mildred, until 11:00 p.m. the night before. They wanted to wait to hear from Grant Russell on his sister's condition before they left. Apparently, Chennelle had been justified in her concern. X-rays of Anne's left cheekbone showed a very tiny hairline fracture and she had a mild concussion. The doctor admitted her for observation. He wanted to do an MRI before he would agree to send her home.

Michael and Justin had fallen asleep on the carpeted floor of the family room near the fireplace. Mildred placed blankets over them, saying she didn't want to wake them. She planned to sleep on the couch so she'd be near them if they woke.

"I don't know about you, but this emotional stuff drains me," said Barnes as she sat down and took a sip of her coffee. "Now that poor kid has to deal with shooting his father on top of everything else."

"That family's been through enough. I wonder if we can throw in assaulting a police officer on top of the attempted rape charge." Chennelle glanced over her report. "I just think it's funny Michael shot him in the ass."

Barnes laughed. "I know, but did you hear him howling about it? The way the bullet hit him, it just went through some of the fat and wound up in the wall. *Oh, God, that little shit tried to kill his own father,* he says. *He could have crippled me for life. I want him arrested for attempted murder.*"

"I'm just glad Sanchez and Lloyd got there in time to get the boys out of the house before Aaron started ranting. Michael feels guilty enough."

"Okay, where are we on Kelso and Winston?" asked Barnes. "I don't suppose we've got DNA results from the skin under Winston's fingernails yet?"

"Nope. I doubt we'll see any before next week. I don't even have the energy to call over there and ask how much longer they think it will take."

"Good morning, Detectives," said Adams as he approached. "I was coming into the building when the sergeant at the desk asked me to bring up someone who says she's a friend of yours, Barnes. Her name's Amber Mc-something."

"McManus?" asked Barnes.

"That sounds right. I put her in the conference room for you."

"Thanks, Adams," said Barnes, standing and heading for the conference room.

Chennelle stood as well only to find Adams blocking her way.

"Can't we just go out for coffee one evening this week? I miss you."

"Get yourself a girlfriend and you won't miss me so much." Chennelle tried to side-step him, but he moved in front of her again.

"Please, Chennelle. Meet me after shift at the Starbucks on the Circle."

His deep brown eyes were burning with passion. She felt heat rising in her body, a heat long forgotten. She looked over towards Major Stevenson's office to make sure they weren't being observed.

"Coffee, and that's all. I need to get back to work, Trevon."

Adams stepped aside. She couldn't believe she'd just consented to a coffee date with him. Was she out of her mind? Did she really want to go down this path again? She had to stick to her word and not allow herself to get involved with him. Maybe she'd get it through that thick skull of his if they had a heart-to-heart.

His beautiful eyes passed through her mind and desire filled her once more. She shook her head, thinking, *Who do you need to convince—him or you?"*

Chapter 41

Chennelle caught up to Barnes before she had a chance to enter the conference room. "Do you think she has something for us?"

"Maybe," said Barnes. "I think it more likely she's scared now that two members of her coven have been murdered. There's only one way to find out."

Barnes grabbed the doorknob and they entered to find a very nervous Amber pacing the room. She didn't look anything like the woman Chennelle had met a week ago. Her hair was unkempt and her clothing in disarray.

"Erica," said Amber rushing over to Barnes. "Is it true? Is some nutcase coming after members of our coven?"

"Amber, let's sit down for a moment so we can discuss this." Barnes took Amber's arm and escorted her to the nearest chair.

Chennelle decided to take charge. "We can't be positively sure of this at the moment. It could be connected or it may be a coincidence. We need to gather more evidence before we can make such an assumption."

"So does that mean more of us have to die for you to come to some sort of conclusion?" Amber laughed hysterically and left her chair, pacing again.

"No, Amber," said Chennelle. "We have collected some DNA evidence, but that takes a while to process. In the meantime, I would advise you and other members of your coven to be extra diligent in making your safety top priority."

"*Really?*"

"Come on, Amber, there's no need for sarcasm," said Barnes. "Detective Kendall just wants all of you to take extra precautions, like never going anywhere alone, or staying with relatives or friends until this is over."

Amber stopped and stomped her foot. "And how long is that going to take? If we're on our guard, won't he just wait us out until he can get to us again?"

Chennelle looked to her partner, who didn't seem to have the answer either. "We realize this is as frustrating for you as it is for us. Believe me, we want this guy off the street and fast."

"I guess," Amber said, obviously not convinced. "Here's a letter from Barbara. She wants you to come to her house tonight. I've got to go."

Amber tossed the letter to Chennelle and without another word swept from the room, slamming the door behind her.

Chennelle glanced over at her partner's stunned face and then down at the letter. It was sealed with wax with a pentagram stamped into the middle. This seemed somewhat medieval of Barbara, but they were dealing with an ancient pagan religion. Breaking the seal, Chennelle opened the envelope and pulled out the letter, which she read aloud.

"Detective Kendall and Detective Barnes,

We would like to invite you to a special meeting of our coven tonight at 7:00 p.m. Our members have many questions for you and would appreciate your presence. You need only respond to me by telephone if you are not coming.

Blessed be,

Barbara Dodson"

"Why do I get the feeling there's more to this than a few questions?" asked Chennelle.

"I know what you're saying. It seems weird for her to send Amber over here with a written invitation when she could have called us on the phone."

"The only way we're going to find out is to accept the invitation."

"I guess we're going to a Circle."

Chapter 42

Shift change came quicker than Chennelle had realized. She and Barnes had been busy making phone calls to parishioners of the Avenging Angels Evangelical Church most of the day, asking if they would voluntarily give samples of DNA. Most were very cooperative, others not so much.

She knew she'd have to petition a judge for a warrant to get DNA from Roman Wagner, but hadn't anticipated Curt Putnam would give her any grief. Perhaps they should be looking at Mr. Putnam more closely. Barnes would check out Putnam's alibi for Winston tomorrow and then question him concerning his whereabouts the night Kelso was killed.

Right now, she was walking toward the center of town to meet Adams for a quick coffee. Barnes was going to meet her later at the Dodson residence so they could go straight home afterward. The closer she got to Starbucks, the more rapid her heartbeat. Was it the walk, or anticipating her meeting with Trevon?

As she approached, she saw him outside the coffee shop talking to Patrol Officer Bays. He wore the leather jacket he knew was her favorite; it enhanced his tall, muscular build. She told herself that it was a sin for anyone to look that good. She took a deep breath and slowed her pace.

"Detective Kendall, good to see you," said Bays. "I was just telling Adams that Samuels went home this afternoon. The fracture in her cheekbone is minute and should heal pretty easily as long as she doesn't receive another blow to the area. She only has a slight headache from the concussion. They're going to watch her eye, though. There's still too much swelling to know if there's any permanent damage."

"I'm afraid the permanent damage was done to her sons," said Trevon. "Even though the kid was trying to save his mother, it will take a long time for him to get over watching his dad hurt her, and the fact that he shot his own father."

"Let's be glad it was just a flesh wound," said Chennelle.

"Better get back in my squad," said Bays. "I'll let you know if I hear any more."

"Thanks, Bays," said Trevon, then he turned to Chennelle. "Shall we?" Trevon held the door open for her. "Since I talked you into this, it's my treat."

"Damn straight it is," said Chennelle before she could stop herself. Warmth flooded her cheeks and she turned away from him, scanning the menu, even though she already knew what she wanted.

"I'll have a Grande Pumpkin Spice Latte, nonfat, no whip, please," she said.

"I'll have the same," said Trevon.

"Sure thing, Detective Adams," said the pretty blonde barista.

Chennelle raised an eyebrow as Trevon turned to look at her.

"What?" he said in his most innocent voice.

"Nothing." She found an empty table near the window. As far as she was concerned, he could cart the things over there. Was blondie another one of his conquests? Chennelle stared out the window, asking herself why she'd agreed to meet him here.

"Here you go," he said, placing one of the lattes in front of her.

"Thanks." She dared not look him in the eye. Closing her eyes, she took that first extremely hot but tasty sip. Then she set the container on the table, both hands wrapped around it to feel its warmth, while keeping her gaze focused on the cup.

"How was your day?"

Looking up at him, she must have had an expression that told him how lame that question was because he immediately snatched up his own cup and took a swig.

"Busy," was all she said.

"Me, too."

Could this be real? Was Trevon Adams actually nervous? This man always had something smooth to say. He truly seemed lost for words.

"So why did you want to meet me, Trevon?"

He took another sip of his latte. "Well…I…um…I wanted a chance to tell you…"

"I don't have all night."

That got his attention. "Why, you have a date tonight?"

"Yeah, with Barnes. We're checking out a lead tonight."

"Oh, I see," he said, looking relieved. "Okay, I'll try to get to the point. Chennelle, you're right, I've always been a player. My dad left my mom when I was four and I guess I just never got to see what a real man…I mean, *how* a real man should treat a woman."

"So you're blaming your father?"

"Come on, Chennelle, this is hard enough."

"Sorry," she said. Of course, after what he'd put her through, she wasn't very sorry. As a matter of fact, this conversation was suddenly giving her a sense of empowerment.

"I guess watching Mom struggle after Dad disappeared, I got all the wrong ideas about life and how it *should* be. It was hard for me to think about settling down, and having kids was really out of the question. That's why I always use protection."

Chennelle sipped more of her latte, but kept her eyes on him now. She wanted to watch his body language because she knew it would tell her as much about whether he was being truthful as his words.

"Then, I met you, and you terrified me. I started to feel like…I don't know…like I wanted to be with only one woman—you. What I did with Tanya was the biggest mistake I've ever made in my life. From the time I met you, I hadn't slept with anyone else, but when you told me you loved me, I panicked. I lost perspective and common sense and went all self-destructive."

He stopped talking. Chennelle could see his eyes tearing up. Was he seriously going to start crying right here in the Starbucks? As Barnes would say, *holy crap.*

"So, are you asking me for another chance?"

"I know I don't have a right to ask, but I can't live without you. Since we split, every time I've asked a woman out, I cut the date short. I take her home, drop her off, and never call her again. The only thing that's missing from pre-Chennelle is the sex. I don't want to be with anybody else. I love you."

Chennelle's heart rate rose as she started to soften. She couldn't let him back in, she couldn't let him hurt her again…could she? Would he actually change?

"Thanks for telling me all of this," she said. "Um, I really have to get going and meet Barnes at the Dodson house."

"Okay, but please think about what I said. I know you have every reason to tell me to get out of your life. I guess after watching what Samuels went through with her husband, I could see that she deserves better, and so do you. If you decide it's not worth it, I get it. Just remember how good we were together and hopefully, we can try again."

"I'll think about it," said Chennelle.

On her walk back to the station to pick up her car, she thought about all Trevon had said and the sincerity of his words. Everything was a risk and she did love him. Now, for the first time, he'd actually said those words to her. If she could just get that image of him in bed with Tanya out of her head, she might be able to forgive him and move on.

Chapter 43

"Are you serious?" said Barnes as she and Chennelle walked up to the Dodson house. "Are you actually considering taking Adams back?"

"I don't know." Confusion tore at Chennelle's brain. "On the one hand, I'm not sure I'll get the trust back, and that would really make for a miserable life. Then I think about the tears in his eyes and the fact that he said I love you for the first time and...."

"I know, I get it. In a way, I guess I understand what Trevon did because I nearly did the same thing."

"You mean when you had the hots for Federal Agent Morgan?"

"Yes. I see lots of guys who are attractive, but at that point in my relationship with Ben, I was terrified of taking the next step. I could tell he was getting serious, but I had my doubts about marrying a fellow cop and having children who might lose both of their parents because of the job."

"There's a difference. You didn't act on your feelings toward Morgan."

"Chennelle, that's not because I didn't want to do it. Morgan turned me down."

"You never told me that," said Chennelle, glaring at Barnes in surprise.

"I was ashamed of myself and embarrassed. Luckily, Agent Morgan was a gentleman and said it never happened."

"Your secret is safe with me."

"So, Chennelle, you need to decide if taking him back is worth the risk of giving him one more chance not to screw up."

The conversation ended as they reached the door. Chennelle rang the bell and an older woman in a deep burgundy robe answered.

"Welcome," she said. "I am Victoria Barker. May I assume that you are the detectives Barbara said would be visiting this evening?"

"Yes, we are," said Chennelle.

"Come in and follow me."

They followed Victoria to a doorway. She opened it and gestured for them to descend the dimly lit stairs. Chennelle's unease from the meeting they'd had with Amber earlier had returned.

"Detective Kendall, Detective Barnes, welcome to both of you," said Barbara in grandiose style. She was wearing an emerald green robe which set off her dark auburn hair. "We first wanted to ask the Goddess for assistance to keep us safe and to aid you in capturing this villain."

Chennelle thought villain was a rather soft term for someone who so brutally tortured and killed these women. Glancing around the room, she recognized Gabriella from Amber's shop and of course, Amber. The others were unfamiliar to her.

"Allow me to introduce our members to you," said Barbara. "We will only use first names here. This is Carmen, Bella, Cathy, Maci, Victoria you met upstairs, Kelsey, Paula, Mya, Gabriella, and you've both met Amber. As you may have guessed, our coven consists of thirteen, but now that we've lost two members, we were hoping the two of you would stand in for them."

Chennelle's mouth dropped open. She looked toward Barnes and found hers to be open as well. This was not what they'd expected to be doing tonight.

"But we aren't Wiccans," said Chennelle. "Isn't that kind of against the rules or something?"

Some of the women giggled. Barbara put on a broad smile. "Hardly, Detective. May I call you by your first names?"

"Sure, I'm Chennelle and this is Erica."

"That makes it a little more intimate," said Barbara. "We welcome all who are willing, but if you aren't comfortable with it we'll understand. However, it does make the circle stronger if we have thirteen."

Chennelle glanced at Barnes again. She gave her the *what do we have to lose* expression. Chennelle nodded at Barbara in agreement.

"Excellent," said Barbara with enthusiasm. "First we must cast our circle. Come, Erica. You stand with Amber. Chennelle, you're with Victoria. Just watch what they do and follow them."

In the center of the room was a short table. On it rested a small caldron, much like the one they found in Sasha Winston's duffle. Next to the caldron sat a bell, a small stick with a crystal attached to the end of it, a small broom, and an athame.

"Stand next to me, child," said Victoria, taking Chennelle's hand and guiding her. "First Barbara will take the athame and will walk around us creating the circle of power. We must all stay inside of the circle or the energy will be broken."

Chennelle saw Barbara pick up the dagger and walk around everyone holding it out as though slicing through the air to make a circle. The she muttered something Chennelle couldn't quite hear in four places around the circle before replacing the athame on the table.

Victoria spoke again in a whisper. "That is our altar. She will light the black candle to banish evil and to bring us protection and then the red to bring us strength in the coming days. That one is especially for you and Erica to help you trap this killer."

Victoria fell silent and Chennelle tried to pay close attention to what Barbara was saying as she started the ritual.

"We burn these seeds of anise and ask you, Goddess, to protect us from this evil spirit who wishes to do us harm," said Barbara after lighting something in the caldron and raising her hands to the sky. "Goddess, protect us. Blessed be."

"Blessed be," said the others.

Barbara lit the black candle. "May this candle of black guide us through the darkness and protect us from evil. Blessed be."

"Blessed be." This time Erica and Chennelle repeated the words as well.

Barbara lit the red candle. "May this candle of red give all of us strength. To those among us who are looking for this evil man, give them extra strength and energy to defeat him. Blessed be."

"Blessed be."

Picking up a purple velvet bag from the table, Barbara emptied the contents on the table. Several colorful stones littered the tabletop. She touched them and came up with two black stones. Barbara approached Erica, handed one stone to her, and then gave one to Chennelle.

"These Apache tears will bring you luck in your endeavors."

Barbara repeated this ritual with an agate that looked like an eye to protect them from evil, something she called a chalcedony to protect them from evil and to bring good fortune, and malachite to avoid forthcoming evil. She gave each detective a small purple velvet bag in which to place the stones.

"You need to keep these with you at all times to protect you."

She then took two large charms dangling from leather strings. She put one around Erica's neck and the second around Chennelle's.

"These amulets contain mandrake. This plant should neither be burned nor ingested. It holds powers to protect you and bring you good luck as long as you are wearing it. Blessed be."

"Blessed be."

Chennelle looked over at Erica who was gazing straight ahead. Did these women seriously believe in this stuff? Were they actually trying to help her and Erica by putting spells on them? This was just too much. She wasn't about to wear an amulet or carry around a bunch of rocks.

Barbara began to speak as she picked up the athame again. "Now let us go out of this circle feeling more protected and energized. Thank you, Goddess, for listening to our pleas. Blessed be."

"Blessed be."

Chennelle started to turn to walk away, but Victoria grabbed her arm to stop her. "We have to wait for Barbara to cut a path with the athame. Then we will exit behind her."

Nodding, Chennelle stood and watched as Barbara made a cutting motion on what must have been the edge of the invisible circle she'd made earlier. They all followed Barbara up the stairs and congregated in the living area.

Chennelle and Erica fielded some questions for about an hour, trying to reassure these women without revealing too much. Certain things, like the branding, had to be kept secret.

They finally left and Chennelle drove home where she tried to process what a bizarre day she'd had. First, the uncooperative church member, then Adams proclaiming his love for her, and now this. Amulets, protective stones, and she'd actually participated in a Wiccan coven's circle.

"God, Goddess, or whoever you are out there, please make tomorrow less crazy. Oh, and a good night's sleep would be great, too. Thanks."

Chapter 44

"Last night was weird, huh?" said Barnes. "I mean, knowing Amber, I had a little idea of what they do, but I sure didn't think they'd bring us in on it. Are you wearing your amulet?"

"Don't be ridiculous," said Chennelle. She tossed a file on her desk and frowned.

"I am. The way I see it, we need all the help we can get," said Barnes with that impish grin she displayed every now and then.

"If things get worse, that necklace thing and pouch are in my purse."

"Excellent. After you left to have coffee yesterday, I called Curt Putnam. He said he'd be over here around nine this morning." Barnes glanced at her watch. "Holy crap! That's five minutes from now."

"Were you able to find out anything more about his alibi for the night Winston died?"

"I can't find anyone who can vouch for him. Even his mother can't say for sure that he was home," said Barnes. "Can you imagine being forty and still living with your mother? Seems like a prime candidate for a psycho serial killer to me."

"I love my parents, but there's absolutely no way I could live with them very long," said Chennelle.

"After being with Pop this past couple of months, I think he's the one who's tired of me, not the other way around." The phone on Barnes' desk rang and she grabbed the receiver. "Hello...okay, thanks." Barnes hung up and gave a thumbs up to Chennelle. "Putnam is in room three."

Chennelle rose from her chair and grabbed a pad of paper and pencil. They always recorded their sessions with suspects, but she liked to take notes. It helped her remember what was said so she could formulate better questions.

When they walked into the room, there sat the almost skeletal Curtis Putnam tapping the fingers of his right hand on the desk. His neatly cut mousy brown hair was combed so not one hair was out of place. He looked up and adjusted his black, thick-rimmed glasses on his nose.

Leaning forward, he folded his hands together on top of the table. "I need to get back to work, so can we make this quick?"

"We'd like nothing better," said Chennelle. She took the seat across from Putnam, and Barnes took the seat to his right. "First, let's start with that DNA thing."

"I don't think I should have to do something like that if I don't want to. It's an invasion of privacy."

"Actually, Mr. Putnam, what happened to Sasha Winston was an invasion of privacy," said Chennelle, leaning in. "A DNA test which could prove you innocent is just an inconvenience."

"Besides, we've obtained a warrant for your DNA," said Barnes as she placed the warrant in front of him. "So, it's a mute point now, isn't it?"

His eyes widened and he looked like he wanted to bolt—very interesting body language. Chennelle was really anxious to have a go at him now.

"We'll have our tech come in and collect it once we've finished asking a few questions," said Chennelle. "Now, where were you this past Thursday night from about eight o'clock to three o'clock on Friday morning?"

She could see Putnam look down at his hands, which were trembling slightly. Then he reached for the warrant and pulled it closer. For an innocent man, he certainly was nervous.

"I…I have to think a minute."

He paused, and the detectives stared at him. Chennelle was hoping this would unnerve him even further. There was nothing like a little fear to loosen a suspect's lips.

"Oh, yeah, I remember. I went to the movies."

"Was anyone with you?" asked Chennelle, poising her pencil.

"No, I always go to the movies by myself. I went to see that new Captain America movie at the theater in Castleton."

"Since you went alone, do you still have your ticket stub? Was there anyone there who you spoke with who might be able to tell us they saw you?"

"I probably threw away my ticket stub," he said, voice cracking with a hint of panic. "I bought a ticket, but so did a hundred other people. I also bought popcorn and a coke, but I doubt they'll remember me."

Chennelle nodded and wrote down his responses. She was pretty sure there weren't hundreds of people at the movies on a

Thursday evening, but she wrote it down anyway. Hearing him shift in his chair, Chennelle waited a few more seconds before looking up to give him a chance to sweat.

"So, it appears once again, you are providing us with an alibi you cannot prove."

"What happened to that woman, happened two weeks ago. Why do I need an alibi for this past Thursday?"

"That woman, as you refer to her, was Sasha Winston," said Chennelle, giving him her most stern look. "A week after her murder, a young woman named Toni Kelso was killed in a similar fashion in her own home."

"And you think I killed these women? I don't know who they are."

Chennelle considered his reaction. If she weren't a cop with twelve years experience, she might have bought his reply. However, she'd known too many killers who didn't know their victims personally, yet they killed them just the same.

"The problem lies in their religion," said Barnes. "Both of these women belong to a Wiccan coven. The church you attend has been quite vocal in expressing its objection to the coven's existence. I think we were pretty clear on that point the day you and your fellow board members stopped by."

"Of course the church doesn't condone their behavior," said Putnam, drips of sweat running down his face. "What they're doing is against God's laws. We want to get them to repent, not kill them."

"It's obvious the person who's doing this wants them to repent," said Barnes. "Thing is, they're not doing a very good job at the not killing them part."

Again, there was silence as the detectives stared at Putnam. Chennelle thought for sure he was going to pass out at any moment. She watched as he licked his lips nervously, his eyes darting from side to side. He pulled out a handkerchief and wiped his brow. Then he suddenly perked up.

"If you're not going to charge me with anything, I think I'm going to go now."

"Not until we get your DNA sample," said Barnes, rising from her chair. "I'll go call for a lab tech to come over."

Chennelle heard the door shut as Barnes left the room, but she kept her eyes fixed on Putnam. He was rocking slightly in his chair and tapping his fingers on the table again.

"Your mom couldn't be sure you stayed home that night. She hadn't seen you since dinner at six o'clock. She went to bed at about eight."

Putnam refused to look up at her. It was as though he'd put himself into a trance. He continued to stare at the table and tap his fingers.

"If it wasn't you, do you know someone at your church that might be just a little over the top when it comes to the religion these women practice?"

Putnam simply shook his head.

There was a knock on the door and then a lab tech Chennelle didn't recognize came in. The name on her badge was Taylor, Melinda. She put on gloves, then pulled out a cotton swab from a sanitary tube and told Putnam to open his mouth. Once she'd swabbed it thoroughly, she returned the sample to the tube and exited the room.

"Well, Mr. Putnam, I guess that does it…for now."

"So I can leave?" he asked.

"I'll have the nice patrol officer waiting outside escort you back down to the lobby. He'll be in momentarily."

She walked out into the hallway and told Officer Lloyd that the suspect was ready to go. Then she went back to her desk to find Barnes waiting for her.

"I don't suppose he said anything else significant after I left," said Barnes.

"No, but his body language was speaking volumes. If that SOB didn't kill these women, then he's done something else he doesn't want us to discover." Chennelle ran her fingers through her hair. "We'll have to make sure we run him through the entire database to find out if there are any unsolved crimes with his marker on them."

"Absolutely," said Barnes. "We could put a tail on him for a while. If our killer has established a pattern, he may strike again in a couple of days."

"That's what scares me," said Chennelle. "At least if we have him followed, we'll soon know if he's the one."

"Too bad we don't have the manpower to have the whole bunch of those parishioners followed." Barnes sighed. "Well, I'm starving. Let's go grab some lunch. I'm buying."

"You talked me right into it."

Chapter 45

He watched the witches in the coffee shop as they leaned in to talk more quietly. Doug was sure they were whispering about the witch, Toni Kelso. He had just prepared herbal tea for each of them. The beautiful witch, Carmen Cortez, had paid for the drinks with her credit card. Now he could access her information. This must be a sign from God that he'd made the right choice of who should be next. He took a rag and went out to the seating area in order to hear their conversation.

"Carmen, you can't," said the dark skinned woman. "We're not supposed to go out by ourselves."

"I've been on my own for a long time now, Maci. Stop mothering me."

Doug was pleased to have another name, but he needed Maci's last name. He'd ask the witch, Carmen, tonight. He continued to wipe the surrounding tables as slowly as possible.

"Carmen, Maci is right," said the pale blonde. "We all need to be extra cautious after what happened to Toni and Sasha."

"We don't know their deaths were related, Bella," said Carmen. "I paid good money for those concert tickets and I'm not going to miss it. It's Paul freakin' McCartney, ladies. Besides, I'll only be alone for a few minutes. I'm going to meet my friend, George, at Veterans Park at seven o'clock, and he's never late."

"I still don't like it," said Maci.

"It'll be fine," said Carmen, sounding exasperated.

Doug saw Maci and Bella look at one another with concern.

"I've got to get going," said Bella, rising from her chair.

"Me, too," said Maci.

"Then there's no reason for me to stick around," said Carmen. "I'll call you tomorrow so you'll know I'm okay."

The other two nodded and they all walked out.

"Hey, Doug," said his manager. "Those tables are plenty clean. Do your girl watching on your own time."

Doug blushed. That idiot didn't realize how important this was to his mission. How could he know what was commanded of Doug?

In his heart, he knew he had to forgive his manager for his stupidity, but he really hated the guy.

Nevertheless, Doug had a calling. He would meet his next repentant at seven o'clock this evening in Veterans Park.

Chapter 46

"You know I would have taken you to a fine restaurant," said Trevon. "I really didn't expect to take you to Potbelly's on our second first date."

"Potbelly's has great food," said Chennelle. "You should be thanking me for saving you some money. Besides, I need to get back to the office and find out who's tailing our suspect, Curtis Putnam."

"You and Barnes think this could be your guy?"

"Would it sound horrible if I said I hope so?" She said the words while staring down at her salad. She felt the back of his hand brush her cheek.

"No, I'd think you were a very compassionate woman. You want to catch the killer so no one else will get hurt or die."

Chennelle looked up into Trevon's warm brown eyes. They were so inviting, but she was scared. She wanted to be sure that she could trust him before jumping in again. But how could she ever know unless she took the risk?

"This guy's been striking in the middle of the night, right?"

She nodded. "Yes, Patel thinks Winston died around one in the morning and Kelso died around eleven at night."

"So let's walk off some of that stress before you go back to your office. It's a pretty warm night. We can walk down to Veteran's Park and back."

Seeing that impish grin on his face was too much. She smiled back and nodded. When she rose from her chair, he grabbed her coat and helped her put it on.

"I've got to get back by seven thirty, though," she said.

"Yes, Detective Kendall."

They followed the Circle around to North Meridian Street and started walking. He reached for her hand and she didn't resist. It was almost as though nothing had happened—almost.

Images of him under the sheets with another woman flitted through her mind. She tried to fight it, even gripping his hand a little harder. He squeezed hers back. He obviously didn't know her response was anxiety, not affection.

"Chennelle, I know this isn't going to be easy. It's going to take a lot for you to trust me again, but I really do want...."

His words trailed off as they heard someone yelling in the distance. They hurried toward the sound and then a voice rang out, "Let her go!"

Chennelle caught a glimpse of a man running north on the east side of the park, still calling out angrily. Then she saw why he was shouting. The small figure of what must have been a woman appeared to be struggling with a tall, darkly dressed person. Chennelle and Trevon drew their weapons and ran towards the melee.

The man doing the shouting reached his struggling friend and her attacker. Chennelle saw a spark of light and the fellow went down, crying out in pain. The assailant must have heard Chennelle and Trevon coming because he glanced at the detectives before pulling the woman in front of him. He kept her firmly in hand until he reached his car, the door of which was already open.

Chennelle and Trevon were still at least five hundred feet away from them. Chennelle heard the woman scream and saw her fall face first onto the ground. The attacker jumped into his car, slammed the door, and sped off. By the time she and Trevon reached the victims, the car was too far away for them to get a plate number.

The male victim was sitting up holding his right arm. Blood spilled down his sleeve. "Carmen, Carmen," he screamed.

The girl was still face down and groaning, the back of her jacket now soaked with her blood.

"Are you hurt badly?" Chennelle asked the man.

"No, I think my jacket kept him from cutting me too deeply. Is Carmen alright? She's not getting up."

Trevon was examining her. He took out his phone and Chennelle heard him call for an ambulance and a crime scene crew. He then pulled off his jacket and put pressure on her wound, glancing at Chennelle with his *"this is bad"* look. She'd have to keep the boyfriend calm.

"My partner is helping her. An ambulance is on its way. Put your hand on your wound and put pressure on it." Chennelle tried to position herself between the man and his sight line to the woman. "You need to sit still and keep pressure on it so you don't cause yourself to bleed more."

"Okay, but I want to know if Carmen's okay."

"She's doing fine, kid," shouted Trevon. "You can help her best by sitting right where you are and telling Detective Kendall what you saw."

"Okay," the injured man said in a shaky voice. "Carmen and I were meeting here to go to the Paul McCartney concert at the Bankers Life Fieldhouse tonight. I was a couple of minutes late." He wiped at tears streaming down his face. "I'm never late. If I'd been on time, he…he…"

"What's your name?" asked Chennelle. She wanted to try to get him to focus on the facts, not his feelings.

"George Smith. What was with that guy? I drove up and saw him grab her. He put something over her face. Then when I got to them, he swung around with this huge dagger and sliced me."

"Did you get a good look at him?"

"It happened so fast, I couldn't tell you what he looked like. His hood was too low over his face. But he was definitely white. I saw his chin and his neck and he was white."

"I don't suppose you got a look at his license plate?"

George closed his eyes momentarily, squinting as though he were trying to squeeze the memory from his brain. "I know it's an Indiana plate, and I think it started with forty-nine, but I can't remember the rest. Car was a dark color, and I saw a Buick symbol on the trunk. Are you sure she's okay?" He shifted his body to look around Chennelle.

Chennelle took his good arm and moved him back into position as they heard sirens approaching. "Detective Adams is taking good care of her. You need to focus on me right now."

George nodded and leaned back to his original position. "I really can't remember anything else. This thing really hurts."

"They're pulling up now," said Chennelle, placing a hand on his uninjured arm. "You've remembered a lot. It will help us get one step closer to nailing this man."

"Good. Tell them they have to take care of Carmen first," he said, frantically pointing at the paramedics. "She's hurt worse than I am."

"Okay," said Chennelle. She motioned for the first paramedics to go to where Adams was still putting pressure on Carmen's back. "Looks like the rest of our team is pulling up."

She saw Sophia Parelli from Crime Scene Investigations and Patrol Officers Lloyd and Sanchez approaching. Sophia went straight to the girl and instructed the paramedics to make sure the hospital collected Carmen's clothing as evidence. She'd have one of her techs go down and meet them there.

"What are those officers doing?" asked George, bringing Chennelle's attention back to him.

"Adams is going to show them the area that needs to be cordoned off, and then they'll put yellow crime scene tape up. One of them will start a logbook and we'll all sign it so they know what police officers were on scene. Ah, here comes the second ambulance."

As the new paramedics came nearer, Chennelle asked George if he could stand. He said yes and she helped him to his feet. "This is George Smith," she told the first paramedic to arrive. "The attacker slit his arm with a large knife. I don't think there's much damage, and he's been applying pressure so I think the bleeding is under control. He's going to need stitches to keep it from bleeding again though."

"We'll get him into the ambulance, take off his coat, and access the wound before we take off," said the paramedic before turning to Smith. "Can you walk to the ambulance?"

"Yes, I think so," said George. He took a couple of steps and turned. "Detective Kendall, thanks. I hope you catch this son-of-a-bitch before he hurts someone else."

"That's the plan," she said.

She turned to see Trevon, his hands soaked in Carmen's blood. He was shaking slightly from the chill in the air.

"Maybe we should ask the paramedics for some water to wash your hands, and for a blanket."

"Yeah," he said, pouting. "It figures something like this would happen while I'm wearing my best jacket."

Chennelle laughed. "Adams, you're pitiful."

"Well, you won't be laughin' when I tell you what the girl said to me before she passed out."

His expression was more serious than she'd ever seen from him. Her heart sank as she waited for him to reveal the girl's statement.

"She told me he called her a witch."

Chapter 47

Instead of going home, Doug went straight to his special place. This was where he'd purged the first witch. This was where he was going to bring Toni Kelso, but she was too heavy for him to lift and put in his car once he'd chloroformed her. Tonight, he'd planned to bring Carmen to this place, but he'd failed. He knew she would be meeting someone and shouldn't have taken the chance of grabbing her in such a public place.

"What about the sign?" he asked himself aloud. "I had to do it on the seventh day. I did exactly what I thought you told me."

He was becoming angry now. Whirling around, he grabbed an axe and threw it at the wall, wedging it there. Howling like a wounded animal, he started wrecking the place. He toppled chairs and tables and emptied shelves. Glass shattered and ceramic broke into pieces.

"No, no," he screamed and fell to his knees. "How could I have been so careless? How can I blame God for my own stupidity? Please, God, forgive me for my anger and failure. Help me to find a way to make this right and do your will."

He bent over, crying into his hands. Doug rocked and sobbed until he was so tired he thought he'd pass out. However, he couldn't rest. First, there was the punishment for his doubting. Then, he had to go home and face Grandmother and try to be cheerful and kind to her. After all, she was the one who took care of him like a mother. She deserved his respect.

Standing slowly, he removed his sweatshirt and his tee shirt, exposing bare scarred flesh. Doug walked over to the back wall and removed a flogging whip from the hook. He stood straight with the whip in his right hand, took a deep breath, and struck himself on the left side of his back with it. He flinched in pain, and then did it six more times.

Doug then took the whip in his left hand and repeated the process until his entire back was bloody and stinging. This would teach him not to question. This would make him stronger.

* * * * *

Doug came into the house by the back door. His back was still burning from his wounds and he knew they'd bled through his tee shirt, but he hoped not completely through his sweatshirt. He didn't want his grandmother to see the evidence of his sin.

Quietly, he walked into the living room to find her fast asleep in her chair. With gratitude, he went to his room and began to shed his clothes. He'd take a shower and then put her to bed.

He checked his sweatshirt. Blood had leaked through it. In the time it took to travel from his special place to home, much of his blood had dried and now his tee shirt adhered to his wounds. He could feel the tugging and the pain, so he took off all his other clothing and wore his tee shirt in the shower.

Although the warm water stung at first, it did help loosen the shirt. He winced as he pulled it away from his skin and finally shed it, allowing it to drop to the floor of the shower. He turned down the water temperature a bit more. The flow of cooler water seemed to soothe the cuts, and soon the floor of the shower was red with his blood.

"God sent his Son to bleed for me, so I must bleed for Him."

When Doug was pretty sure his wounds were no longer bleeding, he turned off the water and got out of the shower. He dried himself, pulling the towel tightly across his back. There was some blood when he pulled the towel away, but not much. Using his hairdryer on a low heat setting, he dried his back more thoroughly, hoping to dry what was still oozing. He put on a clean white tee shirt, a pair of pajama pants, and his robe.

When he reached his grandmother's chair, she was sitting up looking drowsy. "Where you been, boy?" she asked.

"I went to the pharmacy to pick up one of your prescriptions."

"Humph, I didn't know I needed any more," she said, glaring at him.

"You're almost out of your cholesterol medicine, so I had it refilled," he lied.

"Well, I'm ready for bed. Help me out of his danged chair."

Doug retrieved her walker and helped her stand. He accompanied her to her bedroom, making sure she didn't stumble along the way. She got into bed and they prayed together. He kissed her on the forehead before retreating to his room.

When he went to turn off the television set, he decided to wait and watch a bit of the news. He wanted to see if there was a report on the attack. There it was, probably the top story of the day.

"We've been told that Ms. Cortez was grabbed from behind by a tall, white male and threatened with a long, sharp dagger. Her friend, George Smith, came to her rescue and received a wound to the arm. He is in Methodist Hospital in stable condition. Luckily, two police detectives were walking in the park at the time of the incident and were able to chase off Ms. Cortez's attacker, but not before he stabbed her in the back. Methodist Hospital officials tell us that Ms. Cortez is still in surgery at this time. We'll hope to have an update for you in the morning. Live from the scene at the World War Memorial Veterans Park, this is Andrea Atkins reporting."

Doug changed the channel back to Grandmother's favorite station and then turned off the television. The witch was in surgery. He hadn't succeeded in ridding the world of this devil worshipper. People would be watching her now. Those two people running at him in the park were cops. If they'd actually seen him or his license plates, they'd be here arresting him.

George must not have recognized him. He'd seen Carmen in the coffee shop with him on several occasions. But did Carmen see him? No, he decided. He'd grabbed her from behind and she didn't get the chance to turn and look at him. He was safe, he knew it.

It was time to rest. Tomorrow he'd start again. He had to keep going until all were purged of their sins.

Chapter 48

"So, I guess the date didn't go so well last night," said Barnes.

"Dinner was good," said Chennelle. "We went over to the hospital to check on the victims. Mr. Smith had a really nasty cut across his arm, but there wasn't any muscular damage. He was released after they put in stitches and gave him his care instructions. Of course, he didn't leave the hospital."

"He's a good friend."

"If he hadn't tried to stop the attack, that man would have had her in the car in seconds. No way Adams and I could have made it to the other side of the park in time to stop him."

"Good thing you were there or he might have killed both of them."

"As it is, Carmen lost a kidney and they had to repair her liver. If Adams hadn't applied pressure the way he did, she'd have bled out at the scene."

"Did she remember anything?" asked Barnes.

"They wouldn't let us talk to her last night. She was too groggy. The doctor said we could come by this morning and she might be able to give us a statement. I had Donovan Bays guard her room overnight in case the attacker decided to come by and finish the job."

"So Carmen told Adams the guy called her a witch?"

"Yep. She said it just before she passed out. Once I had a chance to get a good look at her, I recognized her as one of the coven we saw at the Dodson place."

"Holy crap," said Barnes. "So this could have been the guy we're looking for. How'd he know she'd be in the park?"

"Beats me. Maybe he was following her and thought this was a good opportunity," said Chennelle. "Another thing Adams noticed. He smelled something sweet and it wasn't perfume. He suspected chloroform and told the paramedics about it. Turns out he was right. CSI found a cloth soaked with it a few feet from where she collapsed."

"So that's how he's subduing them and why there aren't more defensive wounds. Once they're out, he can take them wherever he wants and bind them before they wake up."

"From what Mr. Smith told me last night, the car is a dark Buick. I can attest to the dark color, and it looked like an older four-door model, but that's all I saw. Mr. Smith also noted the license plate was an Indiana plate starting with forty-nine, which fits hundreds of vehicles in Marion County. We just need to find out how many people in Marion County own a dark colored older model Buick."

"That's all?" Barnes chuckled. "What about the attacker? Did any of you get a good look at him?"

"From what Smith could see of his skin, our perpetrator is Caucasian. Adams and I were too far away, but I know he was too tall to be either of our persons of interest. He had to be at least six-foot, two-inches tall. Putnam is only five-eleven, and Wagner is only six-foot. Officer Day was keeping an eye on Putnam last night. He saw him going to a meeting at the church that started at six o'clock and ended at eight thirty. I'd bet you a lunch that we'll find out Wagner was at the same meeting."

"This is so frustrating!"

"I know. It's like the proverbial needle in a haystack, but we know more now than we did before this happened. Let's go over to the hospital and see if Carmen Cortez is awake and talking."

Chapter 49

When they reached the ICU, Chennelle spotted George Smith in the waiting room, his right arm in a sling. She thought he must have stayed there all night. She also saw Barbara Dodson pouring a cup of coffee. Nudging Barnes and pointing them out, Chennelle motioned for her to follow.

"Hello, Mr. Smith. I'd like for you to meet my partner, Detective Barnes."

"Detective Barnes," he said, nodding to Erica.

"Is there any news about Ms. Cortez?" asked Chennelle.

"She's doing better," answered Barbara, coming up behind them. "Of course, they wanted her to save her strength to talk to the police before she gets any other visitors."

"The sooner we find out what she knows, the sooner we can catch her attacker," said Chennelle.

"Detective Kendall," said George. "Does this have something to do with Carmen being a Wiccan? Was this the same guy who killed her friends?"

"We don't know yet, but we think it could be."

"I told her I'd pick her up at her house. I knew we shouldn't meet in that park after dark." He buried his head in his hands. "She said it would be faster and easier. Then I was late. I'm never late."

Chennelle took a seat beside him and placed her hand on his shoulder. "Mr. Smith there was no way you could have known this man would be there. My biggest question is how did he know to find her there? Try to think of places where you discussed going to this concert. Did you notice anyone staring at you when you were there? I know you're tired and weak from your ordeal, but the more you try to remember the last few days you spent with Carmen; the more likely you'll recall something that may not have seemed odd at the time."

"I can do that," he said.

"In the meantime, I think you should go home. You lost a lot of blood last night. I'm sure part of the instructions the doctor gave you concerned bed rest and getting plenty of nutrition to build up your system. You don't want to get an infection by letting yourself get run down, do you?"

"No," he said. "I'll go home as soon as I get to see her and tell her I'm sorry."

Chennelle stood up and addressed Barbara. "I would appreciate it if you could take Mr. Smith home once he's seen Carmen. He really does need to take care of himself."

"I'll be glad to do so. I know Carmen cares very much for him. Please be careful with her. She's such a gentle spirit."

"We will." Chennelle gestured for Barnes to follow her. At the nurses' station, they showed their badges and explained whom they needed to see. A phone call later and the nurse guided them to Carmen's room.

"Hello, Bays. Was it a quiet night?" asked Chennelle.

"Nobody tried to get in. ICU is pretty tight on security, so I doubt he'd try it here. We'll need to take extra care when they move her to a regular room."

"We'll be here for a few minutes," said Barnes. "Why don't you go get some breakfast?"

"Sounds good," he said. "I won't be long."

"Why don't I stay out here while you question her," said Barnes. "Having two of us in there might be too intimidating and tiring."

"Sounds good."

Beeping and humming machines filled the room; it was a wonder anyone got any rest there. Carmen was lying on her left side with her blankets pulled up to her waist and hugging a pillow, probably for balance.

As Chennelle approached her, the girl moved slightly and winced. At first, her eyes opened as slits, then she blinked several times and opened them fully.

"Good morning, Miss Cortez. I'm Detective Kendall."

"You're one of the detectives who chased that guy off, aren't you?"

Chennelle pulled up a chair and came closer. Carmen's voice was so soft she could barely hear her. "Yes, I am. I'm also one of the detectives who's investigating the murders of Sasha Winston and Toni Kelso."

A curious expression came over Carmen's face. "Now I remember. You came to our meeting. You and...Detective Barnes. Was this the man who killed them?"

"We're not sure, Miss Cortez. It does seem to be an odd coincidence for you to be attacked and be part of the same coven as the others."

Carmen took a deep breath.

"Are you in pain? Should I call a nurse?"

"It's not that bad," said Carmen. "Let's get this interview over before I ask for something. I want to be able to think. What they're giving me knocks me out."

"We think this man knew where to find you this evening. Did you discuss your plans in public with anyone?"

"I've done nothing but talk about this concert ever since George bought the tickets. My mom was a big Beatles fan, so I listened to their music when I was growing up. I especially love Paul McCartney."

"Did you notice anyone listening in on those conversations? Anyone you may have seen more than once?"

Carmen winced. "Not that I noticed."

"Are you sure you don't want your pain meds?"

"I'm sure, Detective."

"Do you remember any conversations in which you mentioned going to Veterans Park?"

"George and I talked about it when I met him for dinner last weekend."

"Where was that?" asked Chennelle.

"A Wendy's over on the north side. Oh, and my friends Bella and Maci met me at the coffee shop in the Castleton Mall early Thursday afternoon. They were giving me a hard time about going to the park alone. I guess I should have listened to them."

"Was there anyone in the coffee shop besides you?"

"There were a few people, but I didn't notice any of them looking our way. Then there were a couple of baristas, Doug and Charlotte, and the manager, Bob something."

"You don't know their last names?"

"No, they only have their first names on their name tags."

"Can you think of anything else that happened that night?"

Carmen's eyes popped open wider, fear etched in her face. "The man who grabbed me showed me a knife, but it wasn't an ordinary knife. It was an athame. *And* he called me a witch."

"Did he say anything else?" asked Chennelle.

"Not to me, because then I heard George yelling at him to let me go. But…."

"What? Did you think of something else?"

"Yes. When he stabbed me, he said, *unforgiven.*"

Chapter 50

Monday morning arrived much too quickly. Chennelle had spent most of Saturday Christmas shopping with her mother. Mama always had to finish before Thanksgiving or she'd panic. She said she was getting too old to be in all those crowds, but she'd been shopping this way as far back as Chennelle could remember. At least she'd had Sunday to clean house and get some groceries.

"Hey, Barnes, what's going on?" she asked when she saw her partner had already started without her.

"The DNA tests are back from the Winston case," said Barnes. "They don't match either of our two prime suspects."

"Damn it," said Chennelle. "I guess we knew it couldn't be them after Carmen Cortez was attacked. Neither Cortez nor Smith got a good enough look at the guy to come up with a sketch. Adams and I certainly weren't close enough to get a good look at him before he drove off."

"So all we've got is a dark Buick and a partial plate," said Barnes.

"Smith didn't have enough from the plate to make it distinctive. What we're left with is a white male who drives a dark Buick with a Marion County license plate. That really narrows it down." Extremely frustrated by this case, Chennelle couldn't help the sarcasm.

"It's more than we had two weeks ago."

She was right of course. But then again, Chennelle also recalled how frustrated she and Barnes were when they were investigating the Emerson case. Someone was out there playing God. They had to stop him before he killed the whole coven.

"Did they check the DNA we collected from all the other church members?" asked Chennelle.

"No matches. However, Mr. Curtis Putnam's DNA does match on another open case."

"You don't say." Chennelle perked up. Getting another case off the books was better than nothing. "What was it?"

"It appears Putnam has been out late at night burglarizing houses."

"Is Adams on the case?" asked Chennelle.

"As a matter of fact, he is. I gave him the information before you came in and he's headed out to make the arrest. I wonder what Pastor Green will think of Putnam now."

"I feel bad for Putnam's mother."

"I guess even kids brought up in a good Christian home can go astray. So, what are you doing for Thanksgiving?"

"We're going to Saundra's," said Chennelle.

"Is Adams going with you?"

That caught Chennelle by surprise. She hadn't thought about spending Thanksgiving with Trevon.

"The subject hasn't come up. We just started going out again, so I hadn't really thought about it."

"But you have a history. Don't you think he'll expect it?"

"Well, if he does, he's expecting too much."

"Okay, just don't be surprised if he does."

Barnes was right. Trevon would expect to start where they left off. He might even invite her to go with him to his parents' house. What was she going to say to him if he asked? She wasn't ready for her family to know they were back together yet.

"You know," said Barnes, "you, Trevon, Ben, and I should go out to dinner soon."

"What?" said Chennelle, caught off guard by the suggestion.

"If you don't want to…," said Barnes, frowning.

"That's not it. I was still thinking about Thanksgiving."

"So, what do you think? Want to give it a try?"

"Sounds great. What did you have in mind?"

"We'll go on Thursday after work. We'll talk about where later. It'll be fun."

"I'm sure it will be," said Chennelle.

"You two having fun without me?"

The two detectives turned to see Brent Freeman approaching, all tan and looking relaxed.

"Holy crap, if it isn't our fearless leader back from the Caribbean all smiley-faced," said Barnes, then her eyes turned to slits and she stared at him. "What's new with you?"

"Can it, Barnes," he said, blushing.

Barnes smirked at Chennelle. "I think he still loves me."

Chennelle laughed. Barnes and Freeman had been partners off and on for years and their banter was always fun to watch.

"Now, Barnes, I'm sure Sergeant Freeman is no kiss and tell. Let's bring him up to speed on our latest case. There's plenty of time to interrogate him later."

Chapter 51

"My husband is going to be out of town for a few days. His flight leaves at three o'clock Thursday afternoon," said Bella Fuller while sipping her cappuccino. "I don't want to be alone. I hate being afraid, but after what happened to Sasha, Toni, and Carmen, I can't help it."

"We're all afraid," said Maci. "My husband is thinking about moving."

Doug smiled as he listened to their conversation. They should be afraid, afraid for their mortal souls. He was their one chance to find redemption—their one link to God.

"You should come and stay with us while Stan is out of town," said Maci. "Pack a bag and come to our house until he gets back."

"Really?" Bella smiled, her voice trembling slightly.

"Of course, we'd love to have you." Maci reached over and patted Bella's hand. "What are friends for if not to help one another in times like these?"

"You're the best, Maci. I don't know what I'd do without you."

Ah, such good friends. If I had them both at once, it might be easier to get them to confess if they had to watch one another being persuaded. Of course, he had three more days to make a decision, but this felt like the right thing to do.

"So, what I'll do is come by your house after I get off work Thursday to pick you up. Let's say at about five," said Maci. "That should give you enough time to pack and to give Stan a proper goodbye before he leaves."

"Thanks again. I'll return the favor someday." Bella and Maci rose and they embraced.

Doug watched as they said their goodbyes. If he planned carefully, he was sure it would work. He would go to Bella's house and watch for her husband to leave. Then he would subdue her first. Once he had her in the trunk of the car, he'd wait for Maci to show up at five.

"Bye, Doug," said Bella on her way out the door. "Have a great day."

He nodded toward her. Things were looking up. He'd soon correct the mistakes he'd made with Toni and Carmen. Grandmother would be so proud.

Chapter 52

George Smith had provided Chennelle with the exact location of the Wendy's Carmen had mentioned yesterday. She and Barnes had gone there earlier this morning hoping to beat the lunch crowd. They spoke with the manager who said it would have been very busy during the timeframe our victims were there. He doubted anyone would remember seeing Cortez or Smith. However, he looked up that evening's schedule and gave the names and contact information of those employees to the detectives.

The Wendy's manager was correct. The majority of the employees working that evening were under the age of eighteen. Teens rarely observed strange behavior unless it was directed at them. They'd do a quick background check on them and contact their parents to set up interviews as soon as they got back to the office.

Now they were walking through the Castleton Square Mall looking for the Have a Cup with Me coffee shop where Carmen and her friends met Thursday afternoon. Chennelle hoped one of the employees had seen someone who looked suspicious.

"Maybe we'll have better luck here," said Barnes. "Teenagers are in school at one o'clock in the afternoon."

"Let's hope so. There it is."

The coffee shop was on the corner near the food court. Their logo included two disembodied hands holding coffee cups, tapping them together in a toast. It gave an impression of a friendly place, but was the coffee any good?

There weren't any customers at the moment, so Chennelle walked up to the young girl at the counter badge in hand. "We're from the Indianapolis Police. Is Bob here?"

The girl turned and a short, stocky man of about thirty came up beside her.

"There are three Bobs who work here, but if you're looking for Bob the manager, you've found him."

"It must be our lucky day," said Chennelle. "We're homicide detectives, Bob. We need to ask a few questions. Is there somewhere we could talk privately?"

"Homicide? And you're coming to talk to me." Bob's friendly smile had faded. "Wow, I don't have an office or anything. Malls don't usually have a lot of space for that sort of thing. We can sit over there in the corner."

The round bistro table and chairs was the furthest point away from the mall entrance and the cashier. Chennelle nodded and the detectives followed Bob and took a seat.

"Do you know your customers well, Mr....?" asked Chennelle.

"Marshall, Bob Marshall," he said. "I know some of the regulars by their first names. Sometimes I remember last names because they charge their drinks."

"Have you noticed anyone lingering in your shop? Is there someone who's paying too much attention to your female customers?"

"Not that I recall? What's this about? Did one of my customers get killed?"

"Luckily, no," said Barnes. "However, she was here on the day she was attacked. She and her friends would have been here last Thursday afternoon around one."

Bob's mouth dropped open. "There's a group of three women come in here at least once a week. It wasn't one of them was it?"

"Do you know Carmen Cortez?" asked Barnes.

"Yeah, she's a friend of Maci's," he said. "Maci works at one of the dress shops here in the mall." He paused and looked away, his brow furrowed in thought. "You know, I think they were in here this past Thursday. Carmen, Bella, and Maci."

"Carmen told us that you had two other employees in here that day. She said their names were Charlotte and Doug."

"I can check the schedule, but that sounds right," said Bob. "Charlotte quit on Friday, no notice, no nothing. Doug's not in again until Thursday. I can get their contact info for you."

"That would be great, Mr. Marshall," said Chennelle.

"Do you think someone was stalking them here?" asked Barnes.

"I don't know, but it's a start. It shouldn't have been as busy here on Thursday as it was at Wendy's on a Friday night."

"Let's hope the other employees were more observant than their boss."

Chapter 53

They'd spent the rest of yesterday afternoon calling the half dozen teens that worked at Wendy's. None of the Wendy's employees remembered seeing Smith and Cortez, so it was pretty apparent that they wouldn't remember anyone stalking the pair. They had spoken to Charlotte Holcum from the coffee shop this morning. Again, she hadn't noticed anything suspicious.

The only person they hadn't spoken with was Doug Bronn. When they tried the phone number Bob Marshall had provided, it was disconnected. The address they'd been given wasn't correct either. Apparently, the man had moved without telling his employer his new address. Doug's driver's license had the same erroneous address, so Chennelle contacted his employer again.

Bob reminded Chennelle that Doug was off until Thursday. He promised to get the correct information from him as soon as he saw him, and then he would let Doug know the police wanted to talk to him.

This afternoon, the detectives would be interviewing Bella Fuller and Maci Bradley. Bella didn't work outside the home and Maci had to work until two. Chennelle was able to book a conference room instead of using an interrogation room. The latter was designed for an edge of discomfort in hopes of getting quick confessions.

Chennelle and her partner were in the conference room preparing when they got the call that Maci and Bella had arrived. The asked if an officer could escort them to their conference room and within a few minutes, the door opened.

"Hello Mrs. Bradley, Mrs. Fuller," Chennelle said, motioning for them to sit. "Please have a seat. This shouldn't take too long."

"Is this about Carmen?" asked Bella, her eyes wide like a frightened child.

"Yes," said Barnes. "We know the two of you were with Carmen in the afternoon on the day she was attacked."

"We were," said Maci. "We met in the coffee shop in the mall. Are you familiar with it?"

"We visited the coffee shop yesterday," said Chennelle. "Carmen said you'd all met there early on the afternoon she was stabbed."

"We tried to talk her out of it," said Bella, leaning forward. "Didn't we Maci?"

Maci nodded.

"We told her she shouldn't go to the park alone." Bella's eyes watered and her voice started to crack. "She's so stubborn. George offered to pick her up, but she had to do it her way."

"Did either of you notice anyone staring at the three of you?" asked Chennelle. "Perhaps someone who might have been attempting to listen to your conversation?"

"Detective Kendall, we were much too focused on talking her into changing her plans to notice people around us," said Maci. "Of course, as loud as our conversation was getting, any number of people could have overheard us."

"And we were at the edge of the place so anyone walking through the mall could have heard us," said Bella. "There was a man a couple of tables over working on his computer. I see him in there sometimes. He looked up when our conversation got louder, but he didn't stare at us or anything."

"Doug, Charlotte, and Bob were the only other people in there on Thursday." Maci looked away momentarily. "It was a slow day in the mall that day, so I'm sure they, and the man with the computer, were the only people in the coffee shop."

"We haven't been able to contact Doug," said Chennelle. "What can you tell me about him?"

"He's very sweet," said Bella, smiling. "He always makes sure my cappuccino is perfect, he won't let anyone else make it for me."

"He seems harmless enough to me," said Maci. "He's friendly, very customer service oriented. I've also heard he cares for his sick grandmother."

"What does he look like?" asked Barnes.

"Dark wavy hair, gorgeous deep blue eyes; tall, dark and handsome." Bella's eyes went to the ceiling in dreamy fashion.

"How tall would you say he is?" asked Chennelle.

It was Maci who answered. "Six foot, maybe taller. Wouldn't you say so, Bella?"

Bella nodded.

"Thank you," said Chennelle. "If we have any more questions, we'll be in touch."

Barnes escorted Maci and Bella downstairs. Chennelle returned to her desk, ready to write up their comments. As she sat there staring at her computer screen, she wondered how people could be so unaware of their surroundings. She feels it when someone is staring at her. She hoped this conversation would make these two Wiccans think more about those around them. Especially since this was looking more like some sort of vendetta against their coven.

* * * * *

Doug watched as Bella Fuller's husband arrived home from work. One more day and he'd purge the witch and her witch friend. He wondered if the husbands of these women were under some sort of spell. If they were, he'd set them free of this devilry.

Tomorrow he'd wait until Bella's husband had been gone for a while. This time of year, darkness fell around five o'clock. He could ready the first witch, Bella, and wait for the second witch, Maci. Then he could put them into his car under the veil of darkness.

Happily, Doug started his car and began the journey home. He needed to make sure Grandmother had her dinner and her medication on time. He could not neglect her needs. This was a good day and not even Grandmother's sharp tongue would dampen his spirits.

Chapter 54

"I don't know why I agreed to this," said Chennelle as they walked toward the restaurant. "This makes it feel like Trevon and I are moving way too fast."

"It's just dinner," said Erica. "Double-dating usually occurs in the first phase of dating. It saves you from being alone and keeps you out of trouble."

"With you and Jacobs? Sure."

"Real funny. Besides, we're all driving separately since we all drove to work separately today. Look, there's Trevon."

"Hey, ladies, you're looking mighty fine this evening."

"We're still in the same work clothes you saw us in this morning, Adams," said Chennelle.

He smiled at her and opened the door for them. "I haven't seen Ben yet, but I thought we should go in out of the cold and sit down."

"He's a big boy, he'll find us," said Erica.

"Table for four," Adams said to the host.

They followed him into the restaurant and sat down at a table near the front window. A young waiter hurried over and asked for their drink order. No sooner had he walked away than Erica's cell phone began to ring.

"Hello?" She listened for a few seconds, her expression gradually hardening. "Holy crap, are you kidding?" She locked eyes with Chennelle. "Okay, we're on our way." Placing her phone back in her purse, she turned to Trevon. "Sorry, Adams. That was Ben. He and Mayhew have a new missing persons case. Chennelle and I have to go."

"What does a missing person case have to do with us?" asked Chennelle.

"The missing persons are from the Wiccan coven."

"Missing *persons*?" Erica's use of the plural stunned Chennelle.

"Maci Bradley was supposed to pick up Bella Fuller after work. Bella was going to stay with Maci while Mr. Fuller was out of town. They should have arrived at Maci's by now. With their other friends being attacked, Maci's husband is in a panic."

"I can't believe this guy had the guts to grab two at once," said Trevon.

"It does seem this SOB. is getting bolder," said Chennelle. "He tried to nab Cortez on a public street and now he's taken two of them. It's like he's in a hurry or something."

"They're waiting for us at the Fuller house. Ben's texting the address to me," said Erica. "I'll go tell the waiter to cancel our drinks. Are you staying, Trevon?"

"A man's got to eat," he said.

As Erica walked away, Trevon took Chennelle's hand. "Call me later and let me know what's going on, okay?"

"Hopefully, this won't be our killer. Maybe they simply decided to stop at the store and the husband is stressing out for nothing."

"Let's hope."

* * * * *

Chennelle and Barnes joined Jacobs and Mayhew in the living room of Bella Fuller's house where they were talking to Maci's husband. The poor man was sitting on the couch with his face in his hands, sobbing.

"Oh, good, you're here," said Mayhew. "Mr. Bradley tells us his wife, Maci, belongs to the Wiccan group that seems to be the target of some nut you're tryin' to find."

Chennelle looked at Mr. Bradley and saw how miserable he was. She motioned for Mayhew to follow her to the foyer where she whispered to him. "We've got three victims from the same Wiccan coven—two are dead and one is in the hospital minus a kidney. He's got every reason to be concerned. We believe this nut, as you called him, is a religious extremist. We think he's targeted these women because of their beliefs."

"Man," said Mayhew, shaking his head. "Why can't people just live and let live?"

Chennelle shrugged and then heard Mr. Bradley shouting.

"Sergeant Jacobs, my wife always calls if she's going to be late. She's been very cautious since this maniac started picking off her friends. She would not be gone this long without letting me know. She's not answering her phone!"

Chennelle turned to Mayhew. "Did you find anything in the house to indicate that his wife was here?"

"Bays checked the garage and found two cars in there, both belonging to the Fullers," said Mayhew. "We got a call from a neighbor two doors down, who said there was a car parked in their driveway that doesn't belong to them. The plates belong to Maci Bradley."

"Shit! He moved her car. Does her husband know?"

"I was about to tell him when you came in. There's a broken coffee cup and a vase was knocked off the table in the kitchen area. We also found Miss Fuller's packed bag in the bedroom. This doesn't look good."

Chapter 55

Doug was very pleased with himself. The purging of Bella Fuller and Maci Bradley went quicker and smoother than he'd anticipated. As he had guessed, neither could tolerate watching her friend scream in pain. They'd begged for forgiveness so quickly, he thought there was some good in them.

This was especially satisfying after the witch Carmen Cortez survived. However, he must not question God's decision to let her live. He would wait for guidance on this matter. Besides, there were eight more witches to purge.

Seeing the lights still on as he pulled into the driveway, he wondered if Grandmother had fallen asleep in her chair again. She was normally in bed by nine o'clock and it was now three o'clock in the morning. If he woke her, would she notice the time and question him? He'd have to take his chances. She always got a terrible backache if she slept in her chair over night, causing her to be more abusive.

Instead of pulling into the garage, Doug parked in the driveway. He went to the back of the house so he could go in through the door that led to the kitchen. He hoped not to wake Grandmother right away. He'd use her disorientation while guiding her to bed to keep her from realizing the time.

Creeping into the living room, he noticed the television was still on. He stalked quietly to her side. Grandmother was slumped at an unusual angle. When he moved in front of her, he saw her opened foggy eyes. He'd seen eyes like those before. They were the milky eyes of death.

Doug's heart began to race with realization. He touched her face and it was cold. Shaking her, he shouted, "Grandmother, wake up. It's time to go to bed."

She didn't respond.

His thoughts went wild. What should he do? How was he going to manage without her? This could not be happening, not now.

Doug ran to his grandmother's bedroom and turned down her bed. "She needs some rest," he said aloud. "God would not take her from me, not before I've had the chance to tell her about my work.

She must be in some deep trance. That's it. I'll put her to bed so she can get some proper sleep."

Going back to the living room, he lovingly stroked his grandmother's hair. Then he lifted and carried her to her bed. Laying her gently onto her blue flannel sheets, he made sure her warm lavender nightgown was smoothed down before covering her. Neatly, he brought the sheet and blankets up to her chin. He didn't want her to be too cold.

"Good night, Grandmother," he said in his sweetest voice as he gently closed her eyelids. "You sleep well and I'll tell you all about God's plan for me in the morning."

* * * * *

Doug spent a restless night and woke with a start, sweat soaking his pajamas. He'd dreamt that his grandmother had reproached him for not sharing what God had asked him to do. She was so angry that she'd started beating him with her cane, screaming she would beat the devil out of him.

It was still dark out. Doug rose from his bed and went to the bathroom. He needed a shower in the worst way, but merely rinsed his face in lukewarm water. Raising his head, he caught sight of himself in the mirror. Like a curious dog, he tilted his head one way and then the other.

"Yes, Lord," he said. "I hear you. It was her time. Now she's with you and I don't have to worry. She'll know and understand what I'm doing."

Doug's muscles relaxed in the realization that it didn't matter about his grandmother's death. His mission was clear. He would clean up the urine from the area where Grandmother died and put that chair of hers in the garage. Then he'd call an ambulance for her.

Later, Doug would call a preacher and make sure his grandmother had the grandest funeral possible. God had taken her home.

Chapter 56

Saturday had been so pleasant. Chennelle, Trevon, Erica, and Ben had taken the opportunity to have a do-over double date. They had all pledged to eat, drink, and be merry with absolutely no shop talk. They had succeeded beautifully. At the end of the evening, she could tell Trevon wanted to stay with her, but she wasn't ready to restart the intimate portion of their relationship yet.

Unfortunately, her Sunday wasn't turning out so well. In the early afternoon she received the call that two bodies were found in the woods on the Dodson property. When she arrived, she could see yellow crime scene tape surrounding the area once more. There were still a few pieces stuck on branches here and there from the day they'd found Sasha Winston's body. Chennelle couldn't believe he'd bring any of his victims back to the same area. She followed the path until she found D. I. Spalding examining the bodies.

"Spalding, can we assume they were killed at relatively the same time?" she asked.

D. I. Spalding looked up at her and nodded. "They were probably killed minutes apart. They've been out here longer than your first victim was because despite the cold weather, there are a lot of larvae already."

"Any sign an animal has been at them?"

"No, and I can tell you why." He motioned for her to draw closer. "See these marks around their necks? They were hanging from that tree."

"Did you cut them down?"

"No, and you're not going to like it when you hear who did. Mr. and Mrs. Dodson had come out here for a Sunday morning stroll. When they saw these two hanging from the tree, Mr. Dodson got a ladder and some gardening shears and cut them down."

"Please tell me you're making that up," said Chennelle.

"I wish I were. I guess Mrs. Dodson was hoping they were still alive. All I know is our crime scene has been badly compromised."

"Did one of them call it in?" asked Chennelle.

"From what I understand, Mrs. Dodson called. Officers Bays and Samuels took the couple back up to their house. They're waiting for you and Barnes to come up there."

"Anything else I should know."

"I checked for the branding. Both of these ladies have been forgiven."

Chennelle sighed in disgust. "Thanks, Spalding. Catch you later."

Chennelle found Barnes talking to Sophia Parelli, who looked livid. She'd never seen Sophia so animated or flushed.

"I can't believe these people were so stupid," shouted Parelli. "Everything is compromised now. I took DNA samples from both of them, but how do we know they didn't do this?"

"Hold on, Parelli," said Barnes. "Mrs. Dodson is the head of this coven."

"That doesn't mean her husband didn't have something to do with it," said Parelli, stomping the ground with one foot. "I've got to get over there. It looks like they're getting ready to move the bodies."

"I think I understand why Bays and Samuels took the Dodsons back to their house," said Chennelle as she watched Parelli stomp away. She certainly wouldn't have wanted to be in the path of hurricane Sophia.

"From our conversation, I learned Parelli didn't arrive until after the Dodsons were whisked away," said Barnes. "Good call by whoever made it."

"Looks like you and I need to take a short hike," said Chennelle. "I'm just glad we don't have to trek through snow."

* * * * * *

Having been greeted at the door by the Dodson's housekeeper, the detectives entered and she took their coats. She indicated they should go into a room to the right. There by the fireplace stood a man Chennelle assumed was Mr. Dodson. He was tall and thin, with salt and pepper hair neatly trimmed. He turned as he heard them enter the room.

Chennelle barely noticed Bays approach as her eyes met Mr. Dodson's and the older man held her gaze.

"Detective Kendall," the officer said.

She swung around at the sound of her name, but was distracted by Barbara Dodson. She sat on the couch crying while Anne Samuels attempted to comfort her. Barnes asked Bays the question Chennelle was about to ask as though she'd read her partner's mind.

"Did you get their statements, Bays?"

"Yes, but Mrs. Dodson has been crying most of the time. These were friends of hers, right?"

Chennelle nodded. It was bad enough Barbara had to attend two funerals and visit another badly injured friend in the hospital, but now, to find these two women on her property hanging in a tree. What could Chennelle say to her? Nothing was going to make this okay. She motioned for Barnes to take the husband and she went to sit on the other side of Barbara.

"Mrs. Dodson," Chennelle said gently. "I'm so sorry you are going through this. I need to ask a few questions."

"I have one first," Barbara said, standing and glaring at her. "When the hell are you people going to find out who's doing this? Do we all have to die before this maniac is caught?"

This caught Chennelle off guard. Barbara Dodson had seemed to be such a together person. She was someone who never seemed to let anything faze her. Obviously, this was Barbara's last straw.

"The people who've been protesting against your coven don't match the DNA the perpetrator left on the victims. I wish I could say something encouraging right now, but I can't. All we have is a vague description of the man and his vehicle, plus his DNA."

"So it looks like we may have to take a long vacation, Harold." Barbara began to sound slightly hysterical. "How far is far enough away, Detective? Will he follow us to the ends of the Earth to save our souls?"

Harold Dodson walked over to his wife and took her in his arms. "You must understand, Detectives, this has been a horrible experience for Barbara. She should lie down and rest. I'd like for you to leave now and I'll call you tomorrow."

"No problem, Mr. Dodson," said Chennelle. "We'll ask for extra patrols to run past member's homes."

"Thank you," he said. "You know the way out."

With that dismissal, Chennelle motioned for Barnes, Officer Bays, and Officer Samuels to follow her out. The housekeeper was waiting in the foyer with their coats in hand. Chennelle wondered if the woman had even bothered to hang them up.

Once outside, Chennelle shook her head, frustrated with this whole case.

"Holy crap," said Barnes. "Can't blame the woman for feeling the way she does. Are we ever going to catch a break with this one?"

"I don't know, Barnes. It sure isn't looking good, is it?"

"Detective," said Samuels. "Do you want us to take first watch on the Dodsons?"

"Yes, and welcome back, Samuels." Chennelle glanced at Bays. "Call this in to your sergeant and tell him we need around the clock surveillance on this house. Tell him I'll be in touch about a few other extra patrols."

"Will do," said Bays.

"You doing okay, Samuels?" asked Chennelle once Bays was out of earshot.

"Yeah, it's good to be back on the job despite the fact that everyone is staring at my face. Michael and Justin are in counseling, and Mom has been great. I feel bad sometimes because she's taking care of me when I should be comforting her."

"I'm sure taking care of you is comforting to her," said Chennelle. "Detective exam is next week."

"I'm ready for it."

"Glad to hear it," said Chennelle smiling at her. "Take care."

"I will," she said before heading to her patrol car.

"Okay, Barnes, let's get back to the crime scene and see if there's anything new."

"I'm right behind you."

Chapter 57

Everyone had been very helpful Friday when they took Grandmother away. The paramedics were very gentle with her and showed her proper respect. The funeral director was kind as well. He helped Doug pick out the perfect casket for his grandmother. It was a beautiful dark cherry with soft periwinkle blue interior—her favorite color. He'd also recommended a pastor who might be willing to do the funeral service. This afternoon he was driving over to meet with Reverend Jeremiah Green of the Avenging Angels Evangelical Church.

Doug felt God had used the funeral director to guide him to this church. After all, he was one of Gods' appointed avenging angels. He was sure this Reverend Green must be very special to lead such a group.

As he pulled up to the church, he saw a tall gray-haired man unlocking the doors. The man turned as Doug slammed the car door shut.

"Is that you, Reverend Green?" Doug asked.

"Yes, my son. Do come in."

Doug walked quickly towards the door, anxious to hear what God's messenger had to say.

"Generally, I spend a lot of time in my office in the parish," said the reverend. "However, I thought you might be more comfortable meeting in my office here in the church. You see, my wife has a tendency to fuss too much over people, and many who are grieving don't want or need that much attention."

"I understand, and thank you for meeting me on a Sunday afternoon."

"As I told you on the phone yesterday, we usually do services for members of our congregation only. However, I spoke to our board after I received your call yesterday. Once they heard of your grandmother's inability to attend church services due to her health, they agreed we should make an exception."

"Thank you so much, Reverend Green. I appreciate your help since I wasn't able to give you a lot of advanced notice."

"Your dedication to your grandmother in her time of need is very admirable and your sacrifice was a selfless act of Christianity. We are very happy to assist you now in your time of need."

Doug's heart swelled with pride. Reverend Green really understood him. He saw Doug's devotion to do God's will and appreciated it fully.

"Since I didn't know your grandmother, please tell me a little bit about her and her life. I want to make sure my tribute to her points out her good deeds."

Doug thought for a moment about where he should begin. He, of course, didn't know much about her life before he was born; except that his grandfather was a no good womanizer and his mother deserted him. He decided to be straightforward.

"I don't know much about Grandmother's life before I came into the world. My grandfather left her for a younger woman. Then her daughter, my mother, took off after I was born and left me with Grandmother."

"That's a good start," said Reverend Green. "It must have been very difficult for her to raise you with no husband."

"Yes," said Doug, hanging his head. He always felt guilty about how much she'd sacrificed for him. "My mother didn't have a husband when I was born and never told Grandmother my father's name. That meant no support checks."

Reverend Green leaned back in his chair, his fingertips together.

"Grandmother did some waitressing, and her neighbor looked after me when she was working. I called our neighbor Aunt Ilene even though she wasn't related to us. She passed away a couple of years ago, so Grandmother didn't have anybody besides me."

"Don't worry, Mr. Bronn. Members of our congregation will be there to support you. We'll be your family now."

Doug's eyes filled with tears. The sudden realization that he was alone in this world began to nag at his brain.

"Cry if you need to, Mr. Bronn. It's God's gift to us to help us wash away the pain. Of course, it takes a while for this pain to go away, but it will, and then you'll smile when you think of her."

Not likely, thought Doug. Grandmother's verbal bashing wouldn't bring a smile to his face. The times he'd felt one of Grandpa's old belts cross his buttocks wouldn't bring a smile to his face. The times she locked him in a closet and told him to think about his sins wouldn't bring a smile to his face either. No, the only thing for which he grieved was the missed opportunity to share his mission with her. God would take care of that now.

"I'm all right," said Doug, wiping his tears. "Grandmother taught me all about God. We read the Bible together all the time. We did go to a church down the street for lots of years until she got sick and they moved to the southwest side."

"I see."

"She helped me when I was in school to see that some of the people I made friends with were not good for me. She said they were druggies and thieves and I'd end up in jail if I continued to be friends with them."

"So you didn't have a lot of friends?" asked Reverend Green.

"Not really. It seems like there wasn't anybody who believed like I do. But I had Grandmother and she kept me straight."

Now for the real test of Reverend Green's character. "Of course, she being a devout woman, was very upset when she heard of the coven of witches in our area."

"Yes, that has been very disturbing for our congregation as well. We've spoken with the police on several occasions and even had a protest march around the Circle downtown. The police say they can't do anything about it because they haven't done anything illegal and are within their rights to practice any religion they choose."

"Really?"

"I'm afraid so. However, this country was founded on good Christian principles, and these women aren't abiding by God's laws. Therefore, there should be some way of stopping them from this spell casting and devilry."

"I agree."

"Now, in regards to your grandmother's service, I think I can come up with something very nice for her. If you want to make a list of hymns that your grandmother enjoyed, I'll make sure they are played."

"That would be wonderful," said Doug. "The funeral is tomorrow at one in the afternoon. Again, I'm so sorry this is such short notice."

"Don't worry. God takes us when it is our time. It isn't something we can plan."

Reverend Green stood and held out his hand. Doug took it firmly. He turned and left the church feeling as though a ton of weight had lifted from his shoulders. Looking up to the sky, he simply said, "Thank you." Then he got into his car and drove away.

Chapter 58

"Barnes! Kendall! In my office," shouted Major Stevenson.

Chennelle turned to Barnes, who shrugged. Rising from their desks, they hurried to the Stevenson's office.

"The mayor's breathing down the chief's neck about these Wiccan murders," he said, pacing and indicating for the detectives to sit. "He's afraid we're not going to be able to keep a lid on the particulars with the press much longer. Sergeant Baxter has done her utmost to appease the press, but they suspect there's more to it than we're willing to tell them."

"I've been wondering when Andrea Atkins was going to come knocking," said Chennelle.

Stevenson frowned at her. "She's already knocking, Kendall. She decided we weren't worthy of her call this time. Atkins went directly to the mayor's office."

"That woman has some nerve," said Barnes.

"We've all experienced her sharp tongue at one time or another," said the major. "What I need is an update from you two. Where are we with this case?"

Chennelle looked at Barnes, who was biting her lip. Then she turned to Major Stevenson. "Sir, we've eliminated several suspects through DNA analysis. Of course, you know we found Curtis Putnam's DNA matched in an unrelated case."

"Yes, that solved one for Adams."

"Precisely," said Chennelle, dread tensing her gut as she formed her next sentence. "Unfortunately, that didn't get us any closer to finding the perpetrator in our case. The person doing this obviously knows who these women are and has studied their movements. Somehow he knew Carmen Cortez was going to be at Veteran's Park and we think he knew Bella Fuller's husband was going to be out of town."

Major Stevenson finally went around his desk and sat down hard in his chair. Silence ensued as his gaze drifted off somewhere else. Chennelle had worked for him long enough to know she needed to keep quiet during these moments.

The major leaned forward with his arms on his desk, folding his hands together. Now he was ready to speak.

"So, what we have is this. There is someone murdering members of a particular Wiccan coven. We feel he is doing it for religious reasons because of the words he is branding on their chests. He's also getting braver, having dumped his last two victims in the woods in the same approximate location as the first victim."

Chennelle nodded. "We also have a sample of his DNA, which tells us our killer is definitely a male and he doesn't care about hiding his identity. He doesn't have a criminal record where DNA was recorded."

"The thing I find strange," said Barnes, "is the way he's leaving them afterwards. He laid Winston on the ground and covered her with leaves. Kelso was left in her house and he cut her throat, probably out of anger. Then Fuller and Bradley were hung post mortem, as if they were put on display. Do you think he hung them there for Barbara Dodson's benefit?"

"If he knows she's the leader of this coven, that's a good possibility," said Stevenson. "How many more of these women are there?"

"There were thirteen and now there are nine living," said Chennelle. "He could very well go after Carmen Cortez again. I'm sure he won't be happy that she survived his attack."

"I know you talked patrol into putting extra cars near the residences of these women, but we can't do that forever," said the major. "The dollar figure is too high. This killer seems pretty smart—crazy, but smart. He'll just watch for our patrols to stop and then he'll start over again."

"Some of the ladies are talking about taking leaves of absence from their jobs and going out of town for a while," said Barnes. "They're terrified now that two more of their coven have been murdered."

"Can't say I blame them," said the major. "He'll slip up eventually, they always do. I just wish it would happen before he kills someone else. Even if all of these women leave town, he'll find some other "sinner" to *forgive*. Dismissed."

Chennelle and Erica jumped up at the dismissal and went back to their desks. There stood Trevon, smiling at Chennelle.

"Bathroom," Barnes said, leaving them alone.

"She's so subtle," said Trevon. "I did want a private word with you since we haven't talked since Saturday night."

Chennelle smiled and nodded.

"My mom and step-dad are having a big Thanksgiving dinner this year and my brother and sisters will all be there with their families. I was hoping you'd come with me. They'd love to see you again. Mom said I was a fool for letting you get away."

She knew this might be coming, but Chennelle thought he'd make a phone call or something, not ask her here in the office. Discussing it here didn't make it very private, and she knew Trevon wasn't going to like her answer.

"I'm sorry. I've already told my sister I'd be coming to her house this year. They'll probably be discussing my parents' anniversary party. Maybe I can go with you another time."

That wiped the smile off his face. Barnes was right after all. He did want her to drop her plans and go with him. It was too much for him to expect at this point in their relationship, so Chennelle had decided to stick to her guns.

"So, that's it. You're really not going to spend the holiday with me?"

"I can't," she said.

Trevon pursed his lips and nodded. She thought his head was going to crack, as tight as his jaw was at this moment. Then he walked away, head still bobbing up and down, and nearly walked into Barnes.

Barnes watched him breeze by. "He didn't look very happy."

"You pegged him. He did want me to spend Thanksgiving with him. I can't tell my family about us yet. He says his mom would love to see me. Well, my parents don't exactly feel the same way about him."

"I get it. He'll just have to get over it. If he cares about you, he won't put demands on you."

"That's right," said Chennelle, feeling vindicated. "You and I have better things to do. We have a case to solve."

"Darned right we do. Now where do you think we should start?"

Chennelle looked at Barnes and all her bravado fell away. "I'll be damned if I know."

Chapter 59

His grandmother's funeral would be starting in a few hours. Doug had not slept well again. He thought the lack of cruel criticism from Grandmother would be a relief, but somehow he missed it. Despite the way she dished out his punishments, he knew she meant well. Grandmother loved him and didn't want him to be like his parents and grandfather.

He'd been going through some of his grandmother's things, something he was terrified to do while she was still living. Of course, yesterday he had to find her favorite dress for the funeral director, but he was also curious about a lock box he'd found in the closet. He would search for the key later. He was sure there were private papers in it and maybe some special jewelry.

Now, he needed to get ready to say his final goodbyes. He put on a crisp, white dress shirt to go with his charcoal gray suit. Charcoal gray socks, black polished shoes, and a black silk tie completed the ensemble. Peering in the mirror, he slipped his tie into a perfect knot. He was amazed because Grandmother always told him he wasn't doing it right. He smoothed his hair and took one last look.

In his closet, he found his grandfather's old black overcoat. He'd discovered it in a box in the garage several years ago. Doug had taken it to the cleaners and then hid it in the back of his closet. He'd kept it in hopes that someday his grandfather would see the error of his ways and come home begging for forgiveness. That never happened.

Never daring to wear it before, he slipped it on and it fit perfectly. He and his grandfather must have been the same height and weight. Maybe that's why Grandmother always suspected Doug was like his grandfather. If Grandmother knew he was wearing this coat, she'd be very angry. However, it was very cold and he didn't have anything else nice enough to wear over a suit.

Grabbing his car keys from the table, he set off to say his final goodbye to his Grandmother.

* * * * *

The funeral director had done a marvelous job of grooming Grandmother and making her look happy. Doug couldn't remember how long it had been since he'd seen her smile. She was always so intent on him taking the right path, her expression never seemed to change from stern.

It was good to be alone with her for a few minutes. He looked at her peaceful face—no pain, no more sickness.

"Did He tell you yet? Have you seen Him?"

Of course, Grandmother wouldn't answer. Was her spirit still here waiting for a send off? Some people believe we see our own funerals. Of course, how would anyone really know?

"I arranged for a nice preacher from that church near us. You remember. It's the one whose congregation has been speaking out against the witches." Doug straightened Grandmother's collar and kissed her forehead.

"Ironic, isn't it? God has set me the task of working to get the witches to confess and be forgiven, and this church wants the same thing. I'll see you in a bit. I have to get ready for Reverend Green to arrive."

He turned away from her. Reverend Green would be showing up at any moment. Doug was anxious to meet Mrs. Green. She must be a fine Christian woman to be married to a preacher.

Footsteps approached. He looked at his grandmother one more time and said, "Showtime."

Reverend Green and a lovely woman who looked curiously familiar walked in together. Doug approached the reverend with an outstretched hand.

"Hello, Mr. Bronn. I hope my wife and I didn't disturb your time with your grandmother."

"No, Reverend Green," said Doug, unable to keep his eyes off Mrs. Green.

"This is my wife," Reverend Green said in introduction.

"Hello, Mr. Bronn," she said. "I'm so sorry for your loss. If there's anything we can do for you, please let us know."

Doug blinked. Her voice sounded so familiar, but he didn't remember ever meeting her before. She probably sounded like dozens of other people he'd met along the way. His grief must be addling his brain.

"Would you like to see her?" Doug asked the pair. "They've made her look so lovely. Her last few years of illness took quite a toll on her."

Mrs. Green smiled at him and nodded. She took his arm and he escorted her to the casket with her husband following them. As she looked down at his grandmother, Doug noticed her stiffen, then she let go of his arm and dropped her purse.

"Are you alright, Mrs. Green?" Doug asked.

"Oh, I'm so sorry, Mr. Bronn," she said, her face reddening as she grabbed her purse from the floor. "I'm so clumsy sometimes. The reverend told me your grandmother's name is...was Opal Bronn."

Doug watched her curiously. If she knew his grandmother's name, why the need to confirm it? Why was she so nervous? "Yes, that's her name."

Mrs. Green looked away and turned toward her husband. He looked rather gruff, as though he was looking at a naughty child.

"Why don't you go check with the organist to make sure she has all her music, my dear?" said Reverend Green. "Then perhaps you can start greeting people while I speak with Mr. Bronn."

He'd dismissed her. Doug wondered what the reverend would have to say to her when they got home. Reverend Green and Grandmother would definitely have gotten along.

"Sorry for my wife's behavior," said Reverend Green. "She does get a bit clumsy from time to time."

"No problem," said Doug, glancing over his shoulder just in time to see her exit the room. It certainly didn't take long for her to scurry away. Something was strange. This was more than being clumsy. This woman actually became anxious when she looked at his grandmother. Mrs. Green practically stopped the blood flowing in his arm before she let go of him.

"Are you sure your wife is okay?" Doug asked.

"Of course, she is. You should sit in front and let the visitors come to you. Would you like for me to stay with you or to assist my wife with greeting people at the door?"

"Stay with me, please. I won't know anyone, so you can introduce me. That is, if you don't mind?"

"Of course I don't mind," Reverend Green said with enthusiasm. "By the way, we have a special sunrise service at six o'clock Thursday morning to celebrate Thanksgiving as a congregation. You are welcome to join us, if you feel up to it."

"I'll think about it."

Doug smiled at him, and then his thoughts went back to the very nervous Mrs. Green. Something about her seemed so familiar. Perhaps he should consider going to the service on Thursday so he could spend a little more time with her. For now, he just needed to get through today.

Chapter 60

"This case is going to go cold," said Chennelle, sitting back and tossing her pencil onto her desk. "It's been three weeks since Sasha Winston's body was found and we've got zilch. I called Bob the manager again and this Doug Bronn still hasn't shown up for work. This is so frustrating!"

"I know, I feel the same way," said Barnes. "That's the way some cases go."

"The problem lies in the fact that there are still more women in this group. I don't think he's going to stop until he's killed them all. He's been grabbing someone every Thursday. Do you think he'll take Thanksgiving off?"

Barnes' desk phone rang and she grabbed the receiver. "Barnes." She paused, her eyes widening, then turned her glance to Chennelle.

"What?" Chennelle whispered.

Barnes held up her index finger and Chennelle waited.

"Tell her we'll be right in," said Barnes before she replaced the receiver. "We have a visitor."

* * * * *

"Mrs. Green, what brings you here this afternoon?" asked Chennelle. Mrs. Green was sitting at the conference table breathing heavily and looking as though she might cry.

"Hello, detectives. I came here today because I heard the DNA evidence you collected didn't match any of our male parishioners."

"That's correct," said Barnes. "Is there someone we missed?"

"I think so," said Mrs. Green. "You didn't test any of the women."

That was not what Chennelle expected to hear. "But the DNA showed the perpetrator to be a male. Why would you think we should test the women in your congregation?"

Mrs. Green adjusted herself in her chair and sat up straighter, looking more dignified. "What if the person who's doing this doesn't go to our church? There are many people who attend church, but their children do not."

"Is there something you want to tell us, Mrs. Green?" asked Barnes. "Do you suspect someone's son or brother is doing this?

"I'm not sure, but I think it's worth testing everyone. I think what's happening to these women is horrible. It specifically says in the Bible not to judge others or kill them. I think this person is using religion as an excuse to murder innocent people."

Now Mrs. Green was crying. Chennelle grabbed a box of tissues and set them in front of the distraught woman. Perhaps Mrs. Green was correct. Maybe they were looking at this from the wrong angle. It certainly would be worth a shot.

"Can you convince the women in your congregation to come in and give a DNA sample?" asked Chennelle.

"I believe so. Of course, you don't need to bother Mrs. Putnam."

"How is she doing?" asked Chennelle.

"About as well as can be expected." Mrs. Green had stopped crying and wiped her face. "It's very hard on her to realize her son has gone astray. I'm sure it would be horrible for any mother to discover her child has become a monster."

Chennelle thought that was an odd description of a man who was burglarizing homes. He was certainly not in the monster category.

"You can start with me," Mrs. Green said with determination. "Who should I talk to about it?"

"You stay here and we'll call down to the lab to see if someone is available to do it now." Chennelle nodded at Barnes to go make the call. "In the meantime, I'll give you a pad of paper and you can make a list of the other women you think we should test."

"That will be fine. I hope you can put a rush on it. I don't want to see anyone else hurt."

"We'll do our best. Of course, Thanksgiving is day after tomorrow, so it could be three or four days before they can start testing. You have a good holiday, Mrs. Green, and thank you for coming in."

Chennelle left Mrs. Green in the conference room. The urgency in her request had Chennelle baffled. She didn't think the Greens had any children. Looking around the Greens' living room in her mind's eye, she didn't recall seeing any photos of children. If there were no children, why would Mrs. Green want to be tested? Did she have a brother?

"I've got Mark Chatham coming down," said Barnes. "What was that all about?"

"Don't know, but I intend to find out."

Chapter 61

It had taken nearly all afternoon on Tuesday and all morning on Wednesday to get in touch with all of the female parishioners on Mrs. Green's list. The rest of Wednesday was spent interviewing them and taking their DNA samples. All of them were cooperative, and some Chennelle had turned away because they didn't have sons or brothers.

Thanksgiving had finally arrived and it was time for Chennelle to see what Saundra had up her sleeve. Chennelle pulled up to her sister's beautiful two-story home with its neatly trimmed everything right at noon. She dreaded going in because she knew Saundra was going to make a last effort to convince their parents to let her invite the world to their anniversary party.

Of course, heavy on her mind was the look on Trevon's face when she told him she couldn't join him at his parents' house for Thanksgiving dinner. She not only told him she couldn't go with him to celebrate the holiday with his family, but she also didn't invite him to come with her. She hadn't told her family about her reconciliation with Trevon and didn't want to spring it on them today.

Turning off the engine, she resigned herself to her fate. "We'd better get in there," she said to her famous cranberry salad, picking it up and cradling it in her hands.

As she approached the door, it opened. Her eight-year-old niece, Malea, came running out to greet her.

"Auntie Chennelle," she shouted. "I thought you'd never come."

"How's my favorite niece?" asked Chennelle. She bent over and kissed the girl on the forehead.

"I'm your only niece," said Malea, her hands on her hips.

"Oh, yeah," said Chennelle. They both started laughing.

"Come on, everyone is waiting." Malea grabbed the hem of Chennelle's coat and pulled her toward the door.

"Hey," said the deep, smooth voice belonging to her father. "Girl, it's been too long. Come give your papa a big hug."

"Malea, would you please take this bowl into the kitchen for me?" asked Chennelle.

The girl took it gladly, freeing Chennelle to wrap her arms around her father. She and her father had always been close. When she announced her intentions to become a police officer, her mother was terrified, Saundra thought it not *lady-like*, and Carl stayed neutral like he always did. However, it was Papa who'd supported her and made the rest of the family realize this was a good choice for Chennelle.

"How you been, Papa?"

"I'm doin' just fine, Nelle."

He was the only one she allowed to call her Nelle. Somehow, that made it special and something between them.

"Where's Mama?"

"Where do you think she is, child? In the kitchen drivin' your sister crazy with all her advice."

They both laughed and Chennelle slipped off her coat and threw it over the stair railing. Then they walked arm in arm to the kitchen.

"Look who it is," her father announced.

Chennelle glanced at the flustered, sweaty face of her sister. She was such a perfectionist and Mama always tried to tell her how to do it better. She almost felt sorry for her. That is until Saundra opened her mouth.

"It's about time you got here," Saundra spluttered. "The turkey's been done for twenty minutes and it's going to dry out."

"You told me to be here at noon," said Chennelle in her own defense.

"That's beside the point," Saundra said in a dangerous tone.

Chennelle decided not to argue, but to start helping take bowls of food to the dinner table. In no time, Papa had the turkey carved, prayers were said, and everyone was settling down to a great meal.

"Auntie Chennelle, are you working a case?" asked ten-year-old Jamar.

"I'm always working a case. This one is kind of hard, because we think people are being killed because of their religion."

"Really?" he asked with wide-eyed curiosity.

"I think it's hard because a lot of the people I'm meeting in this case are good people. They just disagree about whose religion is the true one. Unfortunately, we think someone has taken a more radical view."

"That sounds like those terrorists we've been studying in school," he said.

"You're right," said Carl. "Most people of that religion are very peace loving. They believe that everyone should get along and allow others to believe as they wish, just like we do."

"Let's talk about something more pleasant," said Saundra. "Mom and Dad's anniversary party is only a few weeks away."

Not even ten minutes into dinner, and there it was. Chennelle looked at her father who rolled his eyes. When she glanced at Carl, he was not smiling and appeared to be rather tense.

"I thought we'd already settled everything," said Mama. "We're having a small group at the restaurant, just family and a few of our oldest friends."

"You know, I didn't cancel the reservation for Stonegate. We could still have it there."

"What?" shouted Chennelle, Carl, Terry, and Papa in unison. Carl's wife simply shook her head and Mama sat frozen with a piece of turkey clinging to a fork that had almost made it to her gaping mouth.

"Saundra, you agreed a couple of weeks ago to do this at the restaurant," said Terry. His face was flushed and his brows nearly met in a scowl. "Stonegate banks on December Christmas party rentals. You'd have had to make a substantial deposit to hold it."

Saundra's expression became angry as well. She slammed her fork on the table. "This is their fortieth wedding anniversary. I want it to be special."

"Did you just hear yourself?" asked Terry, gritting his teeth. "It's *their* anniversary. Your idea of special isn't what they want. They think an intimate gathering is special."

Glaring at each adult at the table in turn, Saundra's eyes started to fill with tears. Then she set her sights on Chennelle. "This is all your fault. You've been against me from the beginning. You never like my ideas, and Papa always takes your side."

This attack took Chennelle by surprise. She knew her sister was jealous of her relationship with their father, but not to the extent of blaming her for somehow influencing her parents to reject Saundra's ideas.

"Mama and Papa told you that they didn't want a big deal," said Chennelle. "That happened before I got involved, so don't blame me for what you perceive as ruining your plans. Terry said it, it's *their* anniversary and they should have what *they* think is special."

"Fine, fine," said Saundra, tears flowing down her cheeks. "I'm not hungry. You all finish. I'm going to my room." With that, she stormed out and up the stairs.

"I'm so sorry, everyone," said Terry. "Please finish your dinner and I'll go talk to her."

After Terry left the room, all of the adults seemed to lose their appetites. Chennelle noticed that her six-year-old nephew, Rashan, who had been very quiet up to now, was staring at her father. Looking very serious, Rashan set down his fork and linked his fingers.

"Grandpa," he said.

"Yeah," said Papa.

"Did you spoil Auntie Saundra when she was little?"

Papa broke into a wide grin. "I didn't think so, but now that you ask, she used run off to her room when she didn't get her way. But we never gave in."

"Oh, so she isn't really grown up yet," said Rashan.

There was one second of silence, and then everyone burst out laughing.

"Out of the mouths of babes," said Mama, holding up her glass to toast her grandson.

Glasses clinked and then everyone resumed eating and talking about everything except the anniversary party.

Chapter 62

It was quiet in the house, much too quiet. Doug had attended the sunrise service at the Avenging Angels Evangelical Church that morning where it was noisy with music and good preaching. It was so nice of Reverend Green to invite him. However, it seemed to him that Mrs. Green had intentionally avoided him.

There was something about that woman—something familiar. It was the same feeling he'd had when he met her at the funeral home. Was it her eyes or her dark features? He simply couldn't place her.

He jerked at the knot in his tie and went toward his bedroom to change into something more comfortable. Stopping outside of his grandmother's room, he peered inside and looked around. There was the picture of Jesus hanging over the head of her bed. She'd said he was smiling down upon her and keeping her safe at night.

Doug stepped into the room. On her dresser was a photo of him and her together when he was six. He was getting ready to go on the school bus and start first grade. Grandmother was actually smiling in this picture. He hadn't seen that smile of hers in years.

As he turned to leave the room, he spotted the lock box sitting on the bed. He was so tired and so busy taking care of things since the funeral, he'd completely forgotten about it. Curiosity got the better of him and he decided to start looking for the key.

Where did Grandmother put the key? *Perhaps her jewelry box*, he thought as he went back to the dresser. After a few minutes, he decided that was much too obvious. He looked through her dresser and even checked to see if it was taped to the undersides of the drawers. It wasn't there either.

After searching every drawer, every pocket of her clothing, between the mattresses, and on the closet shelves, he'd nearly given up when it came to him. He walked over to her bed and took the portrait of Jesus down. On the back of it was a small envelope and in it he found a key.

Trying his find in the lock box, it opened easily. As he thought, there were lots of papers. Life insurance, old deposit books from the bank, her will, and a couple of envelopes.

He separated them into piles. One of the envelopes felt like it contained photos, so he opened the other envelope first. In it was a birth certificate. The child's name was Douglas Gene Kirkpatrick, born July 10, 1978. Doug stopped. July 10, 1978 was his date of birth.

Continuing to read, he found this child was born to Heather Jean Kirkpatrick and Douglas Gene Morris of Lexington, Kentucky. Why wouldn't the boy have his father's last name—unless…..

It dawned on him at last. This was why his grandmother was so angry with his mother. This Heather Jean Kirkpatrick had become pregnant while a teen. Her date of birth was April 8, 1962, so she was only sixteen when he was born. Is that why she didn't want him? She was too young to be a mother. Was his grandmother too harsh with her?

He grabbed the second envelope and spilled its contents. As he'd suspected, it contained old looking photos. The first one he picked up was of a baby boy being bathed. You could only see the bather's hands and arms up to the elbow. He turned it over to find it said, "Baby Dougie taking his first bath at home, 7-12-78." Tossing it aside, he grabbed another one. A young woman in horn rimmed glasses sat in a rocking chair with a baby wrapped in a blanket. Written on the back was "Heather rocking Doug after his feeding, 7-15-78."

Doug peered at her. It was taken from a distance that made the girl and the baby very tiny. The girl had dark hair and creamy white skin. He wondered what she was thinking. Had she already decided to get rid of him? She didn't appear unhappy. This Heather was smiling in the loving way most new mothers do.

The next photo he picked up was upside down. He read, "Heather, age 15, September 1977." This would have been taken before she was pregnant with him. Doug flipped over the photo and took a good hard look. This was a head shot and showed every feature of her face. Now he knew why that other face looked so familiar.

Chapter 63

"So, how was Thanksgiving dinner?" asked Barnes. "Did Saundra do as you predicted?"

"Oh, yeah. If nothing else, Saundra is predictable," said Chennelle. "If it weren't for my nephews and niece, it might have been a disaster. Kids always help keep things in perspective."

"What happened?"

"Saundra announced that she hadn't cancelled Stonegate, and her husband almost blew a gasket. His face turned so red I thought he'd have a stroke."

"That doesn't sound good."

"We let her have her little temper tantrum and Terry assured us he'd call the Stonegate and cancel it himself. He said if he couldn't get the deposit back, he'd just eat it. I felt kind of bad for him, but he does love my sister. When she decided to go into this bi-racial marriage, I wasn't sure it would work, but he's really very devoted to her."

"That's great. There aren't too many marriages like that these days, bi-racial or not. Did you tell them about Trevon?"

"Not a chance," said Chennelle, raising an eyebrow. "Saundra's antics were enough for one day. I'll tell them soon—if he forgives me."

"Haven't you talked to him since Monday?"

"No, but he can't avoid me forever."

"He can't avoid you at work, but it's been four days since you turned him down."

"I know. I've thought about it every day. I don't want to push it. If he wants this to work, he needs to realize he can't always have everything his way."

"Okay, if you say so. Now back to what we get paid to do. I received an email from Chatham about Mrs. Green's DNA swab. Since she seemed so anxious to have it done, he started the test before he left Wednesday. It will probably be ready by the end of next week."

"Chatham's great. He knows we're under a lot of pressure now that the mayor is involved. I still can't quite understand Mrs.

Green's insistence about the test. I mean, she might have a brother, but I don't recall her mentioning children."

"No, I don't either, and I don't recall seeing any photos of kids or of Reverend Green saying they had any. That is bizarre."

"I think it's about time we did a background check on the Reverend's wife," said Chennelle, scooting up to her desk and signing into her computer. "What was Mrs. Green's first name?"

"Not sure," said Barnes. "I think it started with an H. Give me a minute to go through my notes." Barnes pulled up her reports on screen and did a quick search. "Heather."

"Well, now Mrs. Heather Green, let's see what went on in your life before you came to Hoosier land."

* * * * *

After about three hours of internet research, Chennelle's eyes were getting tired and her head throbbed. She'd found a marriage record for the Greens in a Lexington, Kentucky database, but it had been hard to find a birth record for Heather, so apparently she wasn't born in Lexington. However, by adding her middle and maiden names, which were listed on the marriage certificate, Chennelle was able to find a Heather Jean Kirkpatrick born in Arlington, Virginia on April 8, 1962, to an Opal Braun Kirkpatrick and Kenneth James Kirkpatrick. Further investigation showed a military record for her father. Kenneth Kirkpatrick served in the army and was a Viet Nam veteran.

"That was a waste of time," said Barnes approaching her desk. "I get to court, have to sit there for over an hour, and the defense convinces the judge to grant a continuance."

"And you're surprised, because…?"

"I'm not, I'm just aggravated. So, how was the rest of your morning? Did you come up with anything on Mrs. Green?"

"She and the reverend got married in June, 1980 in Lexington, Kentucky, and she was born in Arlington, Virginia, April 8, 1962. I haven't found any information on Reverend and Mrs. Green having any children. So basically, I spent the last couple of hours giving myself a headache."

"I'm back now, so I can help. Why don't I make some calls to the Lexington P. D. to see what they have? Take a break and get a cup of coffee. Better yet, go see if Adams is at his desk."

Chennelle smiled at her. "Thanks Barnes, I think I'll do that."

Chapter 64

"Ah, the Reverend Jeremiah Green has taken Miss Heather Jean Kirkpatrick in holy matrimony in a small ceremony at the Church of Christ in Lexington," Doug read aloud. "You've got to love the internet. It's so much faster and more intimate than running all over the countryside asking questions."

Now he had his first verification the woman in the photos was Mrs. Green. Grandmother had told him she moved them to Indianapolis from Cleveland, Ohio. Had they moved from Lexington, Kentucky to Ohio first? Since his grandmother and Aunt Ilene were gone, there was no one to ask—except Mrs. Green.

Obviously, his mother never married his father. Did the Reverend Green know about his wife's indiscretion? Did she tell him she had a child?

Did his mother think that marrying a preacher would absolve her from the sins of fornicating and then deserting an innocent child? What sort of woman would toss away her own flesh and blood? There were so many questions.

It was obvious to him now that her reaction when she saw his grandmother in the casket wasn't clumsiness, but recognition. Mrs. Green knew that Opal Bronn was her mother. She knew, but again she walked away from him as though he didn't exist.

Mrs. Green was the only one with any answers. He would have to keep watch and look for an opportunity to speak with her alone. As a preacher's wife, she would have to go out making calls on the sick and those who were grieving. Perhaps he was on her list, but would she dare to visit without her husband? He thought not. Doug would come up with a solution. He always did.

* * * * *

He'd decided to rent a car instead of using Grandmother's Buick. It was much too big and obvious, and he knew too many people had seen it the night he tried to take Carmen Cortez. The rental was a nice silver Focus, small and inconspicuous. This was the perfect vehicle to begin the surveillance of Mrs. Green.

It had been almost two hours and she hadn't emerged from her house. Doug imagined that perhaps Reverend Green was writing his sermon for the upcoming Sunday service and so his wife had to be close by in case he needed anything. If he only knew of her sins, the good reverend would preach about the sins of the flesh this Sunday.

Doug could have forgiven this woman for succumbing to temptation. What he couldn't forgive was how she could take her shame out on an innocent baby by casting him aside like garbage. No wonder his grandmother was so tough. She didn't want him to go the same way his mother had gone. He would never leave his child, never.

A slamming door brought his attention to the front of the house. Mrs. Green was getting into her car—finally. He would follow her and seek an opportunity to approach her. He could use his grief to lure her into speaking with him. Maybe this time she would break down and confess who she was to him and beg for his forgiveness.

Once she'd pulled out of her driveway, Doug slowly followed her. He tried to stay at least two car lengths behind so she wouldn't know he was there. Soon he realized they were heading for the heart of the city. It was early afternoon. There would be too many people.

When they had reached the center of town, he saw her turn down Alabama Street. Then she went into the parking area for the City-County Building. The police were in that building.

Anger started to swell in his chest. He'd waited all this time and she led him to the police station. What was she doing?

His heart rate rose as he wondered if she suspected. She was his mother, after all. Did she have some sort of motherly instinct about him? If she did, she would ruin everything.

He had to go back to his house and pack up his tools and a few clothes. Doug couldn't allow her or the police to stop him from finishing God's work.

Chapter 65

Chennelle had discovered that Trevon was out on a call and was on her way back to her desk when one of the clerks stopped her in the hallway.

"Detective Kendall, there's a Mrs. Heather Green in the conference room. She says she needs to talk to you. She looks pretty shook up."

"Thanks, I'll go see her now." Two visits from Mrs. Green in less than a week seemed strange to Chennelle. The woman must have something she wanted to tell the police, but was terrified to say it.

"Mrs. Green, I'm surprised you're back so soon," said Chennelle as she entered the conference room. Hopefully, this meant she'd decided to disclose whatever secrets she'd been hiding.

"Detective Kendall, I know you couldn't have those test results back yet."

"Our lab put a rush on it, but it takes several days to get the results. It will probably be Thursday or Friday of next week before we get anything."

"I see. Are you sure it will be that long?"

"Yes, Mrs. Green, I'm sure." Chennelle could tell that Mrs. Green was nervous. Her face was paler than normal, her expression one of anxious worry. "Mrs. Green, if there's something you'd like to tell me, I think you should do it now. So far, we haven't found any new victims. It appears our killer decided to take Thanksgiving off. However, he could strike again at any moment."

Mrs. Green sighed and closed her eyes, pain etched on her face. Letting out her breath slowly, she reopened her eyes and looked directly at Chennelle.

"This is a long, bizarre story. I've never told anyone about it, not even my husband. As a matter of fact, I'm not sure how he'll take it when he finds out."

"We hear a lot of long, bizarre stories, and I'm always willing to take the time to listen if it will save lives. Please don't be afraid to tell me what you know. We have to stop him before he strikes again."

Heather Green nodded at Chennelle, took another deep breath, and began to speak. "When I was almost sixteen years old and living in Lexington, I thought I was in love. His name was Douglas Morris. He was tall with dark hair and eyes, and as handsome a man as I'd ever seen. We'd been dating for only a few months when he convinced me to have...sexual relations with him. The next thing I knew I was pregnant." Mrs. Green paused.

"Go on." Chennelle was pretty sure she knew where this was going. She wanted to encourage Mrs. Green to disclose all of the details.

"Well, as you can imagine, I was terrified. When I told Doug about it, he told me it was my problem. My mother was very religious and constantly hounded my father concerning his whereabouts every day. She was downright obsessive and jealous where he was concerned.

"When I finally got the courage to tell her, she was extremely angry and called me every name for a whore she could remember. She told my father and he said they'd simply send me to a home for pregnant teens and the baby would be put up for adoption."

Mrs. Green's voice cracked with her last few words, so Chennelle retrieved a bottle of water from the small refrigerator in the corner and a box of tissues for her. Taking it with a thank you, Mrs. Green swallowed a few sips of water before continuing.

"My mother went nuts. She told him there would be no adoption. She said I was going to keep the baby and raise it because God wasn't going to let me off that easy. So, that's what I did.

"Three months after I turned sixteen, my son was born. He was healthy and beautiful, with the same dark hair as his father and me. His eyes were a darker blue, and I knew they would be just as gorgeous as Doug's. I named him Douglas after his father, but he had my maiden name, Kirkpatrick."

It hit Chennelle like a smack on the back of the head. Mrs. Green's anxiety to have the DNA test, her nervous manner, and the way she'd spoken about how awful it would be to be told your child is a monster...it all made sense now.

"Do you think *your* son is doing this?" asked Chennelle.

"I'm not sure. I hadn't seen him since he was six months old."

"But you suspect it's him for some reason, don't you?"

"Detective, my mother wouldn't allow me to be a mother to my son. She criticized me daily, telling me I wasn't holding him properly, or burping him enough, or changing his diaper quickly enough. One day I'd had enough and I told her I was going to quit school, get a job, and take Dougie with me. Three days later she disappeared with him."

"And for some reason, you think they moved to Indianapolis?"

"I know they did."

"How long have you known this?"

"I found out just before Thanksgiving. My husband was asked to preside at a funeral service on Monday for an elderly woman named Opal Bronn. She and her grandson weren't members of our congregation, but she'd been ill and he'd been caring for her, so our board voted to allow it. When I went with my husband the day of the funeral, I thought the young man looked familiar. He was tall, about six-two, dark wavy hair and big blue eyes. I had this weird feeling about him that I couldn't explain—until I saw her."

"You recognized the deceased?" asked Chennelle, her heart pounding. From the description of the man Mrs. Green had met, he could be the Doug from the coffee shop.

"Yes. I'd never forget that face. It was definitely my mother lying in that coffin. Her true maiden name was spelled B R A U N, but she must have decided to spell it B R O N N to keep us from finding her. I put two and two together and realized that Doug Bronn was my son, Doug Kirkpatrick."

"I guess I'm still not sure why you suspect he could be involved in these killings," said Chennelle, wondering if Mrs. Green was still holding back something.

"I know this sounds strange, but I had a feeling about him—something ominous. After the service when I was fixing dinner for my husband, he told me that Doug was very interested in his opinion of the witches. Jeremiah told me Doug had heard of our congregation's protests of their existence. When I heard all of this, my skin crawled and an uneasiness came over me."

"You were hoping the DNA would prove one way or another whether the killer is your son."

"Yes, and if he is the one involved, his DNA should have characteristics found in mine, right?"

"That's correct," said Chennelle. "Do you have any idea where Doug Bronn lives so we can go have a talk with him?"

"I wrote it down for you," she said, picking up her purse. Mrs. Green rummaged through it for a few seconds and came up with a wrinkled piece of paper. "Here is the home address my husband got from him after he agreed to do the funeral."

"Thank you, Mrs. Green. I know this is very hard for you."

"I always hoped I'd find Dougie someday," she said, tears forming in her eyes. "This certainly wasn't what I had in mind."

Chennelle smiled weakly at her, feeling Mrs. Green's pain as her eyes released drops of sorrow. "Wait here and I'll find someone to escort you out."

On the other side of the door, Chennelle brought the page with Doug's information up to eye level and saw the address was different than the one his employer had provided.

If he truly was her killer, what had the grandmother done to turn him into such a zealot? If Doug was treated the same way Heather Green was treated growing up, perhaps he thought this was the only way to please his grandmother. Whatever his reasons, she needed to find Barnes so they could find Bronn and bring him in for questioning.

Chapter 66

After stopping to visit one of the parishioners at St. Vincent Hospital, Heather Green pulled into her driveway exhausted and fearful. What had she done? She couldn't stop the heartbreaking thought of her son hating her. If he wasn't guilty and she sent the police after him, would he ever forgive her?

She got out of her car and felt the chill of the late fall air sweep across her face. Then a chill went down her spine that had nothing to do with the cold air. Heather turned quickly, looking at her surroundings. Was someone watching her?

Shaking her head, she started walking toward the house. "I mustn't let this get to me. I'm just feeling guilty and paranoid."

Entering the house, she heard her husband's gruff voice calling her. "Where have you been all afternoon? Surely it didn't take three or four hours to make one visit."

"Mrs. Smeltson was very chatty today," she shouted at him as she hung up her coat. "Her children don't visit very often and I felt sorry for her."

"You're a good woman," he said, coming up behind her and giving her an affectionate kiss on the cheek. "I know I'm testy sometimes, but I do love you."

"I know you do." That didn't help her anxiety level. She wasn't so sure he'd still love her once it came out that she'd had an illegitimate child, especially if her son was found to be a murderer.

"I'll have something ready for us to eat in a few minutes," she told him on her way to the kitchen. "I'm going to heat up some of that beef stew you like so much. I'll bake some biscuits, too. How does that sound?"

"It sounds great. I'll go take a peek at the news and you can call me when it's ready."

She pulled out the utensils she needed and had dinner ready in less than an hour.

After dinner, there was one more thing she needed to do. Heather would go visit Barbara Dodson tonight. She must be warned.

* * * * *

Doug had parked his car down the road from the church and watched as Mrs. Green went into her house. She was probably making dinner for the reverend right about now.

Her latest betrayal only compounded his resentment over being abandoned by her as a child. Now that she'd talked to the police, he was forced to leave his home and settle into his secret place. She took away his first home and now she'd taken this one.

He would wait for a while and see if she left the house again. Perhaps God brought her back into his life for a reason. It surely wasn't to punish him. He'd been doing everything he was told to do.

Of course, he had made some mistakes, but he'd made up for that with the last two witches. They had confessed and he was able to put them where their leader would find them. Close to the evil place, right where God could flaunt his victory in Satan's face.

Then it came to him. His mother had sinned long ago. Perhaps becoming a preacher's wife wasn't sufficient to bring her to God. She came to him for a reason. Heather Kirkpatrick Green was brought to him to be purged.

Chapter 67

"I wished it hadn't taken so long to convince the judge to sign off on the warrant for Bronn's place," said Chennelle, peering out the car window. "I hate going to a suspect's house after dark."

"You've got to admit, we have some pretty flimsy reasons for asking," said Barnes. "We have a woman who thinks this might be her son and is having a bad feeling about him because of something he said to her husband. If the mayor wasn't so hot on this case, the judge probably would have told us to get a brain."

Chennelle sniffed, trying to keep her sarcasm in check. "There have been plenty of instances where a woman's intuition should have been followed. I bet if we'd had a woman judge, we wouldn't have met with so much resistance."

"If you say so," said Barnes, giving Chennelle a sideways glance and smirking. "There's the house." She stopped and looked into the rearview mirror. "Good timing. Lloyd and Sanchez just pulled up behind me."

"The house looks dark. He's probably not here, but let's go check."

They got out of their car and Chennelle instructed Officer Lloyd to knock and announce their arrival. However, when they reached the door it was ajar. All four drew their weapons and small flashlights. Officer Lloyd looked to Chennelle for the go-ahead and she nodded at him.

Shining a flashlight and pointing his gun, he pushed the door open with his foot. "Mr. Bronn, Indianapolis Police," he shouted. Silence. Officer Lloyd walked into the house followed by Officer Sanchez and the detectives

The place was a mess. They found magazines and newspapers strewn about, a chair knocked over, and what once had been a ceramic cross lay broken on the floor. Each of the officers scanned the room before Sanchez went to the right and Lloyd to the left down a hallway. Chennelle chose to follow Lloyd.

He stopped at the first door and pushed it open while Chennelle followed the hallway to the next doorway. This room appeared in worse shape than the living room. Men's clothing covered the bed, haphazardly thrown there in loose bundles. Empty drawers hung open in the dresser, and the closet door stood ajar. She moved into the room, trying not to trip over discarded T-shirts and socks, and found another door. This one led to a bathroom where trashed cabinets indicated most of their contents were gone.

Chennelle noticed the bedroom light go on behind her. Walking back into the room she found Barnes, Lloyd, and Sanchez standing there.

"I checked the garage," said Sanchez. "There's a chair out there that stinks of urine and an ancient dark blue Buick."

"We're going to have to call CSI out here," said Chennelle. "If that's the car Detective Adams and I saw the night of the Cortez stabbing, her blood has to be in it. Even if he tried to clean it, he probably didn't get it all. When he pulled that knife out of her, it would have spattered his clothes with blood. The knife must have been dripping with it."

"Sanchez, why don't you call it in. Then run the plates on the car," said Barnes.

Sanchez nodded and went out to her squad.

"Glove up, Lloyd, and start in the kitchen," said Chennelle. "It looks like our perp took off in a hurry. We need to find some clue to where he may have gone. Barnes, you take the living room and I'll start with this bedroom."

Chennelle turned and scanned the room, barely knowing where to start. Bronn probably took everything significant with him, but there was always the possibility he forgot something. She started with the dresser.

A bulletin board hung on the wall above the dresser. Pins from it lay all over the top of the dresser and on the floor. Whatever was on the board must have been very important to him. She checked each drawer carefully, pulling them out to see if he'd taped anything to the bottoms. Nothing. Chennelle got down on her hands and knees and looked under the dresser. She noticed a piece of paper about the size of a small index card. Rising, she pulled the dresser away from the wall and took a closer look at the card. The word PURGED was written across it in large red block letters.

"You son of a bitch." Chennelle left the dresser pulled out so the crime scene crew could take a photo and bag the card as evidence when they arrived.

She decided to look through the nightstand next. A small reading lamp and gold cross on a stand sat on top of it. Chennelle noticed a Bible in the partially opened drawer and wondered why someone who was so religious would leave something so vital behind. Perhaps he thought he was equal to God now and didn't need it.

When she walked over to the other side of the bed, she noticed another corner of paper peeking out from beneath it. Kneeling, she found a photograph of a familiar looking woman holding a baby. Chennelle flipped it over to see if they were identified on the back.

"I looked all over the living area and came up with nothing," said Barnes. "What do you have there?"

"He knows who his mother is."

Chapter 68

"I was about to give up on you," said Doug as he watched Mrs. Green get into her car. "Where are you off to now?"

Mrs. Green pulled out of her driveway. He'd already started his engine a few moments ago, ready to go to his special place and come back tomorrow. Slowly, he pulled out from his hiding place and followed her from a distance.

"Where are you going, sweet momma?"

He hoped she'd stop at a store or gas station. There he could persuade her to accompany him. During Doug's short trip to his special place after vacating the house, he'd grabbed the .22—the up close and personal weapon of choice. It was easy to conceal, so no one would know she was leaving under duress.

To his disappointment, Mrs. Green continued to drive past all of his desired locations. It appeared she was headed for Geist. Had she received a call from an ailing but substantially wealthy church member? If so, why wasn't the good Reverend Green with her?

Then Doug saw her turn down *that* street. Surely she wasn't going there. He continued to follow her past house after house thinking this was a coincidence. But no, Mrs. Green turned down *that* driveway.

Doug drove on to the public parking area. He leapt from his vehicle and ran just inside the boundary of the woods. He got there just in time to see Mrs. Green walk into the house of the witch, Barbara Dodson.

"How convenient."

Chapter 69

Barbara's husband had just left for the airport. She was settling down with a glass of wine and the latest novel by her favorite mystery author, Sue Myers, when the doorbell rang. "Who on Earth could that be?"

She turned on the outside light and looked through the peephole to see Mrs. Green on her doorstep. Shocked, she took a step away from the door, wondering why the preacher's wife would be paying her a visit this late in the evening. Gathering her senses, she turned off the alarm and opened the door.

"Mrs. Green, to what do I owe the pleasure?"

"May I come in?" Mrs. Green asked as she peered over her shoulder. "I'd really like to talk to you."

"Of course, how rude of me. You are most welcome in my home."

Mrs. Green walked in and waited for Barbara to close the door, then followed her to the living room.

"I was just having a glass of wine when you arrived. Would you care for some, or perhaps a cup of coffee or tea?"

"I'm fine, thank you."

"Please have a seat then," said Barbara, pointing to a side chair. "You seem nervous. Don't worry, I'm not going to put some evil spell on you. That would get me in a lot of trouble with the Goddess, just like sinning gets you in trouble with your God."

"I think I may be paying for sins from my past...and, unfortunately, so are others."

Mrs. Green's face screwed up in pain and tears began to flow down her cheeks. Barbara felt for her, but wasn't sure why she chose to come here to unburden herself.

"My husband presided over a funeral this past Monday. I always go with him on the day of the funeral to make sure all the music is right and to greet the mourners."

Now Barbara was really confused. "Did something happen there?"

"Yes. This was the funeral of an elderly woman named Opal Bronn. When I stopped by the casket to pay my respects, I thought she looked familiar. Then I realized she was...."

Mrs. Green didn't get the chance to finish her sentence. There was a crash from the back of the house. Barbara jumped to the edge of her seat, suddenly realizing she hadn't reactivated the alarm. Standing quickly, she grabbed Mrs. Green's hand, pulling her from the chair.

"Let's go to my bedroom and we'll lock ourselves in. I can call the police from there."

They ran up the stairs together. Barbara would look back occasionally to make sure Mrs. Green was keeping up. "This way," she said, allowing Mrs. Green to pass her. Once inside the room, Barbara shut the door and locked it.

"That lock isn't going to stop him," Mrs. Green sobbed. "He's determined to kill you."

"How do you...I'll call the police," said Barbara, fearful now and wondering what Mrs. Green meant. When she lifted the receiver, Barbara found the line dead. Dread overtook her as she realized she'd left her cell phone on the kitchen counter when she'd poured the glass of wine.

"Do you have a cell phone on you?" asked Barbara.

"No, Jeremiah doesn't believe in them." Then a panicked look of realization came over Mrs. Green. "The phone isn't working, is it? Oh my God, he's going to kill you and probably me as well."

"Who's going to kill us?" It sounded to Barbara as though this woman knew exactly who was out there. "Do you know who...?"

A loud banging on the bedroom door interrupted Barbara's question. She and Mrs. Green found one another and clung to each other as though this would protect them. He banged again.

"I'm sorry, I'm so sorry," wailed Mrs. Green.

Barbara couldn't understand to what she was referring. The woman was bordering on hysteria.

Then it hit her—the fire ladder. She turned Mrs. Green to face her, put her index finger to her lips, and pointed at the window.

"We can't..." Mrs. Green started to say.

Barbara placed her hand over Mrs. Green's mouth to stop her saying anything further and guided her to the window. She showed her the ladder stashed away in a chest under the windowsill. She pulled it out and then opened the window, knocking out the screen.

She almost had the ladder secured when the bedroom door crashed open. A tall, dark haired man entered the room and grabbed Mrs. Green from behind. He held what Barbara recognized as Sasha's athame to the woman's throat.

"Now, I would suggest you step away from the window, witch," he said in a sinister, triumphant voice. "If you don't, I'll cut her throat, then I'll thrust this dagger into your back before you can get one foot out on that ladder."

Obeying, Barbara moved away from the window. She caught the terrified expression on Mrs. Green's face before looking into her capture's wicked eyes.

"What do you want from us?" she asked.

"Repentance."

Chapter 70

"I know Mrs. Green doesn't want her husband to know about her son yet, but I don't think we have a choice," said Chennelle as Barnes sped toward the Green's house. "We've got to warn them that Doug Bronn knows who she is and they may be in danger. If he thinks these *witches* are bad, what's he going to think about a mother who he may think abandoned him?"

"Who knows what kind of stories his loony grandmother told him over the years," said Barnes. "His religious references make sense now. Did you see how many crosses there were in that house? You'd think they were terrified of vampires or something."

"Leaving all the religious symbols, and especially his Bible, seems strange to me," said Chennelle.

"Why?"

"The Bible is God's word. It's supposed to be our guide to live the type of life God wants us to live. Yet he didn't take it with him."

"You remember how screwed up Emerson was. He couldn't even remember what he'd done on his trek to Indy. Bronn's granny did a real number on him."

"That's obvious," said Chennelle. "You can't mix religious conviction with hate. It's like trying to mix oil and water. From Mrs. Green's description of her mother, the woman was full of spite and anger."

"There's the house and lights are on. I'm glad. I hate rousting people out of bed."

"Barnes, it's only seven thirty. Just because he's a preacher, doesn't mean he goes to bed at dusk."

Barnes parked and shut off the ignition. They exited the car and walked up to the house in silence. The television was loud and the Wheel of Fortune was spinning. Chennelle rang the doorbell, hoping the Greens could hear it over the noise of the television.

After ringing it a second time, she heard Reverend Green yelling for his wife to answer the door. Chennelle glanced over at Barnes, who shrugged. Ringing it a third time was the charm.

"Heather, why aren't you answering the door?" he yelled.

Then the door flew open and the reverend stood there scowling at them. "What are you doing here this time of night?"

"It's rather urgent that we talk to you and Mrs. Green," said Chennelle. "Is your wife home this evening?"

"Of course, she is," he said and waved them in. "Heather," he shouted as he walked down the hallway. "Heather!"

The detectives waited in the foyer. They heard him open and close several doors. When they saw him again, his expression had changed to one of confusion.

"Is something wrong, Reverend?" asked Chennelle.

"This is odd," he said, and walked quickly through a living area. The detectives followed close behind.

"Reverend Green," said Barnes. "Where—"

"I'm going to look in the garage," he said, cutting her off before she could finish.

Chennelle glanced at her partner. Silently, the two detectives followed Green into the empty attached garage. He punched the garage door opener and stepped out into the driveway. Now he looked panic stricken.

"Her car is gone. Where could she be?"

"When did you last see your wife?" asked Chennelle.

"At supper time. She came home a little late from her visitation. She fixed us some stew and biscuits." He started to pace, his right hand absently stroking his cheek. "After supper, I sat down in my easy chair to watch the evening news."

"She didn't say anything to you about going back out tonight?" asked Barnes.

"No. She was doing the dishes and I guess I fell asleep," he said, each word difficult under the stress. "The next thing I knew, you two were ringing my doorbell. What's going on? Is my wife in some sort of danger?"

"Let's sit down," said Chennelle as she led Reverend Green back through the door connecting the garage to the kitchen. She pointed to the kitchen chairs. "Your wife came to see us a few days ago to tell us that she thought we were remiss by not testing the females in your congregation. She hinted the perpetrator could be someone's son."

"That's preposterous."

"She also visited us around noon today." Chennelle paused and looked into the pastor's befuddled face. Then she told him the whole story.

"I can't believe this," he said. "Why wouldn't she tell me something like this? She told me she couldn't have any children, but she hadn't told me why. I didn't mind, because the life of a preacher is so full of doing for others sometimes the children don't get enough attention."

"I'm sure Mrs. Green was ashamed and scared," said Barnes. "Since she was so young when her mother kidnapped her son, she probably had no resources to help find him. There was no internet at the time and no Amber Alert system. Getting a private investigator would have cost a lot of money that she didn't have. She'd given up by the time she met you."

"Reverend Green," said Chennelle. "Do you have any idea where your wife may have gone this evening? Had she mentioned anyone in the past few days, someone she had concerns for or a friend who is sick?"

Reverend Green leaned forward and placed his face in his hands. He rubbed his eyes and then his cheeks. Then his eyes widened, and he dropped his hands to the table with a thud.

"That Dodson woman," he said. "A few days ago, we'd seen a reporter on the news who was trying to get Mrs. Dodson to answer questions about all the bodies being dumped on her property."

"What did she say about Barbara Dodson?" asked Chennelle.

"Heather felt sorry for her. The woman had lost four friends. Then she said the killer was very cruel. Leaving those bodies on her property was like telling her she's next. Do you think my wife believes Mrs. Dodson is next?"

"That's a good possibility," said Barnes. "We'll go out to the Dodson house and see if she's there."

"I'm going with you."

"We need for you to stay here in case she calls or shows up," said Chennelle sternly. "Here is my card and that is my cell number. If she comes home, I want to hear from you right away."

Chennelle could have sworn she saw the glimmer of a tear in the reverend's eye. He nodded in agreement, and then the detectives were out the door and on their way to who knew what.

Chapter 71

Barbara saw a large duffle bag sitting on her kitchen counter. He'd apparently brought along his instruments of destruction.

"Now, witch," he shouted, and then he pointed toward the kitchen table. "Bring two of those chairs over here and sit down on one of them."

Barbara did as she was told while looking deeply into Mrs. Green's eyes. Once seated, he grabbed Mrs. Green's arm and dragged her over next to Barbara, where he pushed her to the floor. That's when Barbara saw a glint of steel as he put a gun to her face. It was in his right hand and the knife in his left.

"Get up and go over there, Mrs. Green. Take the duct tape from my bag and then please assist me in making sure the witch doesn't get up from this chair."

"But…please, she's done nothing wrong."

"This coming from a good Christian woman!"

"Christians are kind and loving. They don't torture and murder," said Mrs. Green, visibly trembling.

Barbara watched the gun he continued to point at her face until she heard Mrs. Green gasp. Glancing in her direction, Barbara saw her holding what appeared to be a legal document. The multi-colored paper reminded her of a car title or a birth certificate.

"You know, don't you, Dougie?" she said, still holding the document. "You found out who I am."

The man Mrs. Green called Dougie smiled at her. He didn't speak at first but cocked his head one way and then the other, looking at the woman as though she was something curious.

"Yes, I do know. I found that birth certificate amongst Grandmother's things after she went to be with God. She told me all about you and your evil ways. How you deserted me when I was a baby because you didn't want me. She told me how my grandfather doted over you, because he was just like you. Yes, Mother, I know who you are."

Tears formed in Mrs. Green's eyes and she was shaking her head violently. "No, Dougie, you don't…."

"DON'T CALL ME THAT!"

"I'm sorry, I'm sorry," she wailed. "It's just that I haven't seen you since she ran off with you and that's what we used to call you."

The stunned look on this Dougie's face told all. Barbara wondered if he'd believe what Mrs. Green was saying. She was still trying to grasp the fact that the woman was this man's mother.

"Doug, please believe me. I never, never would have deserted you. I loved you."

"Liar! My grandmother was a fine God-fearing woman. She protected me from the likes of you and my grandfather. She wouldn't lie to me."

"She berated my father constantly. He left because he couldn't take it anymore. You need to listen to me. I'm telling you the truth."

"Get over here," he said through gritted teeth. "Bring that tape here and shut your blasphemous mouth."

Mrs. Green pulled the duct tape from the bag and walked over toward Barbara. Their eyes met briefly and she mouthed the word *sorry* before kneeling and putting the duct tape around Barbara's left ankle, fastening it tightly to the chair leg.

"Is that too tight?" she asked.

Barbara shook her head. She felt a mixture of sympathy and anger toward the woman for bringing this blight upon her and the coven. She couldn't believe a sweet woman like this spawned such a monster.

"The chairs don't have arms, so you'll have to wrap it around her arms and torso several times," the man instructed. He pocketed the gun and transferred Sasha's athame to his right hand. Then he brought the knife down to Barbara's chest area just above her breasts. "Don't put any tape here. I have something special for this area."

Mrs. Green sobbed the whole time she was wrapping the duct tape around Barbara, securing her to the chair. Barbara closed her eyes. There would be no escape from this maniac. He would torture her into confessing her sins, and then would kill her as he did the others. She wondered if she should confess right now. He wouldn't have any reason to torture her if she repented quickly. She heard the other chair scrape the floor and opened her eyes.

"Sit still, *Mother*."

Barbara was startled at the pure evil in the man's face. He'd finally discovered his mother's existence and refused to listen to her explanation of what happened. Now he was sitting on Mrs. Green's lap, gripping the hair at the nape of her neck and tilting her head backward. She watched as he slid the flat part of the blade back and forth on the woman's neck as she wept.

"Why are you doing that to her?" asked Barbara, no longer able to keep her silence. "She's not of my religion."

"She is a sinner. She abandoned her own child, and then dares to lie about it. God will not tolerate such wretched behavior."

"From what I've been told, humans aren't supposed to judge other humans. Your God does that."

"Shut up, witch," he said, rising and striking her across the face with the back of his hand. "You do not have the knowledge or the right to tell me what God does or does not do."

"I'm not a witch. I'm a human being, just like you." She thought he was going to strike her again, but he turned and walked up behind his mother.

"She's your mother! You should at least give her the chance to give you her side of the story." Barbara waited for a reaction, but Doug acted as though she wasn't there and began wrapping the duct tape around Heather without saying a word.

In one more desperate attempt, Barbara tried again. "Your grandmother was also human. Humans make mistakes and make bad decisions. There must be a reason. Your mother's a good person. She married a preacher, for goodness sake."

Doug whipped around and was on Barbara in a flash, the knife poised over the artery in her throat. "Shut up or I'll do it now and you'll go straight to Hell."

"Go ahead. I'll be waiting for you."

Chapter 72

Doug went to his duffle and began to rummage through it. Heather heard the clink of metal on metal. She watched her son, terrified of what he might do next. His calm demeanor was more frightening than his anger.

"Ah, here they are," said Doug.

He had pulled out two long metal T-shaped objects that looked like wrought iron and quite heavy from the way he was handling them. Smiling, he went to the stove, turned on the flame, and put the T-ends of the rods on it.

Then in a loud commanding voice, he said, "Witch, are you ready to confess your sins?"

"I can't confess to something unless I know what it is I have done," said Barbara.

Heather watched her fellow captor. Barbara seemed so calm, so sure in her convictions.

"You have denied the one true God and worship a goddess who is of the devil," he said, getting extremely close to Barbara's face. "Now, repent so God can forgive you."

"If the devil exists," said Barbara, glaring at him, "then I must be looking at him right now."

The athame seemed to come out of nowhere. He plunged it into Barbara's left thigh and she screamed a horrendous, gut wrenching scream.

"Stop, Doug...please," Heather shouted as she listened to Barbara whimper in pain. "This woman hasn't hurt anyone. She doesn't deserve this."

Doug turned on her, his flaming eyes boring into her soul. "You dare to plead for the witch and say she's done nothing wrong."

His laugh chilled Heather to the bone. Her stomach roiled as she watched Doug. What had her mother created?

"You are just as corrupt as this witch. She at least admits her guilt. You continue to deny yours."

"My mother was hurt and confused when she took you from me. My father decided to leave us when my mother refused to force me to give you away. She couldn't stand the thought of some stranger raising you."

Doug peered at her, less furious now and apparently curious enough to listen. "Grandmother did say he took off with a younger woman."

"If he did, I never knew it, but he did leave us without much money, and I always felt like it was my fault. I think deep down Mother blamed me, too. That's why she decided to take you away."

"You should not have lain with a man before you wed," he said, red cheeked with renewed anger. "Shut up or I'll cut you, too."

She glanced over at Barbara, whose injury oozed blood which spilled to the floor. Barbara slowly raised her head. The two women's eyes briefly locked in a moment of understanding before Doug stepped between them and broke the connection. They were both going to die tonight.

"How many sacrifices have you made to your goddess on the altar in the woods?" Doug asked Barbara.

"We don't sacrifice the way you mean. We only place our tools, and sometimes flowers, and fruits or vegetables there during harvest time."

"Liar," he screamed and plunged the knife into her right hand.

Heather heard the sickening sound of bones cracking in two before Barbara's screams rent the air. Nausea overwhelmed her. It was all she could do not to vomit. Closing her eyes, she tried to block out Barbara's anguished wail.

Heather burst into tears. Why did he have to torture these women? Looking up, she silently prayed for God to send help before he could kill Barbara. She should have called Detective Kendall before she came here. Now all seemed lost.

Doug retrieved a thick silver mitt from his bag and then went to the stove. "These should be ready now. Since the witch will not ask for God's forgiveness, I will have to mark her as *unforgiven*."

"No, please, no more," cried Barbara, sobbing uncontrollably. "Just kill me…please, no more."

"But you are the worst of all because you have led others into this devil worship." With that, he ripped her shirt away and branded her.

This time her screams were so loud, Heather thought the neighbors would hear even though they were acres away. She had to do something. She had to stop this madness.

"Sacrifice me," shouted Heather over Barbara's continued cries. "Take me instead."

Turning, he cocked his head again. It was as though he'd never seen such a thing before. He walked toward his mother and took her chin in his strong left hand and roughly tilted it upward.

"Are you daring to compare yourself to Jesus and his sacrifice?"

"No," she said, having a hard time speaking with the grip he had on her face. "Not compare, but Christians are supposed to try to be Christ-like."

"Sacrifice," he said, letting go of her. "Yes, I will sacrifice you, just as Abraham was to sacrifice his son. If God stops me as he stayed the hand of Abraham, then you may go free. If not, you die."

Chapter 73

"What made you think Mrs. Green would go over to Barbara Dodson's house?" asked Barnes, as she drove towards the Geist area. "Have they ever met?"

"I don't know," said Chennelle. "I don't think they've met face-to-face. However, Reverend Green said his wife was aware that Mrs. Dodson is the leader of the Wiccan coven. Unfortunately, our suspect may have seen that same TV broadcast and may go after Mrs. Dodson next."

Sirens came up behind them. Chennelle looked back and saw a fire truck about to catch them. "Better pull over."

Barnes pulled to the right and stopped. Not one but three large fire trucks and a rescue squad passed them. Barnes had just pulled back out into traffic when they heard more sirens and she pulled off to the side again. This time it was two IMPD squads and an ambulance.

"Must be a hell of a fire," said Barnes, pulling onto the road once more.

Ten minutes later, they were on the road to the Dodson house. People wrapped up in coats, hats and scarves were looking down the street from the ends of their driveways. Many were chatting and looking worried.

"You don't suppose those emergency vehicles were coming down here, do you?" asked Barnes.

Chennelle's heart began beating faster, and despite the cold, she felt a trickle of sweat roll down her armpit. She was terrified they had arrived too late to help Mrs. Dodson and Mrs. Green.

"I have a bad feeling about this," she said as they approached the end of the street and saw brilliant red and blue lights flashing in the night.

People were shouting and rushing around. Firefighters pulled hoses and set up their ladders to spray water on the roof. Patrol officers were on the front line trying to keep the press and neighbors out of the vicinity.

The back half of the house was engulfed in flames and Chennelle's heart sank. Barnes parked the car on the street and they both got out and ran toward the house.

"Hold it right there," said a female officer Chennelle didn't recognize. "Nobody goes past the tape."

"We're detectives, I'm Kendall, this is Barnes." They both showed her their badges.

"You the investigators they're sending?"

"Yes," Chennelle lied. Well, it wasn't really a lie. They would be assigned to it as soon as Major Stevenson found out this had to do with their Wiccan murders case.

"See Officer Bays over there. He's got the log for you to sign."

"Thanks," said Chennelle.

She motioned for Barnes to follow her as she'd spotted Bays only a few feet away.

"Officer Bays, do you know if there was anyone in the house?" asked Chennelle, taking the log from him and signing in.

"There was one woman, I think she's the owner," he said. "She's burned pretty bad and is having a hard time breathing. A neighbor was walking with his dog through the woods when he spotted flames at the kitchen window. He called 911 from his cell and then entered the house. He was able to pull her out before the fire got too bad."

"That was lucky," said Chennelle as she handed the log to Barnes. "You said she's bad. Is she awake?"

"They're working on her in that ambulance over there." He pointed to their left.

"Thanks, Bays. Come on Barnes. We've got to find out if Mrs. Green is still in that house."

They ran over to the ambulance as fast as they could. One of the paramedics exited the back of the ambulance and slammed the doors shut. He started to go around to the cab, but Chennelle stopped him.

She breathed heavily, but was able to ask about Mrs. Dodson's condition. She asked if they could talk with her for just a moment.

"Sorry, Detective, this patient is in really bad shape. She has second and third degree burns on her lower extremities and was barely able to breathe. We had to intubate her. We really need to get her to the hospital."

Chennelle followed him as he walked to the cab of the ambulance and opened the door.

"Did she say anything to you?" asked Chennelle, hoping against hope.

"Yeah, she did. It didn't make sense though. She kept saying *sacrifice* and *in the woods*. That's all. Now we've really got to get her out of here."

Chennelle watched as the ambulance pulled away. She turned to her partner. "What do you think that means?"

Barnes shook her head for a few seconds and then got that wide-eyed look she always got when she'd figured something out. "Where do people perform sacrifices?"

"In the woods?" Chennelle said, and then it came to her. "Not just any woods, this one. The Wiccan coven has an altar out there. You don't think he took his mother…?"

"Yes, I do. Don't ask me why. People like him don't think the way we do."

"We'll ask Bays if he can spare a couple of uniforms to go out there with us," said Chennelle. "Let's put a stop to this once and for all."

Chapter 74

"Strip," he commanded as though he were God Himself. "You will lie naked before God and He shall tell me your fate. I said, take off your clothes."

Heather was already shivering more from fear than from the cold. After setting fire to Barbara's kitchen curtains, he'd cut Heather's bonds and dragged her out to these woods. He'd pushed her toward a stone table and she scraped her knee, tearing her pants. She could feel a trickle of blood running down her leg.

"But you're my son," she whimpered. "I can't take my clothes off in front of you."

"I have no mother," he shouted. "I am God's avenging angel. He has commanded me to purge those on Earth who have sinned so they will have a place with Him in Heaven. Either you strip or I'll cut them off of you."

She started to cry as she took off her left boot. The warmth of her tears on her frozen cheeks felt good at first, but soon her face was cold as ice and burned. She continued to take off her clothing one piece at a time. Duct tape still clung to the front of her sweater.

"If you don't go a little faster, I'll have to help you," he said with the most evil smile she'd ever seen. Maybe Barbara was right. Perhaps he was the devil.

Once her clothing was shed, she tried to hide her nakedness with her hands, but then he grabbed her and forced her to lie down on the stone table. She knew she was going to die in a very short time, but wondered if it would be from his blade or from the hypothermia setting in. She'd prefer the latter.

He took her arms and legs, one at a time, and tied them to the stone legs of the table. All she could do was lay there and shiver violently while he made his preparations to sacrifice her to a god she knew was not her God.

Her tears were beginning to choke her, so she turned her head to the side and watched him as he started a fire. Doug had brought his branding irons with him. Would he brand her as forgiven or would he continue to believe she wasn't telling the truth and use the one for those who were not forgiven?

"Doug, please. You don't have to do this," she said, her voice shaking. "Please stop this while you can."

"You still don't get it, do you? The reason God brought me into this world was to give me this mission. If God wants me to stop, He'll tell me to stop." He paused and looked at her, cocking his head as he'd done so many times that evening. "I believe if I were you, I'd stop talking to me and start praying to Him."

Doug walked back to his fire and fanned it so it would take off. He must have done this many times, because the fire was burning hot in no time. Then he placed the branding irons in the flames and approached her, bringing the knife with him.

"Did you have other children after me?" he asked.

This question seemed strange under the circumstances, but she decided to answer if it might make a difference in how things turned out.

"No, unfortunately my uterus ruptured when I gave birth to you and it had to be removed. That's why it hurt so much when my mother took you from me."

"You keep saying that," he said gruffly. "It's easy to accuse when the accused is dead and unable to defend herself."

He took the athame and ran the sharp tip lightly in an arc from hip to hip. She winced in pain and soon she could feel warm blood dripping down each side of her body. He hadn't cut deep, just enough to draw blood.

"Tell me about my father. Did you love him?" As he asked this question, he ran the tip of the knife up her torso from her belly button to her sternum, barely cutting her skin.

Tears started to flow more readily from Heather's eyes again. The pain was almost bearable as her skin was numbing with cold, but the danger in his eyes was palpable.

"I did love him. I made a mistake by letting him convince me to have sex with him to show him how much."

"So you admit you didn't want me."

"No sixteen year old girl wants to be pregnant, but once I was, I never thought about giving you away. I wanted to raise you even if I had to quit school and get a job. After Dad left and I started to show some independence, Mother couldn't bear the idea I might leave with you some day, so she took you and left me behind."

"It's time." He moved away from her side and took a place at her head. Then he raised his arms and spread them like angel wings.

The flickering flames made him look monstrous. The athame shone bright in his right hand. He closed his eyes and raised them to the sky. "God in Heaven, please tell me now, do you want me to give you this soul, or do I spare her?"

After a few seconds, he lowered his eyes and without saying a word, he walked over to the fire. He picked up one of the branding irons and came back to her.

"No, no, please, Doug, please don't..."

His eyes were wild and his smile vicious. Doug brought the iron down on her chest and she screamed as Barbara had screamed. The shock of heat on her cold blue skin was horrendous. She could smell her flesh burning and feel a searing pain no one should ever have to endure.

"Oh, God please, please make him stop," she shouted to the heavens.

As he pulled the iron away, he stooped low until they were almost nose to nose and said, "Unforgiven."

Chapter 75

"Holy crap, did you hear that?" asked Barnes. "He must be torturing her. I heard it coming from over there."

Chennelle had heard it as well and the panic she'd felt before just multiplied by about a thousand. She motioned for the two patrol officers who'd accompanied them to follow. It was really dark in these woods and difficult to see despite the fact that each had a flashlight. They had to be getting close, because the screaming and crying grew louder.

Then she saw it. There was a fire burning and she could see the tall dark figure standing over Heather Green, who was lying naked and bleeding on a slab of stone. She was sobbing and pleading for her life. Chennelle's only thought was that Doug Bronn was totally insane to do this to his own mother.

She motioned for the officers to circle to the left while she and Barnes went to the right, trying her best to approach quietly. Of course, as much noise as Mrs. Green was making, it wasn't very difficult.

Doug Bronn moved to the head of the altar and said a few words Chennelle couldn't understand. She could see he had the athame grasped in both hands and was raising it above his head, ready to strike the death blow.

"Please, God," said Mrs. Green, sobbing. "Please forgive my son for what he's about to do and for all those others he's killed. It's not his fault, it's not his fault."

Surprisingly, Doug stopped, lowered the dagger, and looked down at his mother. Then, he knelt down closer to her and said, "There you go being Jesus-like again. He asked for the people who were killing Him to be forgiven."

"I've been trying to tell you all this time, as Christians we should always ask what Jesus would do and try to follow his example. You may not be able to forgive me, but I am going to forgive you, because I love you."

"Doug Bronn, drop your weapon and step away from Mrs. Green," shouted Chennelle. Hers and three other guns were pointed directly at him.

Instead of dropping the athame, he brought it up to Mrs. Green's throat. "You can shoot me if you want, but this dagger is extremely sharp. I'll cut her throat before I hit the ground."

Chennelle could see his point, but she wasn't going to give up. He fully intended to kill his mother, so she'd have to try to persuade him to do otherwise.

"Doug, nobody else has to die. All you have to do is put the weapon on the ground and step away from Mrs. Green. If you die tonight, who'll be around to tell your story? The police and the news media will just paint you as a cold blooded killer."

"I'm not," he said. "I've been given a job to do."

"I know you have, but are you listening to everything God's telling you? Why would you need to kill the women who you labeled forgiven?"

He stared at Chennelle for several seconds, cocking his head one way and then the other. Doug looked down at his mother for a few more seconds, deep in thought, and then he looked back at Chennelle.

"I was afraid they'd stray again or the witch, Barbara Dodson, would convince them to come back. I had to send them to God before they became evil again. I purged them and sent them to God."

"Maybe you should ask Him again about killing Mrs. Green," said Chennelle. "If you're supposed to kill her, why did He send us here to rescue her?"

Chennelle was pleased to see the look of confusion forming on his face. As long as she kept him engaged in conversation, he wasn't thinking about killing his mother.

"God sent you?" he finally asked. "How do you know?"

"The same way you do…He told me where to find you."

Again, he looked at Chennelle with curious, confused eyes. She could see his grip on the athame loosen a little. She had to keep talking.

"God gave me a mission, too," she said. "He told me to be a police officer and to help the righteous stop those who want to break his sixth commandment—thou shalt not kill."

"No, no," he said, shaking his head. "This is some sort of devil's trick. It's this place. It is full of evil. You probably aren't real."

"We're very real," said Chennelle. She took a quick glance at her partner to signal they'd have to do something soon. "You've got to listen to what you're being told. Did you pray tonight? Did He give you a true answer, or did Satan trick *you* into thinking he was God?"

"No, no, I know it wasn't Satan. I do what God tells me. He wanted the witches purged and He wants this woman purged. I don't need a cop interpreting what God wants me to do."

Then a deep voice from behind Chennelle said, "But would you listen to a man of God."

Chapter 76

"Reverend Green, I thought I told you to stay at home," said Chennelle, keeping her eyes on Doug Bronn.

"Yes, you did. However, when I saw the breaking news on television, I knew my place was here."

"Did God send you to help me, Reverend Green?" asked Doug. "I can tell that you are a very devout Christian, and this woman has deceived you."

Chennelle realized this could be good. If this man respected the good pastor, he might listen to him.

"Yes, He did," said the reverend in a calming tone.

Of course, Chennelle knew that most pastors were very good at calming others. They had to deal with much of the tragedy in people's lives as well as the joys. She only hoped it would work this time.

"May I come nearer?" asked the reverend.

"Reverend Green, you shouldn't do that," said Chennelle. She'd expected him to talk Doug down, not put himself in danger.

"I know you are concerned about me, Detective, but God will be with me." His eyes connected with hers and Chennelle knew what he was about to do.

"Reverend, please," she said, but he'd already started walking towards Doug.

Chennelle saw one of the officers move, but caught his eye, shaking her head slightly. He looked towards his partner and raised a hand. She then gave her partner a glance and moved her head slightly to tell Barnes to move further around the circle.

"Do you know what she's done, Reverend Green?" said Doug in an almost childlike manner. "Do you want to hear her confession? She's been telling me lies about my grandmother. She's not respecting her own mother, and it says you must in the Bible, right Reverend?"

"That's true, my son."

"I know, God told me she's not to be forgiven. You see, she's been branded a sinner."

"I do see," said the reverend, looking down at his naked, sobbing wife.

Chennelle could see Reverend Green bite his lip slightly. Then he looked up at Doug.

"Doug, this woman has sinned against us both and that is why God has sent me to you. He wants me to do it. He feels you've carried enough of this burden and should rest."

Doug looked at the reverend with confusion. "But, I think I should do it. She sinned against me first."

Doug's reactions were getting more childish by the minute. Chennelle knew that Reverend Green was trying to get Doug to hand over the weapon. Once he had the athame, he could run far enough away that the officers could subdue Doug and take him into custody.

"Are you sure you're listening to the entire plan God has set forth for you?" asked Reverend Green. "Are you sure you aren't looking to please yourself and not Him?"

Doug stared at the preacher for quite some time. He got up from his kneeling position and turned the knife so that the hilt was towards his mentor. Reverend Green took it from him.

Wisely, he walked a few feet away from Doug and acted as though he was preparing to kill his wife. Meanwhile, the two patrol officers grabbed Doug from behind and wrestled him to the ground. It took both of them to cuff the struggling man, but they finally got him under control.

Without a word, the good reverend started cutting the ropes that bound his wife to the altar. Her wounds were still leaking blood and her lips had turned blue. He grabbed up her sweater and pulled it over her head, forgetting her bra. He pulled her socks onto her feet and her slacks onto her legs. He lifted her and started to carry her back to the Dodson house and an awaiting ambulance.

"You liar, you liar," shouted Doug at the reverend. "You tricked me. You're as full of the devil as she is!"

Reverend Green ignored him and kept walking.

Chapter 77

Chennelle paced in the waiting area of the emergency room at Community North Hospital. Heather Green was in one of the examining rooms, her husband at her side. The wounds she received were superficial, but needed to be cleaned and bandaged. The big concern was hypothermia. Temperatures had dropped to twenty-eight degrees by the time Doug Bronn took her out to the woods and forced her to lay naked on a freezing cold slab of rock. By the time the paramedics got her into the ambulance, she was incoherent.

Detective Barnes had stayed with the team at the crime scene, but Chennelle wanted to be here when Mrs. Green came around. She wanted to know exactly what happened. Her stomach turned every time she thought about Barbara Dodson and the fact that this maniac decided to burn her alive, like they did during the witch trials centuries ago. How could a sweet woman like Heather Green have given birth to such a monster?

At least Chennelle had been able to contact Mr. Dodson's employer and discover he'd gone on a business trip to China. His plane hadn't even landed yet when this all went down. She couldn't imagine the horror of being stopped at the airport and told his wife had been attacked. Would they give him details? At least she was taken to Richard M. Fairbanks Burn Center at Eskenazi Health— one of the best burn units in the country.

Her cell rang and she got the evil eye from the nurse at the trauma station, so she walked out the door to take the call. "Kendall."

"Kendall, it's Freeman. I'm at the Burn Center. Stevenson sent me here to question Mrs. Dodson since you're there and Barnes is still on scene."

"How's she doing?"

"She died ten minutes ago. The doctor said she'd inhaled too much smoke and gases from the stuff that was burning in the house. Her lungs and trachea were so damaged there was nothing they could do for her but keep her comfortable until she passed."

"Was anyone with her when she died?" Chennelle's chest felt heavy with pain at the idea of Mrs. Dodson dying alone.

"There were a couple of her friends—Amber and Victoria. The nurses weren't going to let them in, but I explained that Mrs. Dodson didn't have anyone else who could be with her, so they bent the rules."

Chennelle's eyes filled with tears and her voice cracked. "Do you know if she ever regained consciousness?"

"The doc told us she was in a coma. He didn't think she was aware of her pain. It's too bad her husband couldn't get back in time to say goodbye."

"Yeah, well, I'd better go. They could call me in to talk to Mrs. Green any moment now. I need to hear her side of what happened tonight."

"Do you want me to come down there?" asked Freeman.

"No, I can handle it. Thanks for offering." She disconnected, unaware of whether or not he'd said goodbye.

Chennelle went back inside. She found a vacant chair away from everyone else and sat down hard. Leaning forward with her elbows on her knees and her head hanging, she started to shake. She didn't want to give into the tears, but if she didn't she'd burst. Finally, she covered her face with her hands and let loose.

She heard someone sit down in the chair next to her, and then felt a gentle touch she knew so well. Face and hands soaked in tears, she looked up into the warm brown eyes of Trevon Adams. He pulled her close and she sobbed hard into his shoulder. She cried until she thought every muscle in her body would seize.

"Chennelle, baby, don't worry. I've got ya," he said. His voice was soothing, exactly what she needed right now.

When she finally stopped crying, she pulled back and smiled at him. He got up and crossed over to an end table and brought back a box of tissues. Chennelle must have used a dozen by the time she'd wiped her hands, face, and blew her nose more than once. She looked at him again and noticed a large wet circle on the shoulder of his coat.

"I've probably ruined your coat," she said.

"I don't think a few tears will cause much damage. Besides, this isn't one of my favorites."

Chennelle smiled at him again, and then remembered her grief. "Mrs. Dodson didn't make it, Trevon. He burned her."

"I know. I was at the station when the calls started coming in. I was on my way here to see how you were getting along when I got the call from Barnes. She was glad to hear I'd be with you when you found out."

"Was she?" Chennelle grinned at him again. "I'd better pull it together, because I can't go in to see Mrs. Green with my face all swollen up, now can I?"

"Why, you afraid she'll figure out you're human?" asked Trevon.

"Very funny," she said. "I'm going to go splash some cold water on my face. Will you stay here and listen in case they call me in?"

"Of course, I will. I'm not leaving you alone tonight."

Chapter 78

Chennelle blew a strand of hair away from her lips to no avail because it returned. She growled, set down her knife, and pushed the pest behind her ear. She then commenced with dicing onions and green peppers. The smell of freshly brewed coffee was calling her.

A knock came at her front door. She tied her favorite purple robe more securely around her naked body and walked to the door, curious to know who would dare bang on her door at six thirty on a Saturday morning. Chennelle took a peek through her door-side window to see Erica Barnes on her doorstep with a Dunkin Donuts bag in her hand.

"Barnes," she said as she opened the door. "What brings you to my door so freakin' early?"

"Is that any way to greet your partner when she comes bearing gifts?"

"Chennelle, you know what I....Whoa." Trevon Adams had just appeared, and disappeared, wearing nothing but his boxers.

Barnes peered at Chennelle with a sly smile, nodding in understanding. "I heard you'd been at the hospital until two in the morning. I figured you'd be up anyway, but I didn't know you'd have such a good reason."

"Shut up," said Chennelle, smiling and pushing the door shut. "What kind of donuts are in that bag."

"Only your favorite—Boston Kremes."

"Want some coffee?"

"I thought you'd never ask."

"I was getting ready to make a couple of veggie omelets. Do you want one?"

"Sounds healthy. I think I'll stick to my donuts like a good little cop."

Chennelle pointed her spatula at Barnes and gave her a stern look. "You know, that kind of talk is what keeps those nasty stereotypes alive."

"Lighten up. We've caught the bad guy and he'll be going away where he won't be doing any more witch hunting. Of course, once he gets to prison, he'll have plenty of people to purge."

"If they don't purge him first."

Both women turned as Trevon came back into the room, this time with his jeans and tee shirt on. "Good morning, Barnes. Why you up so early on a Saturday?"

Barnes chewed a piece of donut slowly, giving Trevon an appraising look. She picked up her coffee and took a long swig. "I wanted to write up the report on the Bronn case while it was fresh in my mind, so I decided to go in today. Ben and I have plans later on. Looks like you two might be up to something yourselves."

Chennelle could have sworn she saw a blush in those dark brown cheeks of his. She decided to rescue him. She handed him a cup of coffee and changed the subject. "Did you and the troops find anything more at the crime scene after I left?"

"We found his murder kit," said Barnes, setting her donut on her napkin and taking another sip of coffee. "I don't know why he needed to use Winston's athame, because he had plenty of tools—a butcher knife, rope, those branding irons. The athame must have symbolized something to him."

Chennelle nodded. "He probably thought it humiliated them more to use their own religious object against them."

"That makes sense. Then I got a call from Parelli about what the CSI team found. She said they found a rental car in the public parking lot. The keys we'd taken from Bronn on scene were for that car. In it, they found a box full of photos of our victims, the other living coven members, and some older ones that were probably his mother and him when he was a baby. They also found a deed transfer for some undeveloped land out in Hancock County. A woman named Ilene Baker was the previous owner and signed it over to Douglas Bronn."

"Did they send somebody out there last night?"

"Stevenson got hold of the County Sheriff's office and you won't believe this."

"I think we will," said Trevon.

"They found an old hunting shed out there. In it were tools, knives, guns, and one of those whip things with a bunch of leather strips with dried blood on it. There was also a throne-like chair with remnants of duct tape on it and lots of dried blood around it."

"That's probably where he took Sasha Winston," said Chennelle.

"Then he brought her back to the woods and dumped her," said Trevon. "What a sick bastard."

"No kidding," said Barnes. "As much blood as they found, he probably took Fuller and Bradley there, too. Hancock County secured the scene and we're sending a CSI team up there today. I just wonder if our victims' blood is the only blood we'll find up there."

Chennelle started beating eggs a little too vigorously. She finally stopped before she wound up with meringue or something and poured them in a hot frying pan.

"So how did it go with the Greens last night? I take it they were able to bring Mrs. Green out of the hypothermia."

Talking about the Greens only led Chennelle to remembering what happened to Mrs. Dodson. This time, Trevon rescued her.

"Reverend Green came out to the waiting area at about midnight to let us know she was beginning to stabilize. It took about another hour before the doctors would allow us to see her."

"How is the good reverend taking all of this?"

"I don't know what Chennelle thinks, but I was surprised. He must really love that woman because he had nothing but praise for her. From what Chennelle told me, he went right up to the perp and talked him into giving up the knife, dressed his wife, and carried her to a waiting ambulance."

"That's exactly what happened," said Barnes. "That was the greatest act of bravery I've ever seen from a civilian. How did the interview go?"

Trevon glanced at Chennelle, who nodded at him to continue. "The first thing she wanted to know was did Mrs. Dodson get rescued and was she okay. We'd already told Reverend Green that Mrs. Dodson had passed and we'd all agreed not to tell her, but Mrs. Green got very agitated when we hesitated. Her husband had us go ahead and give her the information."

"That must have thrown everything into the toilet."

"We thought it would, too," said Chennelle, folding the omelet. "However, Mrs. Green simply closed her eyes for a few minutes and when she opened them, her tears fell and she told us that Mrs. Dodson was okay now. She'd made it to Heaven."

"Holy crap! Did she give you any more details about what happened before we got there?"

Chennelle set the plate with the omelet on the counter in front of Trevon and turned off the stove.

"Aren't you having any?" he asked.

"Not hungry right now," she said, and then explained everything to Barnes in detail, from Doug breaking into the house and holding them at gunpoint, to branding both of them alive, and then deciding to burn the witch and sacrifice his mother on the witches' altar.

"This guy's worse than Emerson," said Barnes. "So, the doc says Mrs. Green will be okay?"

"Physically, yes. Mentally, not so much." Chennelle turned to place the pan she was using in the sink. She really didn't want to talk about the case anymore. Although she and Trevon had fallen asleep the minute they hit the bed last night, they'd had a wonderful morning of sweet love making before breakfast.

Barnes apparently took Chennelle's silence as a hint. She crammed the last bit of donut in her mouth and gulped down the rest of her coffee.

"Got to get downtown," she said, her words muffled by the donut still in her mouth. Barnes headed for the door. "See you Monday morning."

"You bet," said Chennelle, watching her partner scurry out the door.

Chennelle moved her gaze to Trevon, who she found was staring at her and smiling. He beckoned her to join him with a wave of his hand. She walked out of the kitchen as he got off his stool. He wrapped his strong arms around her and she felt herself melt into him. The warmth of his body was comforting and welcome.

"Chennelle, baby," he said, continuing to hold her so close she could hear his heartbeat. "I'm supposed to go in today, but I can call and take a day off. You just say the word."

She pulled back from him slightly and looked up into his warm, loving eyes. "I appreciate it, Trevon, but I think I need to be alone for a while. You understand, don't you?"

His face looked a little downcast, but he said, "Of course, I understand."

"It would be really nice if you'd come back later this evening. I could probably have a nice supper ready by seven."

Lips curling into a wide grin, he pulled her close again and held her for a long, long time—and she loved it.

Chapter 79

Chennelle approached Mrs. Green's hospital room slowly. She was in a quandary. For some reason she was taking this case personally. Mrs. Green was as much a victim to her mother's crime as all those murdered by Douglas Bronn—aka Douglas Kirkpatrick. The difference lay in the fact that Mrs. Green had suffered all her life wondering what had become of her son, and now she had to live the remainder of her life knowing.

Peeking in the doorway, she saw Reverend Green holding his wife's hand and stroking her hair. She also heard a familiar voice.

"Thank you for letting me come visit today," said Amber.

"Barbara Dodson was a fine woman," Heather said, her voice raspy from last night's cold temperatures and her pain driven screams. "She tried to get Doug to see reason and to spare me."

Amber wiped away a tear and smiled. "That sounds like something Barbara would do."

Chennelle entered the room quietly and was glad to see there was no roommate. Upon her approach, the conversation ceased and the reverend rose from his chair.

"Detective Kendall, I hope you aren't going to ask Heather anymore questions today," said the reverend, in a friendly but stern voice. "As you can see, she's quite exhausted."

"As a matter of fact, I wanted to stop by to see how you're doing, Mrs. Green."

"How sweet," Heather said. "Please, do come in. Jeremiah, pull up a chair for the detective. Have you met Amber McManus?"

"Oh, yes," said Amber. "Her partner, Erica Barnes, and I went to school together."

Reverend Green had done as his wife asked and brought a chair for Chennelle. Then he sat down next to his wife and took her hand in his. Trevon was correct when he said the pastor cared very much for his wife. She guessed first impressions weren't always correct.

"How are you feeling today?" asked Chennelle.

"As I'm sure you noticed, my throat is still rather raw, but that will heal in time. The cuts are sore sometimes, but they have a nice numbing cream that helps. The doctor wants to keep me in for one more day to make sure I don't have any residual effects from the hypothermia."

Chennelle nodded and glanced at Reverend Green who was fully focused on his wife, smiling at her and rubbing her hand between his. He'd almost lost her. Those times really make a person look at life and figure out what's important.

Mrs. Green smiled up at her husband. "He's my hero, you know?"

Chennelle nodded.

Amber stood. "I'm glad you're doing well, Mrs. Green. Our coven members were very concerned about you."

"Must you go?" asked Heather.

"I'm afraid I must," said Amber. "We're having a meeting today. We'll be selecting a new leader and then helping Harold Dodson with arrangements for Barbara's funeral."

"Please tell him we're praying for him," said Reverend Green.

Amber nodded, then left without another word.

"I know my son has done horrible things, Detective. He was raised by a spiteful, hate filled woman who morphed her religion into something vile. She was my mother, so I know what she was like. Fortunately, for me, I had my father—until I disappointed him. And, of course, my son didn't even have that."

Her eyes filled with tears as she looked into her husband's face. "We've decided we must forgive him, because he had no chance to learn to love or to find the right path. We know other humans won't forgive him, or understand his illness, but Jeremiah and I are going to stand by him."

Reverend Green turned to look at Chennelle. "This has been a real test of faith for me. People think their pastor is perfect, sometimes the nearest thing to God. We're not. The congregation holds us to a higher standard, but we're just human beings like everyone else. This man is my wife's only child, her flesh and blood. We realize he will probably be sent to a maximum-security mental facility for the rest of his life. I've contacted an attorney to take his case and we plan to visit him and try to help him find the true path to God."

"Detective Kendall," said Mrs. Green, caressing her husband's cheek. "I'm very lucky to have found this man. I think he'll be preaching more about love and tolerance from now on. Amber's visit has shown us that they hold no ill will toward us. Therefore, it is our duty to do the same for them. You won't be seeing members of our congregation protesting against those of other religions."

Chennelle smiled at them. "You may lose some of your followers."

"Yes, we probably will," he said. "They'll search until they find another pastor who believes as they do. As I said, we're all human."

"I'm going to leave now so Mrs. Green can rest that voice of hers," said Chennelle, rising from her chair. The reverend rose as well.

"Thank you for coming," said Mrs. Green.

Chennelle patted her on the arm and nodded to the reverend. No verbal communication was necessary.

Walking back down the hallway, she couldn't help but wonder how Harold Dodson would feel when he found out Reverend and Mrs. Green were going to forgive the man who brutally murdered his wife.

Chennelle chose not to think about it right now. She would just relish the thought that this mad man was behind bars and would never be on the streets of her town again.

Chapter 80

Two Weeks Later

Her father practically jumped up from his chair and went around the table, grabbing Chennelle in a tight hug. "It's about time you two showed up. I'm starvin'."

"Yeah, you sure do look like your starvin'," exclaimed his wife. Everyone laughed.

"Ya'll can laugh, but you're gonna get old and fat too someday," he said, and then he offered his hand to Trevon. "Good to see you."

Chennelle could have sworn she saw that look her papa always gave the boys who came calling. The one that warned them not to hurt his little girl, or else. Trevon must have received the message, because his smile seemed a little forced.

"I've never been to the Carolina Grill before," said Trevon. "This is a nice place."

"Hmph."

There was Saundra. Chennelle knew she'd have to get in at least a moment or two of her displeasure.

"Saundra!" said Chennelle enthusiastically. "This place looks great. You really know how to throw a party."

Her sister shot her a look which said, *"You'll pay for this,"* so Chennelle grabbed Trevon's arm and led him to a place between her niece Malea and her brother Carl.

"Oh, Auntie," said a gleeful Malea, "I was hoping you'd sit by me."

"Sometimes wishes do come true," said Chennelle, stroking her niece's hair. "You look beautiful tonight."

"So do you, Auntie." Malea motioned for Chennelle to come closer and she lowered her voice. "And so does your boyfriend."

They both giggled like schoolgirls, and then she heard someone tapping a glass to get everyone's attention.

Her brother-in-law, Terry, was standing with his glass in the air. "I'd like to propose a toast to Devon and Mae Kendall. They have endured hardships, softened by love; they've raised three children of whom they can be very proud; and they've been an example for all of their family, showing us what it's like to have an enduring marriage. After forty years, they are the rock and foundation of this family. Here's to you both. We love you, respect you, and wish you another forty years of wedded bliss."

Everyone shouted a different phrase from "here, here" to "I love you" to "Way to go, Grandpa." Chennelle looked around at everyone clinking glasses. She watched her nephews and niece laughing and making faces. Her heart melted as she watched her father kiss her mother with the enthusiasm of a twenty-year-old. Then she looked at Trevon and thought that maybe, just maybe, this would be them one day.

# # #

About the Author

Michele May, whose pen name is M. E. May, was born in Indianapolis, Indiana, and lived in central Indiana until she met her husband and moved to the suburbs of Chicago Illinois, in 2003. Although, she has physically moved away, her heart still resides in her hometown. She has a son, a daughter, and four grandsons still living in central Indiana.

Michele studied Social and Behavioral Sciences at Indiana University, where she learned how the mind and social circumstances influence behavior. While at the university, she also discovered her talent for writing. Her interest in the psychology of humans sparked the curiosity to ask why they commit such heinous acts upon one another. Other interests in such areas as criminology and forensics have moved her to put her vast imagination to work writing fiction that is as accurate as possible.

Michele is an active member of Mystery Writers of America Midwest Chapter, Sisters in Crime Chicagoland, Speed City Sisters in Crime in Indianapolis, and the Chicago Writers Association and its affiliate InPrint.

Her *Circle City Mystery Series* is appropriately named as these stories take place in her home town of Indianapolis. The first novel in the series, *Perfidy*, won the 2013 Lovey Award for Best First Novel, and the second book in the series, *Inconspicuous*, released in July 2013 was nominated for the Lovey Award for Best Suspense Novel. *Ensconced* is the third novel in the series and was released in March 2014.

Made in the USA
Charleston, SC
11 December 2014